Man and Other Monsters

Dr. Candido Diaz Jr.

Acknowledgement

Thank you to everyone who supported me after my first book and told me to keep going. Thank you again to my mother and Aubrey for always pushing me forward. It was during the finishing of this second book that I became fully appreciative of how truly privileged and lucky I am to be able to be doing what I am doing— to have the time, freedom, and support to write down my crazy ideas. I dedicate this book to everyone still working on making their dreams come true and all the people who will never have the time to write down their stories.

Contents

The Historian

The Historian

Deckard sat in his car, a powder blue convertible, and anxiously waited for the right time to leave. The soft white top of the car currently lay open, and the mild spring sun fell onto his pristine dark brown hair. He trimmed it weekly to make sure that the fade was perfect and that the length of his front curl bounced at the right speed.

His car was an old-style vehicle shell with a contemporary engine. As the car sat idling, it was nearly silent. The leather seats were perfectly white and meticulously cared for, recently reupholstered. Deckard's dark brown suit consisted of subtle blue stripes that perfectly matched the tone of his car; this was not by accident. He was a fashionable man, which in this day and age meant he was an individual who dedicated his clothing to a particular style or a particular era. For Deckard, something about the clean and proper 1950s always brought him peace. His grandparents controlled the television growing up and it instilled their fashion into the forefront of his mind. His glasses were simple black rectangles meant to complement the fluff of hair. He was, by design, a professional-looking man.

He checked the clock on his car for the tenth time that minute. He once again saw that it was 3:43. He only had to wait for two more minutes; he used it to prepare. Deckard began to recite his opening speech and muttered it quickly under his breath. "Hi, it's a pleasure to finally meet you. I'm Deckard," he repeated to himself in various happy tones. "It's a pleasure. Wait. Is that right?" he started to question himself. "It's a pleasure. No, it's my pleasure. It's MY pleasure. Too formal? Too much? No, they are by all accounts classy people. It's…my pleasure."

Though he had been sitting in the car for nearly an hour, he had only just realized how warm he was getting. He wondered if it was stress. Deckard touched the top of his hair to check and make sure its perfect shape was not ruined by the heat. He then flipped the switch on the convertible top. While the lid slowly closed, Deckard turned the dial on the air conditioning as low as possible and put the fan on high. He began to fan the cool air into the armpits of his suit, then reached over to the passenger side seat and grabbed a small tome. The book was stout but thick and extremely old. A fancy gold pen was hooked onto the tattered binding. He moved the book to his lap and began to search through a group of folders that sat below it. He rifled through many; labeled with different names; some were thin but others were thick and overflowing with information.

Deckard grabbed the second folder from the bottom and opened it up to find a photo of the house he was currently parked across the street from. He flipped through the pages, which were filled with more photos and files. At the back of the stack, he found what he was looking for—photos of his two interviewees. One was a strong-looking gentleman with a square frame and strawberry-blond hair that fell to his shoulders. His wife sat beside him, a tall, slender brunette, her smile as large as he was wide.

"Chaaaazzz…and…Mah-ria. Chet and Mariaaah…," he said to himself as he scanned the associated file for their last name. "Moore. Chet and Maria Moore. Gotcha. Beautiful."

Though Deckard had done this a hundred times, he still aways got nervous *every* time. It was a sign he was doing something out of passion. Deckard was a man who truly loved to listen, to hear other people's stories. It was such a pleasure, he thought, "To be enveloped in the history of what makes someone who they are." It was something magical you could see in his eyes. Thus, he always chose interviewees whose lives were so vastly different from his. This way he always felt like he was learning. It felt like he was even living a new life; each interview was a life-changing experience.

Deckard looked over the top of the folder to check the clock again. "3:46! Crap!" he huffed. His right hand gripped the key tightly and turned off his car, while his left threw open the door. He then slid back his seat and placed the mass of folders on the floor. He placed Moore's folder into the tome and exited the car. He removed the pen; he placed it into the chest pocket of his suit. Its gold and wooden casing matched the tone of his suit as well. He straightened his suit, he fixed his tie, and then he used his hip to check the door shut.

"Crap…why come early if you're going to be late?" he groaned while he checked his hair in the side mirror of his car. Deckard then patted down his pockets. "Where are they?" He swung open his car door, and he leaned back in. The glove box was the third place he searched, and where he found his small box of business cards. He grabbed a fistful and placed them in his breast pocket. Deckard locked the card and once again used his hip to shut the door.

To make up time, he walked briskly across the street but remained stiff as he tried to appear casual. He reached the door in short order, breathing much heavier than he wished he would. *I really should work out*, he thought. He rang the doorbell, then proceeded to check his reflection in the glass pane on the front door. The tome was in his left hand as he used his right to fix his hair, the angle revealing some unflattering parts. He adjusted the fluff a little to the left, then a little to the right. The sunlight shone off his cufflinks; a symbol of an arrowhead eclipsing a sun reflected back onto the house.

The door was answered by Chet, the fine, young gentleman from the picture. His face had not changed or aged a day from the photos Deckard had seen. Chet wore a light blue sweater with its sleeves rolled up over a white long-sleeved shirt. His pants were a faint white color, cream. His smile was large and friendly but clearly signified confusion as to Deckard's presence.

"Hi, sir? How can I help you?" Chet asked, while he gestured politely with his hands and with a raised eyebrow.

"Hi-hii," Deckard stuttered, as if his voice needed to warm up. Chet's confusion threw a wrench into his prepared speech and tone. "It's a pleasure to finally meet you in person, Chet. I'm Deckard." He reached his hand out for a shake.

"Hi, Mr. Deckard…what can I do for you?" Chet reached his arm into the air and stretched it behind his back while letting out a yawn. After a moment, Deckard began to pull his arm back but Chet finally reached in for a quick shake. "Now, I'm sorry but I don't recognize your name. I am a little embarrassed. Have we spoken before?"

"Oh, no, don't be embarrassed. I am the one who is embarrassed," Deckard said while he put his hands on his hips and let out a deep sigh. "Did you not receive any of the emails or the phone messages about my visit?" His voice was growing a bit panicked. Deckard then pulled out his phone and placed it on his tome. He then began to slide through his emails. "I am so sorry to intrude but I have a confirmation email here from my assistant. It says that they talked to you. Is your number 12a-1293-21?"

"Oh no, my number is 12a-1293-51," corrected Chet. "That must be the problem. Well, Mr. Deckard, what is this about?"

"Well, now I'm very embarrassed and might have to fire my nephew," he joked while blushing. He reached into his jacket's front pocket to retrieve a business card and handed it to Chet with two fingers extended. The man grabbed it and started to inspect it.

Chet flipped it over and admired the beauty and simplicity of the card. The subtle off-white coloring and the tasteful thickness of it. It even had a watermark, the same symbol as Deckard's cufflinks. It read "The Historian" in red cursive letters. Below in bold it continued,

"Your history is a time capsule to honor your life." In the bottom right sat Deckard's name and email.

"Thank you for the card, but I'm still not quite sure what this is about," repeated Chet while he flipped the card over in his hands a few more times.

"How presumptuous of me," said Deckard. He grew more and more embarrassed by the second; his nervous twitch of adjusting his glasses was in full force. "Who am I to assume you know about our little column?" he continued, tugging at his collar. "I work for *The Historian*. We are a small company that runs stories in local newspapers on local people we believe to be inspiring— local heroes. Long story short, my assistant was supposed to reach out to you as we would love to run a story on you and your wife."

"That's an honor, but why would you want to do a story on us?" chuckled Chet. "Honey!" he called to his wife, who was seemingly upstairs. After a brief moment another voice called down.

"Yes, Chet?" Maria's voice was high-pitched. Her body appeared around a corner from the second floor just a moment after. She wore a long white and gold sundress, decorated with wildflowers. Her outfit, like Chet's, was surprisingly fancy for lounging around the house. Maria made her way over to the front door and stood behind Chet, her head easily looked over the top of his. "What's this all about?" she asked as she put her arms around him.

"This man says he wants to interview us for the paper," responded Chet while he looked up to this wife and gently kissed her chin.

"See, it's that right there," Deckard said enthusiastically, pointing his two fingers at the couple. "Our mission at *The Historian*, as I was telling your husband, is really to find inspiring people. To document their impressive lives. To honor those people in the background of our society with so much wisdom to share. If I'm to understand correctly, you two have just celebrated your two hundredth wedding anniversary. Am I right?" The pair smiled pridefully and looked at each other. "In today's world, it is so rare to see a couple who have gone through so many years together. A couple who through all the changes in the world have been able to love each other and stay together. *The Historian* would consider it an honor to tell your story. We're dedicated to bringing uplifting and motivational content. Right here at home." Deckard paused and smiled after his speech. His arms rested on his waist once again.

"Well, we were getting ready to have our dinner date night," Chet said, looking up to Maria. "But I don't know, Maria. What do you think, would you mind?" He then turned back to Deckard. "One of the many things we do is that we check in to each other's emotional needs. You might want to jot that down," he joked.

"Well, we just threw the food in the oven…so it won't be ready for a while. I think we would have time to answer some questions. Do you perhaps want some tea or coffee?" offered Maria.

"Thank you so much, I would absolutely love some tea. Again, I am terribly sorry for the mix-up and lack of communication on our part," said Deckard as the couple led him into their home. Once he entered, the couple gestured to Deckard's shoes. "Oh of course," he said awkwardly as he slipped his shoes off by pressing on each heel with the toe of the opposite foot. The mixture of smooth, clean floor and sock made his movements cumbersome and strategic. He felt like he might topple at any moment.

The group walked into the foyer and Deckard could see the multilevel staircase Maria had just come down. The tan wall was painted with a desert flower landscape that moved up the wall. The full image of the staircase was one giant mural complemented by light green walls that surrounded it.

"What a beautiful home," Deckard marveled as they walked down a hallway, the wall of which was lined with family photos. He stopped to admire them and continued to compliment the style of their home. "We really must do a tour before I leave. I would love to hear the stories behind these photos." He stopped to slowly look at each one, a large smile beamed across his face. The pictures contained Chet, Maria, their children, and a host of family and friends.

Once you were no longer a child, it was often hard to tell your true age. It made understanding family relationships more of a guessing game than an exact science. Fortunately, physical consistencies still existed and could sometimes give a clue. It could often be considered gauche to ask, so Deckard simply hoped and waited to be filled in.

The house was made of many straight hallways and paths, a clean-cut design. As they moved further into the house, some hallways became fully glass on one side. The giant windows showed a view into the back of their property, a small valley. The house sat on the edge of a cliff. A forest of trees was visible below and a wonderfully blue sky was above. The house sat open to nature and felt more like a treehouse than a real house. In the living room this was especially true.

Chet continued to lead the expedition; Maria walked slightly behind him and the two stil held hands the entire way. "We've owned this home for the better part of a century," he began to explain. "We have been fortunate enough to have been able to curate it to our liking. We bought it when we had our second set of children." The three entered the living room to see a giant tree growing through the ground in the center of the room. It gave the room a pleasant and deep wooden smell. "We planted that tree when we first bought the house. It's gotten so large, we've had to expand the floor and fix the ceiling. In the meantime, we figured why not update the rest of the house." Chet then pointed at the tree using his hand that still held Maria's. "The roof is modified to fit around the trunk of the tree. We have a sealant around it to keep out the rain." Within the house, the tree was surrounded by a small railing to keep visitors from falling into its large roots.

The group moved to a set of three couches which were arranged to open toward the tree. In the middle of all seats sat a small transparent glass coffee table decorated with a matching vase that contained fake flowers. There, Maria finally let go of Chet's hand. "I'll start the hot water," she announced. "Do we prefer coffee or tea?"

"Any type of low-caffeine tea, preferably something fruity. Citrus, if possible," quickly responded Deckard.

"I'll see what I can do," responded Maria, surprised by his sudden impulsivity. She then made her way to the kitchen. Deckard and Chet walked forward and made their way to the couches. They sat across from one another. Deckard placed his tome on the glass table in front of him, the reflection of his face gleaming back at him off its impeccably clean surface. Its torn and beaten-up leather contrasted both the table and house as a whole. The binding was blank but decorated with several stripes of gold at the top and bottom. The cover of the book, now neatly revealed face up, was hand decorated; *The Historian* was written in large, decorative, gold calligraphy at the top, and below it was the symbol of the arrowhead eclipsing the sun. A long golden ribbon extended from the binding to act as a bookmark. The pages of the book were clearly worn and tattered. The edges were frayed and stained; patches of brown, burgundy, white, and green tainted them.

"What a unique book," Chet commented. "It's subtly beautiful. Does everyone at your company get one?"

"No, it's my own personal book. Most other people use their phone or a computer nowadays. I just find it so much more satisfying to handwrite things, makes me feel like I remember it better. Feels more personal."

"Plus, who can stand the sound of all the clicking?"

"Now I hope I won't be too distracting, and you don't mind if I am jotting down notes like a madman," Deckard joked. "Some pretentious people may suggest I do fluff pieces, but I consider myself a serious journalist. As such, I would never want to get anything wrong, so I do tend to take a lot of notes. Now, you said you were having a dinner date. I hope I am not intruding too greatly. Am I interrupting anything? Are you two expecting company? Couple or community? Tell me more about this idea— it sounds darling."

"No, no, this dinner is just between the two of us. We started it about 150 years ago, while going through a bit of a slump. Long story short, we make sure that every Sunday we are together for a meal. Tonight, it's dinner," proudly explained Chet.

"Well, there must be sometimes when you two are apart and cannot meet. What about then?" enquired Deckard, both eyebrows raised.

"I'll let Maria tell you about that," laughed Chet. "Very good question." The two sat in silence for a moment before Deckard reached into his pants pocket and pulled out a black ballpoint pen. Picking the tome of the table, he flipped to the furthest page, marked by a flap of gold fabric, and began scribbling. The book's pages were naturally blank, but the pages prior were filled with Deckard's tiny and almost typeset writing. On this new page, Deckard started at the top of the page and wrote the names of his two interviewees.

"Already taking notes? I didn't know the interview had started. I need to be on my best behavior," joked Chet.

"Oh, you know, as I said—jotting down like a madman. I am just writing up a summary of our time up until now. I like to make sure I remember all the details. The beauty of your house. The way you choose to decorate it. The exact way you and your wife banter. Truly try to paint a picture." Deckard never looked up from his pages; too much to write. "Before we start, I'd like to let you know the structure I was thinking we'd take with this interview. If you have any concerns or anything, please let me know. I am quite flexible. I was thinking we make it simple and go chronologically. Let's begin in the beginning when you first met or started dating. Then we can move ourselves forward through your love, stopping at any major events or turning points and end present day."

It was then Maria came into the room carrying a tray with a teapot, three teacups, small individual containers for honey, sugar, lemon, and a larger wooden container that held the tea packets. Placing it on the table she asked, "What have I missed, honey?"

"Mr. Deckard was just wondering what happens when we have to miss Sunday dinner?" Chet said as if setting up the punchline of a joke.

"Oh no no no no no no no no," responded Maria as she moved the teacups off the serving plate and placed one in front of each drinker. While she began to pour hot water into the cups she continued, "What reason could we have for such a thing? Maybe, perhaps…when we first got together but now with technology, there is no reason that you cannot sit and eat some food together on a screen for forty-five minutes. What else could be more important? Even if we cannot be physically together, we can plan a meal together. What kind of tea would you like? We do not have citrus, but we do have a number of other fruits."

"I guess what it comes down to is that we always put being together first. We can do our work a few minutes late if it gives us time to feel connected to each other for the day," interrupted Chet.

Deckard shook his hand; it had already begun to partially cramp. Deckard ignored Chet for the time being. "Please surprise me—I'll take any one with no caffeine. I'm already too excited," Deckard said while continuing to write with his right hand and searching through the tea box with his left. "Actually, do not surprise me. Here is a lone lemon one. That sounds lovely and light." He then took the packet and placed it into his water. He then picked up the small spoon and scooped a bit of honey into his tea and began to stir. "So, here we are, here two hundred years into your marriage at Sunday dinner. But as I mentioned, now that I have you both in the room, let's start at the beginning. They always say a good home needs a steady foundation."

"Well, I believe I speak for both of us when I say that I still can't believe you're interested, let alone excited, to talk to us…well, about us," said Maria as she sat down on the couch next to Chet. She rested her arm on his lap as she stirred sugar into her tea. "What a unique book you have there."

"That's exactly what I said, darling."

"Most people these days just use their phone or computer to take notes. You don't find that more convenient?" asked Maria, now rubbing the back of Chet's head.

"I just find it more pleasurable to take notes in a notebook, makes me feel more connected to my work. This is just for me. You can consider it my own oral history of my cases…of the world and what I've learned. Of course, I'll transfer all my notes at work later…aaannnd of course, I am an excitable person. It slows me down a bit to have to write things down instead of typing. I truly don't know how anyone could not be with my job, though. I guess I am just a person who likes to take down other people's stories," explained Deckard, who then picked up his teacup with two hands. He then brought it up to his lips and carefully blew on it before taking a sip. "I think it's beautiful following people's lives. It's just so much more interesting than what I do. My interviews are the most interesting parts of my life. It's just that each is a new adventure to learn from, a life to imagine. What is the point of spending so much time on this planet if we can't use the wisdom and experience of the world around us to learn how to better our time here? Maybe one day I'll publish it all and you'll be famous." Deckard placed down his tea and returned to writing.

"Besides the article, of course," smiled Maria.

"Yes, which paper did you say it was for again?" questioned Chet, now lightly leaning on Maria.

"*The Historian,*" proudly proclaimed Deckard. He began to gesture putting his hands on his waist in a superhero pose, but gave up halfway through and ended with a smirk.

"I don't believe I've heard of that paper…" Maria continued to think out loud.

"Well, it's not a full paper—we run a column. Sometimes large-scale but often small, going from town to town. The last time we would have written in this area was probably about eight years ago. As you can guess, I travel a lot for it. That's part of what makes listening to your story so exciting. Learn about a life with some stability," he divulged. Deckard slumped back in his chair and then jumped back up and continued. "So please let me start by congratulating you both on two hundred years of marriage. That is quite a feat. If you don't mind me pivoting for a moment before I forget, what were/are your plans for your bicentennial celebration?"

"We actually didn't do anything particularly special that day," Chet explained while looking at Maria and kissing her hand. "We didn't want to put too much weight onto it. To make it feel forced like Valentine's Day or something similar. As part of our vows, we live our days one at a time, with the same amount of love every day."

"That is a beautiful encapsulation, isn't it? I'm going to write that down as a heading. Great quote to start," said Deckard as he quickly scribbled in his book. "So now to start at the beginning of your love story... Where did you meet? How did you start dating?"

"Those are two very different questions. It's actually a rather complicated story. Technically we first met when we were five or so," Chet said while he gazed at Maria to verify his time frame; her head nodded in agreement, a light smile on her face.

"Yes, so we were actually childhood friends. Our mothers had grown up together, but Chet didn't move to town until right around my fifth birthday. Wanting to make the transition easier for him, they asked to put him in my class. Aaannd from then on, he was a pain in my butt," laughed Maria as she squeezed Chet's neck lightly.

"I was not a pain; I was just hyper."

"You were chaos."

"I was fun. Anyway, you always thought I was cute, so I don't know why you would even take that tone."

"Oh, I have a tone," she responded with death stare eyes.

"This was essentially the beginning of our friendship, always teasing each other. We spent a lot of time together. Grew up together. Protected each other. And as we got older, I realized I couldn't live without her," Chet continued. Once again he kissed Maria's hand.

"So, our relationship grew up out of a friendship. Best friends for a very long time. It was actually me that stopped it from happening for a long time; I'll admit I never saw him in that light. Something about being my best friend, the security blanket I had for so long, kind of stopped me from seeing him as a full person."

As they continued to talk, playing off one another with a natural but well-rehearsed dance, Deckard noticed the comfortability and calm they shared. Their mannerisms were that of an old couple. The youth of their faces hid the years of wisdom they kept inside. He took that down as a note before he interrupted them.

"So, you two grow up as best friends. Helping each other through other relationships, important life lessons. You grow close and what happens? How did you realize you loved each other? When did you realize? Especially for you, Maria, who didn't see it for a long time. How do you overcome that fear?" Deckard asked while he pretended to pat his head with a handkerchief.

"Well, *I knew* I loved her when I was about seven years old," Chet started saying. Maria's face was a mixture of surprise and skepticism.

"That young?" responded both Maria and Deckard at the same time.

"Yeah, there was a time when we were about seven and we were playing outside on the lawn. It was me, you, your brothers, and my little sister, I think. My sister, Vivienne, fell out of your tree and broke her leg. It was a bad fall and I panicked at the sight of the blood. All I could remember was that she was bleeding and everyone except you started to freak out. You were so calm and caring. You helped stop her crying and directed us to go get help. I didn't know what it was then by name, but I knew that I admired you. I wanted to be like you and wanted to protect you. Who could help but find that nothing but charming and look up to you?"

"Awwww," responded Maria. She touched her head lightly to his. "You never told me that before."

"Really? I guess I don't know how. Well, I'm sorry I haven't told you every day," responded Chet and the two shared a small kiss.

"Well, if only I knew that, perhaps it wouldn't have taken so long for us to truly find each other. We actually started dating when we were sixteen years old. I was dating a man who you might call…"

"He was a dick," interrupted Chet, who laughed as he bent forward to take a sip of his tea.

"Well…yes, he was a dick," laughed Maria, who also reached for her tea. "Oh, wait, before we continue, should we not be swearing for this interview?" apologized Maria.

"Don't worry, I enjoy the honesty and enthusiasm. I'm sure I can paraphrase and find a way to soften your language if need be."

"Ah, well you know, you're young. You don't know how you should be treated, how to treat people, or just even what it means to be in a relationship. Chet and I started dating as soon as I was aware he loved me. We were at a party and the now ex-boyfriend was treating me poorly, upset at some nonsense. I honestly can't remember. He started an argument and was yelling. He was being so brutish and terrible, and I guess Chet was a little drunk and also got angry."

"I normally had been very good at just playing the best friend, but then he tried to get physical. He grabbed her arm and she resisted, slipping away, but he held onto her coat. I had to step in. I can't stand someone putting their hands on someone else. Well, then he pushed me and continued to yell, now at me, saying things like 'She's *my* girlfriend' and 'Why do *you* care?' I was really just trying to be helpful. I had already seen him act like this at past parties. I insisted I was her best friend, and that honestly, he was being a drunken mess. Obviously, I should have been more tactful because that only made him more upset. He wouldn't lay off of me then, channeling all his attention and rage to me. At some point he said, 'What are you, in love with her?' and I couldn't stop myself. I said, 'YES! Actually I am.'"

"Before that point, I had always kind of felt that the two concepts, a boyfriend and a best friend, were incompatible or generally mutually exclusive. My parents were more old-school. They loved each other deeply but they were not in any way friends; partners and parents. So, I grew up thinking there were just some qualities you wanted in each that were mutually exclusive. It was then I realized I could, or at the very least should, try to have it all with Chet. All of our friendship fell into a new light. It really was like time slowed down in that instant. I've never looked back, though; only hoped I'd noticed earlier. I do, though, think it helped that we grew up with each other…together but separate. It let us know who we were without each other, so we could see how great we'd be together."

"So, then obviously from there you two continued to be high school sweethearts, correct? You graduate high school together, go to the same community college, but then your file here says you went to different graduate programs? How was that and when did you get married?" Deckard's smile was the widest it had been.

"That part of our relationship was actually the hardest. Up until that time, we had spent most of our lives with each other as a support blanket. We didn't know but we still had so much growing to do. Our conflict came when we both wanted to follow our dreams, and we were not able to find anywhere that could fulfill us both," explained Maria as she grabbed and held Chet's hand.

"We needed to find something to support both of our passions, but those were especially different at that time. Maria wanted to be a medical doctor and I wanted to become an engineer. Our acceptances pulled us across the country. We probably would have broken up if it wasn't for the invention of Rejuverron. I'm not sure if you noticed but I do have some wrinkles under my eyes. We were born before Rejuverron and at twenty-six years old, halfway through my PhD, we became part of the many people who started taking it," continued Chet.

"So, while you were apart, the busy schedule and perhaps new people in your life started to create the first real tension in your relationship?" Deckard asked as he leaned forward, his tone much more serious and somber. The couple looked at each other and then back at Deckard. Chet was the first to respond.

"Partially, for me, it was never about being attracted or in love with anyone else. I was so downtrodden, and our schedules were so disjointed. I just truly felt alone and worried about what was really happening in her life. I felt our lives were growing in different ways; we had new friends, coworkers, restaurants, and even pets. With my exhausted brain, I could never keep any of the names of anyone or anything straight. Our shared world was now different in a way I never expected. It felt so much lonelier than before I had her in my life."

"For me, I wasn't even aware of how little time we spent together and how distant I was. I feel like Chet's life was busy, but being in school he had many specific events/deadlines that punctuated his life. He felt the time much heavier than I did. I was doing many shifts at my residency and so many hours in the same white corridors. I was so exhausted that I didn't even realize how many days and eventually months were passing. I heard about Rejuverron first, through work, and got us incorporated into a medical trial. We decided to do it together."

"I was honestly desperate to find a way to stay connected, and I felt like it took away the fear of losing each other forever. In my mind it kind of gave us so much more time than we could ever have hoped. If something happened, if we were truly meant to be together, we'd find each other again. It took pressure off the relationship and helped me to calm down. Helped my anxiety. I didn't have to give up on my dream to stay in her heart."

"It helped us because what we were struggling with was how to follow the paths we wanted for our lives, while still holding onto each other. Rejuverron gave us so much time. It was kind of like, if we lost each other for one reason or another, we had infinite time to rediscover each other," Maria followed up. "Instead of putting one or both of our dreams on hold to be close, we could pretend *our* life was paused. It came down to faith."

"How did the drug help you both deal with the loneliness?" interjected Deckard, his expression confused.

"I barely had any. I just needed to get through. I was asleep, working, or trying to show Chet I still thought about him," answered Maria.

"I hate to admit it, but I honestly drank a lot. I tried to fill my little time with many other things, such as extra volunteering, or even working out a lot. I was so strong but lonely. I had a much harder time than she did. I had to tell myself that in case anything ever happened I would win her back. I had the time. We finally got married after our respective programs ended. I found work at the first firm near the hospital she worked at."

"That must have been a beautiful day. How have your parents felt about this relationship of yours?" asked Deckard.

"My dad was protective but what could he say? Chet was always my best friend. It was kind of like they saw it coming the whole time. We lived in that first house for a few decades. It was where we raised our first set of kids," said Maria, sipping on her tea again. "We were both in a massive amount of student debt, so our wedding was in our own backyard. Our first home was a small one, with a tiny backyard. Our parents did their best to make it fancy. They put up lights and made arches out of broken tree branches. The backyard was actually part of a small parking lot shared with the backyard of the house next door. The family was kind enough to allot us all the space for the day. We had maybe twenty people there? The entire party and reception fit only in our home. My dress was an old one I found at a secondhand store. It was a simple but a little short, white lace dress. It was by no means a real wedding dress, and everything else was borrowed; shoes, makeup, veil."

"Besides having to decorate the backyard, the wedding was a calm and surreal experience," followed Chet, grabbing Maria's hand again. "We got married when we could, through the means we could, with our most important people in the world, and at our pace. If anything, I was just excited to not have to wait to call her my wife. We remained in that house for twenty years before we decided to have any children."

"Ah, yes, I saw that you had seemingly four kids in the hall photos. Is that when you had them all? How much of an age range did you want?" followed up Deckard, now chewing on his pen.

"We actually had our kids in two sets. The eldest and youngest are roughly ninety years apart. Those first two kids were one right after another. After eighteen years they were mostly out of the house, off to college and work. When she was twenty-seven our eldest daughter blessed us with our first grandchild. Our eldest daughter, Phyllis, has always been very motherly; she ultimately had four herself. We spent our time helping raise those children and continued our careers. Then everyone was older, and we weren't sure what to do with ourselves, besides live. So, after another sixty years or so, we decided we had enough independence and to do it again."

"It worked so well the first time that we decided to have two more," continued Maria. "We went on down to the clinic where my eggs are frozen, and we had them fertilized and inserted. I was worried so I instantly put my eggs on ice when we started Rejuverron. I was afraid it might make me sterile, but ultimately that wasn't an issue. It was a little before everyone did it; save your eggs for a later date. Do you have any kids, Deckard?"

"No, no, I don't. I am a person who has spent the better part of my life on work. I still haven't found anyone so in love with me that they are willing to deal with my line of work. Perhaps that's why your story is so interesting. How close and connected you are. We can only inspire to be like you two. The way you balanced work and love and family in this complicated world… So to follow up…you not only are parents, but you are double parents. Wow, that must have been so exciting both times…and such a learning experience. So much time has passed, though. Do you feel like you have forgotten what it was like?" excitedly probed Deckard.

"I think helping to raise our grandchildren, we could see the personalities of our kids coming back. Perhaps it is the Rejuverron—I believe some studies have shown it—but it all feels like it was just the other day. The joy…and the stress," Maria said while she looked at Chet smiling. The two of them held deep eye contact and nodded in agreement. "Our first set of kids were a breeze. Sometimes you hit the genetic lottery. Phyllis and Hunter were fussy babies but once they started to talk, we knew we had two winners."

"As the children grew, they really embraced our hobbies and morals. Both loved school, Phyllis into art and history and Hunter interested in medicine like me. They were just passionate children who were always interested in doing what we were doing. It was like raising two new best friends, with your best friend. The act of being pregnant was terrible, obviously, but I think it was worth the family and experiences we were able to make. It's such a common connection, parent and child, that we sometimes overlook how truly special it is, teaching something so pure and vulnerable about the world."

"That's beautiful. My favorite age is when kids begin to talk and develop their personality. It's so interesting to watch them become full people. It must be so nice to help raise a child so much like you, with the same values," Deckard said, his eyes open and fixated on them like a baby deer.

"Our second set of kids were…to put it lightly…a bit more difficult. The twins had a much harder time establishing themselves as independent from each other. The boys were not nearly as into school as the rest of the family. It was difficult at the time to understand how they could be so different from us. It at first created a rift between us. We just didn't know what to do. We didn't agree on how to help them. I think that difficulty ultimately drew us closer together. Though for quite a while, I felt terrible. We really needed to grow as people from that. Even being so old, we were never able to prepare for that." Maria almost began to cry by the end.

"How did you two overcome this? What did you do?"

Seeing that Maria was a bit overwhelmed, Chet responded instead. "I think we really grew from the experience in a way that we didn't with our first set of children. Obviously, we love all our children, but when someone…when two people…" Chet's voice began to waver. "…are so different from you, it's hard to fully understand them. It's cathartic but scary that you and they are experiencing and interpreting the world in vastly different ways. Our emotions and passions were not theirs. We had to make time for them and ourselves instead of simply being able to incorporate them into everything."

"They were taxing but taught us so much."

"I actually came up with the idea for bio-culture cement because of something our twins did. As children they came in from playing and decided they wanted to bring the beautiful flowers with them. While we were working, the two of them proceeded to stain our walls green." He pointed at a distant wall down the hallway and continued, "When they tried to place them against the wall and it fell, they then tried to hang them, smash them, really every combination. The painting in our foyer is actually a nod to my sons and their mess."

"That shift in family dynamic must have changed how you two related. I suppose on that note, how have things changed in your relationship as it has aged? How is it different now from those days raising the family?"

"It was actually the first time, since our graduate school days, where we actively had to split up. Not always seeing each other, kind of feeling like we were on different teams. That was when we decided to start doing these official date nights again, making them permeant. I think it helped us reignite independence and reestablish how important it was that we have each other. The bond we share. As we have aged, we have worked to keep them/ourselves together. We love our children," responded Maria, her voice heavy.

As the group sat silent in the weight of the moment, a bell rang in the distance, signifying something had finished cooking. "I can see that it is beginning to get late," said Deckard, finally breaking the silence and checking his watch. "I hate to intrude on any more of your dinner. It's beginning to smell delicious in here. But before I go, could I get that small tour?" begged Deckard, who now clutched his tome against his chest like a schoolboy.

"Well, the roast is finished. We really did lose time, didn't we?" Maria said while standing up with Chet and Deckard slowly following suit. "I will go and check on the food and make sure it's keeping warm. How about you and Chet do a small tour and I'll meet you two in a few minutes?" Chet and Deckard smiled in agreement as Maria walked off into the kitchen.

Chet motioned for Deckard to follow him by putting out his arms to his side, and the two made their way toward the entry hallway. "As we take this tour through the house, please point out to me any noteworthy spots. Share with me your story. Such as here, in this hallway. Tell me about these pictures, so I can take notes," suggested Deckard, in an upbeat but almost begging tone.

"You don't mind writing and walking?"

"No, I'm a regular expert. It'll be like being at a museum. Goodie."

The pair then walked down the hallway they had taken to the living room. They moved slowly as Deckard examined each photo and jotted notes the entire way. He paused at one photo in particular. The family on the beach. Deckard spotted six young adults, two of which were Chet and Maria. "Now, I can guess that this is Phyllis and these two have to be the twins, so that makes this Hunter. Am I right? Also, I don't think you ever mentioned the twins' names."

"Oh, that's a bad habit. But yes, you are right. It's funny, they always bothered me about doing that. I always refer to them to others as the twins. Their names are Cory and Shawn."

"Were they not close? Is that why they didn't like it?"

"They were inseparable but different, contrary to their looks. I think, as Maria said, they had a hard time not being forced into a box by us. I think specifically they didn't want to be forced into a box together. They didn't want to be us or each other."

They continued to the end of the hallway and made their way into the grand foyer. The two stood and admired the art on the wall. "This piece of art was actually done by a local artist. We commissioned this to try and get it a little greener in this area of the house."

"You didn't want to use your cement? Make yourself a jungle?"

"Oh, no, this was meant to be a tribute to our children, and what we learned, and honestly, it's a pain to maintain inside. We really did not want to add anything else we'd have to water." Chet chuckled like he was letting out a little secret.

"Well, it's a subtle and wonderful way to honor your family. You do already have a lot of incorporated green space. It's giving me decorating ideas of my own."

"Thank you. I've worked at it for most of our lives. Actually, there is another spot I'd like to show you. It's my favorite part of the house. Follow me upstairs."

The two then traveled up the stairs and reached the second-floor landing. The left side of the house was a regular hallway, not so dissimilar to the ones they viewed below. On the right side, the long wall of large windows continued, allowing the two to see down into the living room.

They walked down the hallway, this one a faint burgundy, and Deckard returned to writing as he admired the art and photos. A number of doors lined the hallway, all closed except one. The two passed the barely open door, as Chet led Deckard to the end of the hallway. When he opened the last door, Chet revealed a porch overlooking the valley, a mixture of city and forest in the distance. The two stood during golden hour, the sun was setting, and color bounced throughout the valley.

"This is where I always come to think and remember how wonderful my life is. It helps to be put at awe. Awe at the world around me and the life we've been able to build."

"So is there anything you'd like me to know about your wife, now that she's not here?" Deckard joked.

"Truly…no. I have not put on airs for you or lied about anything in any way. I never would have known I needed it, but it was actually very nice to have these conversations. Remembering why we do what we do, and how beautiful our life has been together. Thank you, Mr. Deckard. If you want to know how I really feel right now, just know that it is how I always have and always will. I love her with all my heart. In all this time, nothing has changed about that, only what we passions we wanted to follow. I don't know if perhaps we or I are different or if everyone is possible of this, but I have never wanted anyone else. Since the day I admitted I loved her, I have always been content and happy just looking into her eyes."

"A lot of people are capable of love," Deckard replied, "but many people don't know how to hold onto it, or they hold on too tight and let it slip away. I have interviewed many people and I have never had anyone not have anything to say about their significant other. You two are truly special."

Unsure of what to say, the two stood and watched the sun slowly set.

After a moment Chet broke the silence. "Okay, let's go see what's taking Maria so long," he said while he wiped a small tear from his eye. As they entered the house again, Deckard noticed the open door led to the master bedroom and stopped to admire the décor within. He walked into the room with his book still held close to his chest. The room was white and gold themed, creams and tans complementing the shiny detailing. In the hallway, Chet continued for a few feet before he noticed that Deckard was no longer behind him. He turned around and entered his room to find Deckard standing there.

"Oh, sorry, Chet. I just saw the pop of color coming from the room and walked in. Kinda like a bug to a zapper. It's so beautiful."

"Thank you but I'd rather you not be in our bedroom."

"Sorry, Chet. I didn't mean to offend. I admit I get overly excited," he apologized, bowing his head slightly. "That reminds me that I forgot something. Before I leave, I will need you to sign a disclosure agreement, so we can use your story in the paper. Would you mind signing this for me?" Deckard opened the front of his tome to reveal a folded piece of paper. He unfolded it and placed it on top of his tome and turned it toward Chet. Deckard reached into his breast pocket and pulled out his gold pen, then offered it to Chet.

"Of course. Of course. And it was an honor to be interviewed, but again let's please step out of the bedroom. Maria especially likes her privacy." He gripped the pen like a glow stick with both hands and pulled off the top. The removal of the cap unleashed a small blade from the pen's body, which impaled his finger. "Fuck," Chet exclaimed, dropping the pen, and using his other hand to tourniquet the wound. "Wha…wha happennn…ed," he tried to utter, but he was beginning to lose feeling in his body.

Quickly Chet collapsed to the ground, unable to move, his breath shallow. Though he could not speak or move, he could see. Deckard carefully picked up his pen and replaced the cap. A small blade retracted and he safely placed it back into his pocket. He then opened his tome again. He flipped to the back to reveal a small cut-out compartment containing a band-aid, syringe, needle, and small vial.

"Sorry about the cut. There really are very few nice ways to do this," Deckard said as he leaned down to Chet and applied the band-aid to his wound. He then reached back into the book, removed the syringe and needle, and filled it with the same liquid as the pen. Deckard then hid behind the bedroom door and waited for Maria to arrive.

"Darling…Deckard, where has the tour gone now?" Maria called down the hallway, her footsteps echoing toward the men. Once she reached the open bedroom door, she placed her hand on the door frame and leaned in slightly. She peered right, then left. She looked for only a moment before Deckard lunged from behind the door and injected her shoulder.

"Wwwwwhhhhaaaa waahhhhiiiee?" stammered Maria as she attempted to step toward Deckard before she collapsed to the ground. Now lying motionless on the floor, she could see the top of Chet's face; his body was mostly hidden by the bed. Maria could see his eyes and that's all she needed to know what was happening. As they stared at each other, their bodies screamed out to each other, unable to move. Their communication was now only telepathic, through their souls in their eyes. As Deckard moved around the room, they ignored him, their eyes fixated on each other.

"The problem today is that we are not making history," Deckard explained as he moved throughout the room and inspected the framed photos. In the process he stepped over the couple with care. "Most are just gliding through life, and so many people just feel stagnant. They need hope. They need to know it can all go well. You two represent the best of us and the future we all want. The problem is, it's not history until it's finished. It's not a satisfying story until it's over, and your story could do so much good in the world."

Deckard removed a silk cloth from his inside pocket and used it to parse through their belongings. He started his search by walking over to the closet, two large, mirrored doors, and slid them open. At the base of the closet, he saw a basket of accessories and his eyes spotted a pair of fluffy pink gloves. Though his hands were far too big, he partially put them on and stretched them to their breaking point. "Well, these are adorable. You two really have some great style." As he moved past the nightstand, Deckard scanned Maria's collection of perfumes, neatly organized and displayed. "Roja. Sounds nice," he muttered to himself as he selected a clear bottle with a purple crystal top. He first sprayed the perfume on himself, then he breathed it in deeply before spraying some into the air above Maria. "This is an amazing scent."

Deckard shifted to looking through the drawers he found himself in front of. He searched through them and finally found what he was looking for, pajamas. Before him sat the collection of pajamas that Chet had accumulated over his long life; silly pants worn with their kids, the comfiest pants for the sickest days, and the fanciest silk for luxury: a collection of a dynamic life. Deckard then realized he was only seeing Chet's clothes. Maria's were nowhere to be found. "Well, we can't only have one of you be comfy, now can we?" He scanned the dresser, found the symmetric drawer on the other side, and opened it to reveal the other stash of pajamas. "There we go."

Deckard then darted back and forth to compare various pajama combinations, trying to find complementary cloth for the pair. Under his feet still lay both Maria and Chet. "Now what to wear? I think your clothes really should project that love and connection you had. But…do we go with kooky, silly parents? Comfy at all costs? Lap of luxury?" he said rhetorically, as he held up various tops up to his chest. "Now this seems perfect," he said, louder this time, placing matching white satin pajamas onto the counter.

Deckard now drew his attention to the couple for the first time in a while but stepped over Chet. "What if you two were to break up? Then the story would be nothing, a waste of time, in some ways even a lie. Just another relationship lost to time," said Deckard as he grabbed Chet by his ankles and began to drag him toward his side of the bed.

"I really wish I could publish everything about you two. There is so much here, so much more we could go into. We have barely even scratched the surface of what you did, what you have done. It's really a pity. Neither of you happened to have kept a journal, did you?" As he spoke to them, he took his time carefully undressing them. As he took off their clothes, he traveled to the closet to neatly hang up each article of clothing. It was then time to get them ready for bed.

Once he was done dressing them, Deckard unbuttoned his jacket coat to give himself a little more room and lifted them. "Wow, you are much denser than you look," he said as he threw his elbows under Chet's armpits and used all his strength to hoist him into bed. Maria, though taller, was much lighter and easier to prop up. He placed the two under the covers and tucked them in, while he gathered his thoughts. As the couple lay next to each other, he thought, "I should have asked this before—I am such a fool. How do you two sleep? Butt to butt? Cuddle? Who would be the big spoon? I definitely think you're both cuddlers…. You know what, I got it." He attempted to snap his fingers, but the motion was silent in the gloves.

Deckard then arranged them, their arms over one another, holding each other's sides and their faces close. The two lay with their foreheads touching, their eyes still open and staring at each other. Still unable to move. "This is very beautiful, yes. You fall asleep looking at each other. You cannot stand to be apart for even a moment."

Going back to his tome, Deckard stored the small vial of liquid still in his pocket and swapped the used syringe for a fresh one. He then pulled the plunger and filled it with air. He first made his way to Maria. "Thank you so much for everything. You two really are my idols. I hope I find love like yours one day." Then with pinpoint accuracy, he injected a small bubble into Maria's neck. Chet watched her eyes shake in pain as her brain lost oxygen. Without another word, Deckard made his way over to Chet to do the same.

Deckard placed his tools back into his tome before he removed the borrowed gloves and dropped them into the laundry hamper in the corner. Then he grabbed his coat and the book and made his way downstairs. As he walked through the house, he could smell the cooking in the kitchen. *Yes, that is most definitely a loose end,* he thought. Deckard marched back deeper into the house and used his nose to find his way to the kitchen.

The kitchen was a large chrome space with another open floor plan. If not for the delicious smell of food, it would have been sterile and lemony. The dining room was separated by a bar counter and located near the oven where the roast was warming. Deckard followed his nose and peered into the oven. A faint light illuminated the beautiful roast simmering in heat. He gleefully looked throughout the many drawers and found the oven mitts. Carefully, he removed the roast, shut the oven door with his hip, then used his elbow to turn off the oven. Deckard then picked up a spoon and used it to drizzle pan jus on the meat. He then noticed the Brussels sprouts and rice already out on the dinner table. "Those must be cold by now." Deckard served himself a generous portion and heated them in the microwave. While his vegetables were reheating, he carved himself some roast. The ding of the microwave echoed through the silent house. For atmosphere, he lit the candles on the table, and he even dimmed the lights before grabbing his food from the microwave. Lastly, Deckard removed the cork from a bottle of red wine and poured himself a glass.

"This roast is delicious but uhh…these sprouts suck," Deckard said to himself, as he made exaggerated chewing gestures and added more salt. Even so, he sat and enjoyed his meal and his wine. Once he was finished, he rolled up his sleeves and placed his plate into the sink. After scanning for a moment, he found the dishwashing gloves. The remainder of the juicy roast was thrown into the trash before Deckard did all the dishes while whistling a soft country tune. As he walked out of the home, his hands were filled with his book and the trash. He looked up and saw he was standing under a beautiful, glowing night sky, and he smiled.

It was a new day and Deckard rushed toward his car. The frigid winter morning air made its way down his collar and into his back— shivers traveled down his spine. Though the same model, his car was painted lime green today and his suit was now a more muted brown, much lighter than before, to match; his outfit was complete with a green pocket square that complemented the subtle lines within his blazer. He had just exited a bodega. One hand grasped a coffee and the other was in his pocket for warmth. His elbow pinched his purchase, a newspaper. Using his free pinky to open the car, Deckard jumped onto the driver's side quickly and slammed the door shut. He put his purchase on the seat next to him and his keys in the ignition. Deckard attempted to start his car while still rubbing his hands together for warmth and let out a sigh of relief as the cold air was slowly replaced by hot, soothing air.

Now finally comfortable, Deckard picked up the newspaper to admire his work. He hastily flipped through the pages and made his way to the personal ads, pages 56-57. On the left page was only one large photo, one of the many framed photos of Chet and Maria with their family, this one by a river. Deckard had scoured their house after the interview and taken it from their wall. He felt it was the truest expression of the success and outcome of their love. On the right page, Deckard then began to admire his work. What he considered to be a thoughtful and beautifully succinct summary of their conversation. As he read it, he found each word self-indulgent poetry to his ego. Though he had written it, each word he read felt new, and reawakened buried feelings. With each line he met them again.

As he relived that moment, he remembered the Moores deeply and smiled. His heart was once again overwhelmed by the story of their love and how much he had learned from them. He felt a small burst of passion as he once again hoped to one day find such support and love; they gave him hope. At the end he took special care to check for the presence and proper printing of the *The Historian* symbol. After he saw its perfect shape and outline at the bottom of the page, Deckard smiled at another job well done. As he popped the car into drive and went home to plan his next interview, his work sat on the seat beside him.

Chet and Maria "Love Forever" Moore:

There are few things that transcend culture, age, or society the way that the search for love does. As you look through history, there are only a few loves that truly stand the test of time; those that do live in our hearts and minds forever. It is those couples who, beyond all odds, choose each other, that are the beacons of hope for our society. They are the ones that passively scream at us: Yes, you too can do it. You can and will find your soul mate, they say.

Humans are amazing in their unique ability to connect—to nature, to animals but most deeply with one another. It is that deep emotional connection that drove us to create society. It is what drives so many of us to be better. Many cultures believe in the cycle of life, death, and rebirth. Even the luckiest souls find each only over many lifetimes and are then torn apart. The rest are left to try again. It was only until a few centuries ago that we became honored and lucky enough to fight that cycle. We are lucky now that we are granted a life of endless time, as we all search for that. The truly lucky ones are those now who have already found it, with nearly all the time in the universe to bask in it. It is my misfortune to alert you that one such love, perhaps the greatest love of all time, has recently passed—their legacy and connection was hidden by their own modesty.

Chet and Maria Moore passed away this past month, a tragic case of Sudden Rejuverron Death Syndrome (SRDS). The rare but all too real and fatal condition has this time claimed two impassioned victims. Like all other cases, there seemed to be no reason for this sudden and premature ending of one's eternal life, a simple shutdown of the body. The couple had just celebrated their 200th wedding anniversary and had been together for nearly 215 years in total. They were found cuddling in bed, having passed in their sleep. It would seem that when asked to part this world separately, their souls instead passed on together; perhaps like the magic connection of twins. The heart of one sensed the other and the two left together.

The power couple were a masterclass in accomplishment as well as love. Chet had a long career as a city civil engineer, having a hand in designing and building many of the community gardens and public structures throughout his local city of Hunter's Hollow. His invention of plant growth enabling cement is still used to grow beautiful buildings and fill walls with vines and flowers all over the world. Maria was a doctor whose specialization varied throughout her career, but no matter the position, she was dedicated to the health and betterment of society. She spent the last leg of her life managing hospitals as she worked on creating new and safer surgical techniques. Though there is much we can learn from them professionally, this article is not a celebration of their careers and their work. Instead, it is to honor what we can learn from their love.

The two leave behind a beautiful family composed of four children and eight grandchildren. Their relationship spanned over two centuries, possibly the longest ever recorded. They decided not only to raise a family once, but a century later for a second time, decided they were not done giving and creating wonderful people to put into the world. Others have said of their family that the Moores were a blessing to the community.

Even before they dated, their love started as friendship. As children they became friends, then best friends, and lastly eternal lovers. When asked when their love started Chet would always say, "I didn't know what it was then by name [age seven], but I knew that I admired you. I wanted to be like you and wanted to protect you." In a triumphant moment of bravery, Chet professed his love after years of friendship to protect Maria's honor. Her world shattered upon realizing she could have a best friend and lover together. She would say before that, "Ah, well, you know, you're young. You don't know how you should be treated, how to treat people, or just even what it means to be in a relationship.... Before that point, I had always kind of felt that the two concepts, a boyfriend and a best friend, were incompatible or generally mutually exclusive.... It was then I realized I could, or at the very least should, try to have it all with Chet." And have it all they did.

From then on, they both knew they had found something special, and as they aged, they grew to fully understand one another. Perfectly thankful for their time. Their life was not always easy, but they always made sure "to check on each other's emotional needs." The only thing that could pull them apart was the passion of their dreams, but they stated that "Rejuverron gave us so much time. It was kind of like, if we lost each other for one reason or another, we had an infinite time to rediscover each other."

Perhaps all of us can help to keep such hope and faith in the world alive. No matter what, we can at least hope that perhaps their souls are joined in the afterlife or that they will once again find themselves in rebirth and be fortunate enough to spend another 200 years together. Theirs is a story with a truly beautiful ending. We all can only hope to be so lucky.

With honor and pleasure,

The Historian

Voices in the Music

Voices in the Music

Leona, known by her friends as Lee, was a veteran of the party scene. So much so that she, like thousands of others, lived in it. New Dionysus was once only a small collection of bars located in slums—abandoned warehouses were the perfect spots for alterative life-stylers and partiers to have privacy and freedom. With time, some warehouses were renovated into apartments and more clubs were built. In the past as partiers grew older, they moved out and a new influx of youth trickled in. With the invention of Rejuverron, however, everything changed. Now everyone was kept young forever. This meant that many people never lost their energy, and the population of ravers grew as they decided they never needed to leave. The party street became a party city.

Every morning hundreds of bars and restaurants were open, and every night hundreds of dance clubs thrashed—the entire city danced and sweated the night away. Lee had been partying there for nearly eighty years and had lived there for forty; not that she had an apartment. She spent her time in many clubs and over the years had transferred between many groups of friends. Somehow, she always bounced from couch to couch and found a comfortable place to sleep. Not that it was hard to sleep at night when she got all her party favors for free— decadence filled the club scene with generosity. Its patrons readily shared drugs, drinks, and saliva with one another. One thing Lee loved the most was that the dosage of drugs and the combination of tongues for the night was always a mystery. Tonight, like every night, Lee was raving.

Even though her eyes were closed she could still see the pulsating lights of the stage blaring through her eyelids. Her hair was long in the back and short in the front, cut to rise into bangs across her face; her naturally brown curls were bleached, dyed, and faded. The base of it was reddish pink, but green, purple, and blue stripes were scattered throughout. She had a small nose, deep green eyes, strong cheekbones, and a pointy chin. She was wearing a black bra underneath a vibrant silver fishnet shirt. The flashing lights alternated through every color of the rainbow, and her body shimmered into the crowd around her.

Each color of light brought its own emotion and energy to Lee's body. She swore she could feel the difference on her skin—differences in the tingle. She threw her hands in the air and spun. Her eyes were still closed but she felt she could see the room in front of her. Multicolored lights flashed above, and the crowd cast a shadow below. She and the shadow swayed to the beat together, one harmonious family. A soothing and upbeat man's voice spoke words of affirmation to the crowd. As the crowd pulsated and bodies bounced in all directions, his monotone love washed over them.

"Your smile…lights up the room. Those eyes…make heart go boom."

Lee was part of the organism of music. Like the rest, she bounced between others, always on the move but never quite making it anywhere. They circled each other like distant galaxies. Outside of the pit, another group formed, those who grouped together on the outskirts for a brief hit of cold. For Lee in this moment, the pressure of other bodies and the pounding in her chest was revitalizing. Her body was a void, a vessel being filled by the music. It quelled a darkness in her soul; the music was her life. Earlier this evening she had felt nothing, but now while dancing she was alive.

"Our love is forever; our friendship is eternal."

The air in the room was warm and thick, humid from the sweat and body heat of the crowd. Lee's mind was empty, and she was content—she presently imagined herself as a tulip, basking in the sun. While her body swayed violently to the beat, her heart pounded to its own slow and drawn-out rhythm. As the heavy electronica attempted to shake her body, she moved in fierce bliss. Her body was in too much chaos for her mind to properly register if anything was wrong. Between dehydration and the multitude of chemicals pumping through her blood, Lee's joy came from her feeling nothing instead of feeling like she was nothing.

"Let it out, sweetheart."

His words were out of sync with the atmosphere of the music, but that made it cut through to Lee even harder. She unclenched her jaw and moved it side to side. Then she threw back her head. The sudden release from her once scrunched position sent a rush through her body. A sensation of tingling rained down on her as the cooler air from above began to hit her arms, face, and shoulders. The unclenching spread down her body first at her head, then hands, then her legs, then finally her feet. She smiled, and with her eyes still closed she ran her fingers through her hair. Each nail sent an intense tingle throughout her body as it slid across her scalp. Each one was painted a different color; their tone and order were entirely random. The only consistency was the intensity at which they glowed under the black light. Some were a single color of neon green or blue; others were splatterings of multiple colors. What started as an experiment became a mainstay among her friend group. Their fingers dazzled each other as they all clenched to the music. Though she had not seen many of those people in years, she continued to paint her nails in hopes of entertaining those around her.

On the stage in front of her stood two platforms, and atop them dueling DJs. Each set was a hodgepodge of bright and eccentric objects—so unique they were almost the same. The music began to fade as one of the artists handed control to the other; the high-intensity beats of DJ Beauregard bled into the slow, rhythmic trance of DJ Olmec. The softer melodies were aggressive to Lee's mood. *I had just settled into a dance rhythm*, she thought; the first thought to make its way out in a few hours. Her heart had just begun to match up with the tingle in her legs. Instead, the sudden lack of bass released her mind. Lee was now aware of her heart, of her shortness of breath, and her lightheadedness. With her panic came a new singer's voice blaring across the loudspeaker. A couple belted in aggressive tones, once again out of sync with the music around. A deep man's voice bellowed while a high-pitched voice screeched behind.

"Don't you dare, do how you do. We're to be respected. I can't say I'm surprised by you."

"You're sickening us, use your fucking head. We'd rather off you were dead."

The music continued to slow, blue lights filled the room, and isolated white lights turned on—one directly above Lee. Now distracted, she felt like a star. She had to stabilize. She ground her teeth and ran one hand over her neck and jaw. She used her other hand to rub her chest. Her heart would listen. She stared across the shadowed faces of the crowd, unaware that everyone was in their own world. The only thing Lee could make out among the shape of the crowd was a large, square gentleman near the stage; it was a shape she *hated*. She *needed* to ignore it.

Instead, Lee turned her attention to the lights and stared up. The over-stimulation of the light helped to distract her from the beating of her heart. The music was *still* too soft, but the song had changed, and the voice was once again one she found pleasant.

"You are the love of my life and I've never felt this way before. This I say is true, and I owe it all to you you you you you."

She started to spin. Without the bashing of the beat, her dancing was limited by her own lack of coordination. She began to stumble, unable to keep her balance. Then she remembered why she was dizzy. She returned her hands to her side and stopped twirling, then dropped to a crouched position. From the floor, she looked up at the people around her; they were like a vast wall towering over and protecting her while she caught her breath. She grabbed the little tail of her hair and used it to pull herself into a smaller ball—with her knees to her chest, she was calmer under the waves of people. *Much better than at the surface*, another thought escaped.

In her hovel, Lee checked her pulse, and began to bounce in place; the motion felt great on her legs. She checked her watch. It was only 11:30. She began to interrogate herself and checked her wrists and arms for markings. "When did I take my last hit?" she asked the legs of the strangers around her. On the underside of her left arm, she found *10:45* scribbled almost illegibly. On the underside of her right arm were three tallies, one for each drink she had had. Lee looked back at her watch to verify the time.

"I'm still not peaking," she whispered to herself. The realization was more calming than anything else she had experienced so far this evening. "You know what's coming next," she began to repeat to herself in a whisper; each was a little prayer, and she breathed deeper with each one. Her body loosened and adapted. Lee was used to these panic attacks; they came frequently and often. She thus knew how to stop them, but it was their explosive and sudden nature that made it hard for her to remain rational and in control of herself at all moments. It always took her a minute to regain her bearings, but among the legs Lee no longer felt alone— these were all her friends. A weight was suddenly lifted off her chest and her energy began to return. "This is why I come here," she mouthed to herself. Her body was too excited to produce a voice. "I love it here," she mouthed again. "They all love me…and…I love them. What else could I possibly need?"

Lee smiled as tears began to build in her eyes. She stared into the crowd, and even though they were all cast in shadow she could see so many beautiful people. So many different young, happy, beautiful, and bright people. She could not make out faces of anyone, but she could feel their beauty welling up her heart. Finally, Lee stood up and stared at the lights above the stage—she was about to start tripping, and at least she knew what she was in store for. She smiled as she began to move her body in an exaggerated circular motion. Her fingers once again made their way through her hair, and a tingle once again shot through her body. Her mind and her body were lost in the music—her contentment was back. The lights of the room shifted to a deep and soothing pink. Lee could feel the gentle stroke of the pink lights as they shifted and moved over her. She instinctually followed it, flowing left and right in the crowd with its dance. The music continued to be pulsated by words of love and affirmation in a soothing male voice: *"You're my best friend, the only friend I need."*

The shapes and tastes of the lights above her distracted Lee for hours. It wasn't a change in music that startled her mind into consciousness but a sudden drop in joy. She was finally beginning to come down. The effects of her earlier dose did not last nearly as long as they should have, as long as she had hoped—her tolerance was exceedingly high. Lee's head became foggy and all at once she felt sick, nauseous, and weak. She pushed away the dancers around her and created a small circle around herself. The cool air rushed to fill the void, and it chilled her body, which was beginning to be on fire. Now, the cool air felt like frostbite on her skin, in the best way possible. She was dehydrated and she gasped at the air, though her sore throat ached. "I have never been so thirsty…in my entire life," Lee forced out before chuckling to herself. As quickly as the discomfort came, it was gone, and Lee could no longer feel her throat.

Lee stared at the crowd as the entire room swayed and breathed—like an organism she was living within. She stopped dancing and merely stared at the lights of the stage. The DJs had changed, and she did not know who these new ones were. Her nirvana was ruined as her drugs started to wear off and as she came down, her mellowness was harassed by the aggressive duo of voices she had heard before. Now her body was not as numb, and this time she felt their words inside her. *"I can't even look at you,"* bellowed the man while the woman sang *"should have left you in the trash."* Lee's gaze began to drop, and below the stage she again saw a square figure; it was the only thing in her vision not swaying. As the lights danced throughout the room, they gave him an iridescent face, one that swapped between man and goblin. His high cheekbones were complemented by a large and intimidating smile. His eyes pierced through the crowd. The face was one she felt she recognized but…she didn't want to think about it. She wouldn't put in the mental effort. She was growing increasingly distracted by the words that continued to pour through the room. *"You're too stupid to know what you don't know,"* screeched the woman, while the man followed with *"if you didn't come with a check."*

"What? What a weird line," Lee whispered to herself. Her words were lost in the crowd. Her sobering mind recognized something about the voice—about both voices. As the beat pounded, the voices echoed her name. It was the voice of her parents. They were back again.

Their voices carried with them an emotional weight, one that Lee was compelled to silence. She needed to find another hit; the drugs were wearing off and she could feel her spine. She could feel a phantom pain run through her neck and down her back, along an ancient bruise—physical and emotional scars. She was still tripping, and the boxy figure of her father moved his way through the crowd and toward her. She rubbed her head and turned away from him. Her method was to ignore. She started to move out of the crowd, but then she imagined his hand; a claw gripped onto her shoulder and as if he were real, he stopped her motion. Lee stood in fear, refusing to look directly at the tan hand that sat in her peripherals—it shook with the music. *This is exactly what I thought you'd do,"* he whispered in her ear.

"Ignore him," she whispered to herself. As long as he didn't respond, she knew he wasn't real. "I'm just tripping," she began to repeat to herself. The realization grounded her. *Son of a bitch is dead...most likely*, she thought before she choked on the thought of him secretly being out there. Lee gazed out at the back of the club, away from her father and the stage. She closed her eyes, turned, and ran—luckily, she felt no resistance from his claw, only the crowd squirming around her. *Another sign he isn't real.*

She began to push her way through the crowd, but in the distance she saw another familiar figure. Her mother, in her purple and white lapel-neck dress, stood in the crowd with a scowl on her face. Though Lee continued to push toward her, she felt like a child lost and moved on instinct. Her body was shaking, made worse by the still-dancing crowd. As if transported back to her childhood, Lee pushed through the crowd but played with her hair. Her two hands met on the same strand, over her left shoulder. She tightened the piece of hair in her hands, and she pulled tightly on it; then one by one she pulled individual hairs from her scalp. The small feeling of pain distracted her temporarily from her thoughts.

In the distance, she could see the small neon light for the exit sign, an indication of where the restrooms would also be. Lee needed the cool of exiting the crowd, she needed water, she needed to get her mother out of her vision. As she drew closer to all of those things, her body felt much more unsteady as the floor and the room began to breathe. Lee looked down and stumbled as she failed to step firmly—where was she supposed to step? It was still breathing. The breathing contrasted the movement of the music in a way that began to overwhelm her. She felt as if she was in between two worlds. Lee turned her body away from the figure of her mother and anxiously turned toward the stage. Her desperate glances scanned for the square figure, but he was nowhere to be found. *He's not real*, she reassured herself again.

Lee's panic was broken by the sudden warm feeling of fingernails across her arms. From behind her and out of the darkness, long, yellow, neon nails found their way up Lee's arms and onto her shoulders. The nails dragged across and down her back. Her body was still hypersensitive, and every touch shot tingles. The touch of her nails awoke Lee's body; it began to pulsate with the music again. As the nails made their way up her back, and onto her head, Lee's body began to quiver. She purred to herself and leaned into the sensation; she then fell back into her petter.

Her head fell gently against a soft chest, and above her Lee could feel the chin of someone smiling. A gentle female voice whispered, "You okay, beautiful? You look lost." From the side a water bottle appeared, and like someone lost in the desert Lee seized it and began to chug. Lee rocked side to side in rhythm with the nails like a cat against a leg. Then she turned to see her admirer for the first time, her eyes meeting the chest of the woman behind her. She gazed up and could see that the bright yellow nails were complemented by bright yellow lipstick. In the flash of the darkness, Lee could not make out the woman's face; only her plump and delicious lips were visible. Her name was Feenie, which Lee should have known.

As the woman continued to stroke her arms, Lee's eyes were drawn to her mouth, with lips perked up into a smile. "Hi," Feenie said as she leaned in for a kiss. Lee's eyes were transfixed on the lips as they approached her. Her mind raced with excitement as she wondered what the yellow lipstick would taste like. The admirer's lips soft but full. The kiss, passionate but gentle. The last thing Lee noticed before she closed her eyes was the matching bright yellow eyeshadow. As their lips came together so did their tongues, and Lee could feel the tingle of the mint in the woman's gum. As they kissed, their tongues fought over the piece of gum, a little game. The two passed it back and forth before it settled in Lee's mouth. Lee lifted her arms and placed one on the woman's waist and the other on her face. Then Lee slowly ran her fingers along her admirer's jawline. She bit onto the woman's lip, pulled back, and sensually released it. Lee continued to chew the gum and a large smile graced her face—hidden by the darkness of the pit. "I need a hit—you partying?" whispered Lee smoothly, though she was panicking on the inside.

Lee reached back up to grab the woman's face, loudly smacking her gum as she went onto the tips of her toes to get closer to those lips. The woman grabbed Lee's wrists, putting them down by her side, and leaned back in. She whispered into Lee's ear, "Of course," while turning away. She held out one of her hands and pulled Lee back out from the crowd with a gentle tug. The woman looked back on occasion, her lipstick was still the only clear feature and it was always smiling back. The two squirmed their way through the sea of concertgoers, and though Lee could still see her mother in the distance, she pressed on.

The woman led Lee out of the crowd and down a short hallway where the two moved swiftly past a smoking room on the left. Smoking was an especially high-risk activity when one could live forever. Lee wondered why people would do such a thing to their body, destroying it with the risk of cancer. The hallway smelled of smoke as they moved toward the bathroom, and near the exit door stood another woman smoking a small cigar. Her cloud drifted into the hallway in the cold breeze. As Lee passed her, she pretended to cough before she was pulled into the bathroom.

As if staring into the sun, the harsh lights of the bathroom began to burn into Lee's eyes, and with it came an unsteadiness in her legs. The two made their way to the sink where Lee immediately leaned forward and dug her fingers into the cheap countertop. She swayed gently back and forth to brace herself, but after a moment the lights were too bright for her. She closed her eyes and continued to rock back and forth. Behind her, Feenie played with her hair and ran her fingers down her arms. "You okay there, darling?" she whispered into Lee's ear. The gentle wind tickled her earlobe, and as she twitched, she leaned forward. Lee leaned her face into the sink and turned on the automatic faucet. Without hesitation Lee placed her face under the stream and began to chug again—the water splashed onto the already wet counter. After an extremely long thirty seconds, Lee emerged from the sickness and rubbed the excess water off her mouth with her forearm. Slowly, she felt a little better and was able to stand.

Lee checked out herself in the mirror as Feenie stood behind and continued to run her fingers up and down Lee's body. Then she started kissing her neck. Finally, rehydrated and in the bright lights of the bathroom Lee could see Feenie's face. She was beautiful…but of course she was: She like everyone else was timelessly stuck at twenty-five. Her dress was yellow like her eyeshadow and nails, but it failed to glow with the same intensity. Her long brown hair fell down her back, reaching to the bottom crux. It was complemented by her light brown skin and beautiful brown eyes. Though Lee did not recognize her, this was not the first time that she and Feenie had met—in fact, it was not the first time they had kissed.

Lee had no way of knowing Feenie's true age, her true skin, face, or voice—she only knew the beautiful front that Feenie, like everyone, put on at the club. "Arrive beautiful, leave ugly" was a common slogan in New Dionysus. Like Lee, Feenie could be one of the elders. Those who were adults prior to the invention of Rejuverron. Those who were frozen in middle age, forced to watch others live life in their prime forever. Lee's addiction to Rejuverron was exacerbated by her aged body; she was not as naturally energetic as all her friends. By taking extra, however, her cells could be revitalized. The energy and rush of which was a feeling no other drug could replicate. It was a feeling that those who were lucky enough to be frozen at twenty-five would never been able to feel. In that way Lee was lucky. She lived for that feeling, for the beauty it made her see, and the beauty she felt in herself.

Feenie stopped kissing her and started to play with Lee's hair. "Now doesn't that feel better?" Lee ran her hands over her eyes and applied some pressure. She felt a pulsating within her body; it was actually kind of nice. Lee turned to face Feenie's chest once again and attempted to use her arms to climb onto the counter but struggled. After a moment of flailing, Feenie grabbed Lee's waist and lifted her onto the counter. Though her ass was placed promptly onto a wet spot of unknown origins, she was comfortable. This was a place and situation she had been joyfully in many times before.

Unfortunately, the rush of being picked up sent a flash into Lee's head, and she began to pass out, then she slipped backward into the mirror. With a loud thud, she bounced off the wall and awoke. "Hey, sweetie…are you okay?" Feenie repeated, more concerned but still with a smile on her face. She grabbed Lee by the head and rubbed the back of her skull. "You don't seem to be bleeding, but you almost broke the mirror. You cute psycho." Through her haze Lee smiled…*cute but psycho*. It was not the first time she had been called that, but it always felt great to be reminded she was beautiful.

Lee continued to smile but kept her eyes closed. She hoped a few minutes of darkness would help her to readjust. She sat vibing to the music and swayed side to side out of beat. Feenie watched Lee with her arms firmly placed on her sides, ready to grab her if she were to fall in a more dangerous direction. With a drunken grace, Lee ran her arms slowly across her waist and searched for her bag. Along her back she found the fanny pack, rotated it to the front, and started to play with the zippers. In the front pocket she jostled with the contents but failed to find what she was looking for. She grew frustrated after only a few moments and opened her eyes. With a panicked haste, she began to take out the contents—lipstick, an expired crushed granola bar, and a squished and empty water bottle were all she found.

She quickly leaned forward to get a better view and, in her momentum, lost coordination. She gently fell into Feenie's chest; had she not been there, Lee would have face-planted onto the ground. The only thing in the front pocket were a few empty prescription vials with various names along the side—a hundred pills, a hundred refills, Rejuverron. Rejuverron was free to everyone, and it was found to be much easier to give everyone large samples than it was to police its use. Feenie's soothing tone vibrated through Lee's skull and sent tingles through her body. "Hey, what about here?"

Feenie tilted the fanny pack to expose a second set of zippers in the back. Lee smiled at the realization and looked up at Feenie through squinted eyes. Then Lee searched through the new pocket and found what she was looking for, a small brown vial. What Lee had was concentrated Rejuverron, a street variant that was condensed powder, a hundred times the strength. When partying, Lee found it wasn't worth it to waste time on the weak stuff. She was never going for that type of high.

"Oh, you have some good stuff…that looks fancy. What is it?" Feenie asked slowly but excitedly. "I'll trade you," she offered. Feenie reached into her waistband and pulled out a small goodie bag of her own; the refurbished coin purse's psychedelic colors matched Lee's nails and Feenie's outfit. As Lee tried to open her vial, she lost her balance and gently fell backward in her joy. She sat smiling with her head against the mirror behind her, finally opened the jar, and slowly tilted its contents onto the counter; only a few tiny caramel-colored crystals came out. Lee's smile faded and her eyes bulged at the realization that she was out of drugs. She limply used her pinky to crush the few small crystals and they stuck to her finger. She raised her hand to her nose and inhaled it all as one hit.

"Aren't we the selfish brat, huh?" Feenie joked. "You didn't want to share with me? *Fine*." she smiled. "I've got mine right here." From her bag, Feenie pulled out a set of white baggies and laid them out on the counter beside Lee. From one baggie, she dipped her long nail in and raised it to her nose, a small hit. Feenie then pressed her fingers into a small amount of powder remaining on the table and rubbed it onto her chest and pulled Lee's face into her cleavage. Instinctually, Lee began to lick the Rejuverron off her and bury her face into her breasts. Her tongue traveled the length of her body, following each curve until she reached the woman's collarbone, where she bit. Lee looked up at her and the two leaned in for another kiss.

Feenie let out a deep and pleased groan as a jolt of joy shot down from her brain and into her back and continued to her feet. It then returned in a second jolt, and she wiggled, reached back down to kiss Lee again. She moved her lips onto Lee's neck, rubbed her tongue along it, and started to give her a hickey. For Lee, the drugs had done nothing to elevate her mood, her tolerance far too high for the small amount she licked off Feenie. Lee began to drift off and leaned her head back. As Feenie kissed her, Lee stared into the mirror behind her. Her vision was hazy, but she could see the reflection of her father standing in the doorway. Her mind wandered as she started to argue with him in her mind.

Feenie could see the disconnect in Lee's body; she was a million miles away. Feenie tapped one of the bags on the table with her finger and opened it. She placed her finger into the bag and then began to rub it on her gums. "Looks like you could use a little pick-me-up." She then offered the packet to Lee with one hand and used the other to stabilize her. Lee dipped her finger into the bag and scooped up as much as she could get. She then brought it to her nose and snorted as much as she could; the rest went into her mouth. "Oh, holy shit," Feenie said as she pulled the bag away from Lee. "Babygurl, that's way too much. Here, you're gonna need some more water." She took a deep breath. "A lot of water."

Feenie pulled Lee off the counter and propped her up in front of the sink and turned on the faucet. Lee leaned heavily into the counter to support her weight and began to chug, that was thrice this evening. As the water splashed haphazardly in her face she began to laugh incoherently. To test her stability, Feenie let go of her and as she did, Lee felt all the warmth leave her body. Her soul was stealing heat from Feenie, and it was the only thing keeping her distracted. Feenie moved to the side and began to clean up her cornucopia of drugs—with a little snort of molly here and a little more coke on her gums.

With a chill running over her body and the cold of the water running down her throat, Lee felt like a corpse. For a moment she couldn't feel a thing and she was happy, but her tranquility disappeared as quickly as it started. From the hallway, she could hear a set of footsteps coming into the bathroom. The heavy-heeled shoe and stomping of her mother's walk echoed throughout the room. The noise was all too familiar to Lee, who slowly raised her eyes and looked into the mirror again. At the door now stood both of her parents' familiar figures, their eyes fixated on her. As she stared back, her mother made her way into the room, her form flickered in and out as she approached. Lee pulled her head from under the sink but managed to hit it on the top of the faucet with a loud thud.

The noise caught the attention of Feenie, who grabbed Lee as she began to crumble to the ground. Feenie let her down gently, and as she helped her to the ground Lee's hand slid across the countertop. She grabbed a mystery baggie off the counter and held it lightly in her clammy hands. Lee continued to stare absentmindedly into the distance at something past her. Feenie turned her head to look but saw nothing. "Perhaps we'll have to lay you down. Can you sit against the wall?" Feenie inquired. "You okay?" She continued to question her, but Lee only stared into the distance. Feenie got up and filled her hands with some water and splashed it onto Lee's face, but that didn't change a thing.

Over Feenie's shoulder, Lee's father stood with his hand out. His giant frame cast a shadow over the pair, and Lee's body grew colder. She opened the small bag she had stolen and threw back all that she could mouth. As she tried to gum the mystery powder down her dry throat, it snowed out of her mouth and onto her body. "What the fuck?!" Feenie shouted as she swiped back the baggie. "Wait, that's mine. How dare you? Wait, what?" Feenie leaned Lee forward and began to bang on her back. "You gotta spit up some of that. I have no idea what you just did to yourself. Do I need to call a doctor?" she asked all too calmly, as if she had said it before.

Lee smiled and started to fully lose control of her body. The image of her father began to vanish, and the stern tapping of her mother's foot was completely drowned out by the music. Once again, a beautiful voice came through the speakers, and she could hear it echoing in the bathroom. *"Welcome back, my love."* Lee smiled as she swayed side to side against Feenie's attempts to stabilize her.

Lee then finally spoke. "Oh, I do, and it's wonderful, Tina." Lee's body became limp, and she fell to the side.

Feenie began to tap Lee on the face in an attempt to wake her up. "Tina? I know you're fucked up, but do you not know who I am?"

"Yeah, duh." Lee squinted but was unable to see anything.

"What's my name?" Lee hesitated, unable to remember the name she had already said. "Autumn, duh." She smiled and let her body hit the floor. The cold ground was warm compared to her corpse—soothing. The music continued to wash over her.

"How do you not know who I am, Lee? You're scaring me. Are you that fucked up?" Feenie's playful tone was replaced with an upset and angry one. "How many times, Lee? And you don't even recognize me? You need help, my love. You're just wasting both our time."

Without acknowledging Feenie, Lee talked to herself. "No, I actually don't feel good." Her heart was beating out of her throat, and suddenly she felt overwhelmingly sick to her stomach. Somehow, she hadn't felt sick until she was asked. Lee used her little strength to push off Feenie. Feenie watched as Lee attempted to weakly crawl to the stall—she headed in the general direction more than to a particular one. As one last act of friendship, Feenie lifted Lee by her armpits and pulled her to an empty stall, using her hip to throw open the door.

Feenie left Lee lying on the ground, where Lee's arm searched for the cold porcelain in front of her. Like a baby cuddling into their mother, Lee dragged herself toward the dirty toilet and raised her head into the hole. The smell of it rose into her nose and removed any doubt that she was going to throw up. Lee began to vomit violently. She used one arm to brace herself on the toilet while she reached out to the door behind in a weak attempt to close it. She paid no mind to Feenie. As the door slowly shut behind her, Feenie gathered her things and left the bathroom in a huff. Though her heart was still erratically pumping in her chest, Lee passed out.

Lee awoke disoriented. The smell of vomit wafted from below, and she realized her head was still sitting in the toilet; the rim choked her neckline. The bliss of sleep subsided after only a second before her she felt a shock of sickness shoot through her body with a violent pulse. Now that it was awake her stomach was angry again, and she started to vomit once more. A fleeting thought came across her mind: At least she had snorted some of her drugs; she wouldn't be throwing them all up. The music still pounded from the other room—no energy was lost. Lee attempted to gauge her body but didn't know if she was still on her way up or finally on her way down. "Did I sleep through the high?" she worried. The return of the pair of voices alerted her that yes, she had.

From above, her parents watched over the stall walls as she vomited. Each one took a side, and peered down; their bloodshot eyes and noses were all that were visible. She was in too much pain to move and had to listen to their commentary as she threw up. *"Getting all dolled up, just to end up in a toilet stall,"* her mother sang.

"I didn't raise my daughter to be so weak," her father continued. *"Pfft. She can barely crawl."*

With her little remaining strength, Lee placed her hands on the toilet and used it to prop herself up. She sat on the edge and noticed some vomit had dribbled down her shirt and stained her pants. Lee then placed her arms wide and used the two walls of the stall to lift herself up. Her legs were shaky as she worked to regain balance, and her vision was still not completely clear. She leaned against the stall, grabbed the handle, and with the weight of her body falling back, opened it. Just like before she found the bathroom was empty, not a single soul besides her and her parents. Feenie was nowhere to be found. Lee returned to survival mode; she wobbled her way to the sink and struggled to turn on the water.

She waved her hands franticly under the faucet, but it elicited no response. She began to angrily bang on each part of the sink, growing more feral with every tap. As the water finally ran, she reached over to the towels and damped one. She then applied some soap and began to clean her chest and the stained part of her pants. Behind her, the image of her parents still stood in the stalls, one peaked from the top and the other below. Lee knew they were smiling something sinister behind the door. She reached into her fanny pack for her drugs. In her panic she was unsure of where she was in her drug cycle. She then remembered she was out.

A new worry came across her mind: She had to get out of that room. The isolation was killing her. The sound of her parents was drowning out the sounds of the club. *"Why was the music so low?"* Lee worried. She slowly wobbled her way out of the bathroom using the walls to hold herself up. She found her way to the same smoke-filled hallway she had left earlier. The darkness of the club overtook her—compared to the bright lights of the bathroom, she was in an abyss. The wall became important not just for her stability but for guidance. The hallway was significantly longer this time and Lee moved blindly through the darkness. A thick smell of smoke sickened her stomach again.

The stability of the wall gave way and Lee felt herself falling. Her motion was stopped and as Lee's eyes adjusted, she realized she was moving through the crowd again. As she flowed passively through it like a zombie, her eyes scanned through the motions of the dancers. She had to find someone who looked like they were taking the drugs she wanted. She was scanning the shadows for the body movements of someone in the state she wanted to be in. Lee had learned the tell-tale signs of those who *partied* and didn't; as they swayed, she could notice many things in their subtle movements.

"No, not that one…not coke…no extra energy…no, not that one." She continued to scan while grinding her teeth. "No, not that one…moving slow and asleep." She used her hands to push through the people around her. Lee was unable to tell anyone apart. Their faces were all shrouded, but demonic grins flashed across their faces with the movement of the strobe lights. She spun, looking for the exit sign, but only found larger and larger crowds of people. She pushed through them, but failed to see any direction that was not a black sea of bodies. The pace of the strobe picked up and the faces that flashed around her began to turn into her parents—a sea of disapproving faces glared at her. Lee checked her watch. 12:30. *Wait, no? What?* She was confused. *It has to be later than this.* She had taken so much… The lights flashed, now more on than off, and the room started to spin. The volume of the music increased, and it began to scream. She covered her ears and dropped to the ground.

Lee found herself back in the bathroom, still lying on the floor, now unable to move. As her tripping mind attempted to venture into the hallway once again, her body kept her in place. From the corner of her eye, she could see her watch: 2:30. It taunted her. She was going to be tripping for a long time. One worry went through her mind as her eyes were filled with light, and the bass started to beat within her chest. *I need to find some more drugs* is all she could still think.

Lee began to lose consciousness again but this time as she did, she saw people rushing into the room. She watched from above as her body was lifted out of the bathroom by some EMTs and her motionless body was dragged through the crowd. Around her, everyone continued to cheer and dance. As her body was wheeled from the club, the music didn't stop. From the crowd she could hear voices. "HELL YEAH! GO GIRL!!! I WANNA PARTY WITH HER. WHAT A LEGEND." She could see that the cheering crowd and their faces were still monstrous forms of her parents.

In the doorway of the club stood Feenie, who pointed to Lee with a concerned gesture. She attempted to shake the gurney and scream, but nothing came out. The medics asked her, "Are you okay?" as they put her in the ambulance, but still, she could not speak. She pleaded desperately with her body and tried to tell them of her dislike for needles, but nothing—her body wouldn't respond either. They attached wires and an IV to her in the ambulance as she tried to thrash. She knew her high would end even faster now. She begged her body to rip off her tubes, but she was helpless. The ambulance pulled away from the club and was somehow immediately on the horizon. Lee could see the lights of the city bathing the mountains around it. The clubs and casinos were still going strong.

The next thing Lee knew, she awoke in a hospital bed. Her arms were still filled with tubes, the sight of which sent a chill down her spine. Lee's eyes jotted throughout the room. Still, the first thing that came to mind was the throbbing pain in her head. It was the feeling of withdrawal she hadn't felt in months, and with an intensity she hadn't felt ever. The process of taking Rejuverron was swell and beautiful, but like all drugs the withdrawal was terrible. Lee winced from the pain and lay heavily in the bed. The sensation gave way to body aches, and then she became extremely aware of the sound of the lights. The fluorescent lights, even brighter than the bathroom, were screeching with electricity and she could hear every volt. Then she held her hand up to her head, covered her eyes, and applied pressure to her face. Lee looked at her arms and saw that the wrinkles had returned. The sight was even more alarming than the tubes in her arms. In a panic, Lee attempted to pull out her tubing, and this time her body responded, but as she did an alarm went off. She was pumping her muscles as hard as she could, but they moved slowly.

In a rush, a nurse made his way into the room, shouting "hey hey hey hey hey" in a deep and calming voice. His scrubs were light blue and covered in yellow rubber duckies. His face was kept in a tightly trimmed beard, and his eyes were a bright blue made to pop by the design on his clothes. When he grabbed her arm, Lee could see how much more wrinkled her skin was compared to his and she recoiled from the realization.

"I need my medicine…please, I feel terrible." Lee's voice dropped in shame. "I look terrible." Her body had aged back to her fifty-five-year-old self, but the wrinkles were much deeper and her face more haggard than she remembered—it was older and worse than it had been.

"Lee, is it?" The nurse paused. "We were given a name, but we weren't sure if it was real. You have been asleep for a few days. Unfortunately, from what I've been told, you mostly look your age. Well, that and some time." His tone was gentle enough that Lee found it hard to hear him over a loud buzzing in her ear, but brash enough that she knew he was scolding her. "How do you feel?"

"Like shit." Her voice was exasperated and frustrated. "Why does my body hurt so bad?"

"Well, I assume you know it's because you are withdrawing from Rejuverron. Have you not had this feeling before? How long have you been taking this much?" Lee's gaze became a glare. When she realized the face she was making, she turned her head to the side. She didn't answer the question. "Much like a wizard, you're having to grow bone…new old bone. As the extra DNA degrades, your body begins to catch on fire, burning as you return to size. You also have to shed all that extra DNA, and so it has given you extensive nitrogen poisoning in your blood. That's part of why you're especially loopy. Unfortunately, due to your tox-screen, you can't be given any pain relievers." He paused one more time. "So, I think you're all caught up."

The music in Lee's head was gone, and its absence left a deafening silence in her mind. Between the pulses of pain, she was forced to face her own voice—it spoke over all the ringing of her dying ear hairs. "Where are my things? Let me out."

"Not a good idea. I don't think you realize how much you damaged your body. You should rest. Your kidneys and liver have been processing a lot, for seemingly a long time. I'm surprised they work at all. You're lucky. Even at base, you're extremely dehydrated and hurt." Lee began to shift in bed, but she found that her legs were not moving very well. Embarrassed and angry Lee began to get up, but as she tried to step out of the bed, her legs crumbled. The nurse grabbed her and held her up. "We can't help you if you won't let us help you. I think you have a problem. Are you leaving just to get high again?"

"You underestimate my ability to process toxins" was the only thing Lee could think to say. That and "Where are my things?"

"You don't have anything. Only some clothes and an empty fanny pack. They are cleaned and in the bag on the chair next to you." He helped her to sit on the bed. "You've gotten up in a haze a few times. Calling out random names… Is there someone you can go talk to? Someone for us to call?"

Lee grabbed her hair and began to play with it again—an emotionally regressive move. The gravity of her situation had settled in. "I need my Rejuverron, my medicine. I need it, to make them go away." She spoke without thinking about her present company. Then Lee looked around the room and realized she couldn't see her parents. It was only the whisper of their voices in the back of her head at the moment. It seemed she was embarrassed enough for herself—she didn't need them to pile on.

"There's no one here," said the nurse gently, but Lee went back to not responding. The nurse's voice became comforting and supportive in a way he hadn't been yet. He took a deep breath and sighed. "I know I don't know you, but I'm going to take a shot at this… I think we create ghosts in our mind. It's astonishing the way certain people live on as a voice in your head. For better or worse, their soul impacts yours so heavily that you adapt their voice and their physical being into every line your mind delivers. These voices play strongly, like mini-movies, clips in your mind; some of them long enough to stun you. Some souls become a part of you; you talk to them instead of talking to yourself. Our brains have evolved to keep us alive, not happy." Unfortunately for most, and Lee was no exception, the voices that stuck best were the negative ones. For Lee, with age, the voices had only gotten louder. He continued while she sat in silence. "Those people become the voice of your own insecurities; your fears manifested in a cycle of internalized verbal assaults. Everyone's family has tragedy and secrets. The hope is to get to a point where the history of it no longer negatively impacts your life. There are some voices we cannot silence but it doesn't mean we have to listen to them. There are voices that become novels, become law, become religion."

Though his words had struck her, she responded coldly. Lee just needed to be alone, but she still couldn't move. "I'll simply leave when my legs are feeling better. Thank you very much." She began to tuck herself into the bed, refusing help from the nurse. "I appreciate the concern, but I can take care of myself," she stubbornly protested.

"If you keep being awake…you should be able to leave in the next few days. The PT nurse can come in and help work on your legs if you'd like," the nurse said as he left. He shook his head and walked out of the room. On his way down the hallway, he alerted the security guard to watch her.

A few days passed and the hospital bracelet was no longer on her wrist, but there was a scar from the constant rubbing against her frail skin that was still sore. Her body still ached from withdrawal, but the burning in her blood had subsided. Lee could no longer take Rejuverron at a normal dose; the amount left her sick to her stomach—which was one way to curb her addiction. For the time they prescribed her mini pills, an attempt to keep her from continuing to age dramatically. She'd need forty years of prescriptions at this rate to feel anything. She had tried to relapse already, but her body was too weak, making her sick and vomiting up the little she had. She knew she would be stuck like this for a while.

Without anywhere left to go, Lee was forced to live in a shelter. The weather had turned too cold to live outside, and she was too sick to return to New Dionysus. She just needed a warm place to sleep. At the shelter she refused to communicate with anyone she was not forced to. Their group therapy sessions were always open but with an empty chair where she should be.

Lee stuck to taking short walks around the block, trying to clear her lungs and her head. She felt an itch in the back of her mind; to do something that would take a great deal of courage.

Early on October 3, Lee made her way from her shelter and returned to her old home, but only for a moment. She was wearing a winter coat and some spare clothes she had gotten at the shelter's lost and found. She made her way toward the building, which hadn't changed in eighty years. While it stood timeless, she was a relic of her own creation. She could have been decently young forever, but now her body was failing and weak. The voices told her that anyway. Going straight to the door was too forward; there was too much pressure. The driveway was daunting, and the two small steps seemed like mountains. Instead, Lee took to the side of the house and looked through her old windows to see what she was in store for. Her anxiety caused her heart to race, though she appeared stoic and calm—a party power.

She peered in; the kitchen was empty but past it she could see deeper into the house, to the living room. Its lights were low, and a few small candles burned on surfaces throughout it. She saw her daughter, Autumn, sitting in her husband's favorite chair. She could not see what Autumn was doing, but she knew what it meant. The kitchen table was clean, no random scattered papers. On the fireplace she could see a photo of her, her daughter, and Marshall—as if a shrine. Lee began to cry; she knew that Marshall had died, and to Autumn, now they were both gone. There's no way he wouldn't still be in that chair. Lee couldn't feel him there, and she couldn't hear his voice.

Lee came back around the house, toward the front door. Her heart pounded and her cheeks became flush. She wasn't making any noise, but she was crying. Her husband had been gone in bits and pieces for a long time, but now he was completely gone. A voice in her head bullied her for Autumn's smile. Lee hoped it wasn't a rare occurrence…but she couldn't help but hope that her daughter missed her from time to time, not that she deserved it. She looked at the door and she thought of what to do.

Lee took her pulse and breathed deeply, while pacing back and forth. *No*, she thought. She wasn't ready. She wasn't prepared to be there for Autumn—she wasn't even there for herself. She couldn't handle being a burden to a daughter who owed her nothing. Lee placed her hands into her pockets and gripped her coat tightly. It didn't feel right, she was sorry, but she couldn't return to that house. *She couldn't return to the house.* She wasn't strong enough. Lee made her way to the street corner where she found a bus and rode it for five hours to the outskirts of the city.

Lee exited the bus at a lonely corner—the single-lane cement road was surrounded by open, flat land on one side and a mountain on the other. A single gated arch extended with a decorative wall on each side for merely ten feet. A large metal plaque was built into the wall—on its face was carved a welcome and a goodbye in nearly five hundred languages. Its metal was mostly bronze, but brighter touches of silver were shown where it had been adjusted or added to. Another blank plaque sat on the other side anxiously waiting to be written on next. As Lee passed through the gate, she could see the massive set of stairs that etched their way through the mountain. The face acted as a staircase extending to many paved and flattened pieces of earth. Among the wall and open fields were scattered obelisks, mausoleums, graves, and occasionally trees. The largest stood at the top, forever casting a shadow on everyone who came to pay their respects.

The cities were too dense and filled with people for graveyards, so except for some families who had their own small personal shrines everyone was buried there. The infrequency of death left each grave exceptionally from one another; bodies were buried and scattered more like a statue garden than a cemetery. For hours Lee made her way across open space. She wound up and down the mountain, taking a leisurely walk through its many floors. She had nowhere to be.

Even when the sun set, Lee continued to walk through the graveyard. When she grew tired, she rested her head against a large tree in some place she didn't know. When she was hungry, she ate a small bag of powerballs she had made; a simple mixture of bread and vitamins that kept you going, barely. She wandered until the next morning, when she eventually stood above Marshall's grave; she knew from its plain-colored but overly dramatic design it was his, even before she saw the sign. Beside it stood a large tree, providing shade and fruit to those below—peaches. Lee stood in silence with her eyes fixated on the obelisk. This is where he was. If she didn't hear his voice here, where else could she? Lee began to think out loud, to talk to herself. She had so much time to get to this moment, but now that it was here, she wasn't sure what to say.

"You've gotten so big…so fancy." Lee sucked in some snot that began to fall down her face. "You were always so subtle. How did this become your tomb? I mean, it is you…the persona you…the most dramatic you. But you were always subtle and witty. It feels weird to talk to you this way." Lee picked at her sleeves and pockets as she talked. Then she noticed a small glimmer below the tree. She walked over to see a small plaque in the ground, shaded by the tree as if it were sleeping. The small bronze design simply read:

Marshall Oswalt

Beloved Father, Cartoonist, and Friend

"This seems a lot more like you," she said to herself and sat down in front of the tree and grave. They were like two toddlers at their first play date. "You're in a good section. You have some real famous dead people for neighbors… I know you're not really here, but…this feels good. As good as I think it could ever feel… I feel…like we can talk again. I never got to say so much to you. I don't even know when you forgot I was there, but I'm sorry I left you."

Lee began to rub snot from her face, and tears started to form in her eyes. "I loved you too much to be able to watch you be gone. To know you weren't really there. It was so lonely. Without you the voices came back, and I couldn't take that. Not being able to talk to my best friend drove me crazy, and then I got *even* crazier. I took Rejuverron and it was like I was a teenager again, rebelling against everything that attempted to oppress me. And there you weren't. No one to talk me off the edge. No one to stop me from being mad and listening to their voices. I know they were terrible and mean…and their thoughts mean nothing, but I just can't stop from hearing them." Lee got more comfortable and began to lower herself to her belly.

"You were the one I couldn't think of myself living without… Our daughter seems to be doing great. She was smiling and looked healthy, but before you ask. No, I haven't seen her. I couldn't return to that house without you. I was never a good mother; I never wanted it. I held onto her as a little piece of you, but as you left I saw how truly different she was from you. Well…I wanted your child, I wanted more of you, but I learned that the fantasy of children is different than reality. When I saw how poor of a mother I was without you and how good she was with you…I snapped. I couldn't get myself to take care of you, because for me you weren't there, because I couldn't get what I needed from you. I lost my patience, and my heart was on fire, but I knew it was selfish. I started to take drugs, and it only seemed to make the voices worse…but sometimes it made me hear your voice again and I lived for that. Then I took it out on Autumn. I abandoned you. I put all the weight of your decline on her. I can't show myself to her. I'm sure she is at peace thinking I'm dead. I wouldn't take that away from her."

Lee crawled her body toward the gravestone and placed her head on the cool metal. She felt like they were cheek to cheek.

"I loved her…I *love* her…but I never really felt connected to her. It's so fucked up to say…not feeling like your child is the greatest thing in the world. Well, she was, but my heart wasn't in it. I could see it, but I couldn't feel it… It made me feel even worse. Why am I so broken? Why am I so dependent on you to tell me I deserve better and to be happy. That *I am* happy. Maybe…because you were so good at it, I never had to learn to fend for myself. But again…my fault, not yours. I became just like my mom, just like my dad…. Even with you, I was cold and distant. I couldn't treat you the way you deserved, and I couldn't stop hating myself for it. I tried to live for those moments that you would return, joke, and I could hear that presence in your voice, but they were so short-lived. My soul dropped even lower than it already was. I couldn't get myself to know, to lose hope that you wouldn't just be okay one day. You'd return, for good." Lee was now sitting beside the plaque picking at the grass and breaking it with her hand. Her transition was slow and steady.

"The drugs made me so over-stimulated that I don't need to think. I couldn't and didn't need to feel. I wasn't me and the monster wasn't there. When you first got sick, it made me remember your voice so well. It was like you were with me. Then I couldn't find you at home and I stayed away… I really wish you were here. I know you'd be able to tell me why I'm wrong, but as much as I wish I could remember your voice, every day grows quieter. I know how you made me feel. I know the hole I have in my heart, but I don't remember what I miss exactly.

I only know you brought me calm. I need to find a way to bring that to myself, but that's going to be a long process."

Lee turned toward the plaque as if it was going to respond. "Do you think I could come back every now and then? Talk to you some more? If you can believe it, I really need someone." She laughed while wiping some tears from her eyes. "I haven't allowed myself to make any progress on making friends at the shelter yet. I haven't allowed myself to make progress anywhere really. Therapy, friends, eating, hygiene. I know my party *friends* haven't even noticed I am gone. I'm sure someone else will just take my spot on the couch.

"I don't know why but here is the loudest your voice has been in a long time. This place is surprisingly pleasant. I've had some time walking here that has been really peaceful—I think talking to you, thinking about you, and trying to remember have helped. I've tried to forget, like you, for so long. Why don't we do that with people who are still alive? Hold onto the good things. Why is every interaction in my head so negative? I hate to say death is a strange closure, but it's something I have absolutely no control over. Something I just must accept. It's amazing so many people might never experience this. Why can't I…do this with Autumn? Just accept and talk to her. Why am I so afraid she hates me? Why am I so afraid to take that on?

"I don't know what you'd say at this moment anymore. I'm searching my mind trying to come up with your advice and your words but it's so hard. I search and search but only find the monsters. I know I need to find my own voice; my own control, but it would be so much easier if you were here." Lee stood up and looked across the landscape and saw a nearby grave. She rushed over to it and took one of its plastic decorative flowers. She thanked the grave for its sacrifice and returned to Marshall. "I brought you something. Thank you for your time." She leaned down to place the flowers on the grave and began to cry again.

For the first time while sober, Lee could hear a small glimmer of his voice in her head. She repeated it out loud to herself in a strange and silly voice—one that she used to use to playfully mock him when they were together. "You love her in your own way. You don't need to feel something magical to love and have a good relationship with your daughter. We're all emotionally deficient in some way and we're all learning to understand each other. *You are* a heretic, but well, I don't think your symptoms are extensive enough to need an exorcism…. Also, I love you."

Leona chuckled to herself for the first time in a long time; she let out a heavy laugh, as if her tears were being pushed out. "God, you were such a weenie…in the best way." She laughed a long and slow laugh. It relieved tension in a way she never realized possible. In a way only Marshall could do. She could hear his voice again—only a little, but it seemed to be getting louder.

"I'm going to do something good for myself; I think the hospitals have therapy…. I can stay at the shelter…so, I'm really lucky. Perhaps, I'll join some type of AA group…perhaps. I don't know. Maybe helping someone else… Someone I don't owe so much to will be easier. I could, yeah, I think I could start there. I think I need to do something good now, something not for myself. I need to retrain myself if I want to be happy. I know you used to say stuff like that. That still sits in the back of my mind, but it's silently written on a chalkboard. Eventually, I'll find what I'm meant to do. Then one day, I'll be there for Autumn."

Cyber-Disconnection

Neil stood at the front door, nervously clutching a book and notepad to his chest. He wore a bright yellow t-shirt he had purchased online secondhand; the antique's collar was stretched, and the body had a few small holes scattered across it. It was a rare and limited print run from the cult classic cartoon series *Andy Armadillo*. The creature's large, iconic grin was a bit faded but intact, impressive for its age. The show was Neil's current obsession, having discovered the cartoon on an online forum a few months prior. He loved how the bright and flashy cartoon style was juxtaposed with hard-hitting and often sad emotional beats.

Neil had always found watching cartoons the most calming way for him to digest life. Between lighthearted comedies and the deep action of anime, he could always find an animated story to match his mood or to play in the background. Neil had always had issues understanding how others felt, and he appreciated the exaggerated and clear facial expressions often used on those shows. This social disconnect was one of many reasons that he felt most comfortable alone. It's also why he so proudly worked from home. He simply didn't have the social battery for constant interaction and appreciated a stern separation of work and play. His social anxiety made the combination of the two draining.

At the moment, though, Neil's new hobby had given him an uncharacteristic energy. It was one he only really felt when deeply engrossed in something, usually a hobby but on rare occasions could be work related. This excitement bypassed his anxiousness, and he felt his social battery was charged enough to venture out into the real world. That is what brought him to where he stood now. Neil paused awkwardly at the front door of Marshall's house, catching his breath and hoping to calm himself. He didn't get too many opportunities—or should I say, he didn't give himself many opportunities—to practice speaking to others. Thus, he prepped himself, trying to plan out some of his questions.

"Hello…Hi…Hello…*Hello*, I'm Neil. I am Neil. I *am* Neil." He then gulped in an attempt to slow his rapid speech. "If you had to eat only a single meal forever, could you choose? What is your favorite TV show…besides your own, of course."

By talking to himself, and by having a speech prepared, he made sure he wouldn't go too far off topic. When Neil felt he was ready, he finally knocked on the front door, then stepped back. He provided what he felt was a polite distance between himself and the entrance. His heart raced and he began to sweat a bit more as each second passed. He stood there for what felt like ten minutes. There he stood in silence, hoping he wasn't being ignored. Then he noticed the doorbell.

Ding Dong Ding Dong

He once again stepped back.

"I should have made an appointment. I'm so very foolish. Who am I to drop in unannounced to see Marshall Oswalt?" Neil now felt he needed to do something with his hands and began to flip through the pages of his notepad. Every sheet was covered with notes, questions, and comments. There were even a few extra sheets he had forced into it—it was filled to the brim. He pulled out one such sheet and placed it at the top. On it he had created a small outline of conversation starters.

Icebreakers and Important Questions

1) Hi, I am Neil, pleasure to meet you. How have you been?

2) Ice breaker—choose one: weather (recent humidity), video games, food, classic literature.

3) Do you ever think of reviving the show?

4) How did your trauma lead you to making this show? Did you mean for it to be so adult?

5) Do you have any other passion projects?

6) Do you accept gifts from fans?

After reading the last question, Neil padded his back pocket, making sure he still had the small trinket he had brought as a thank you for Marshall. Then he could hear someone at the front door, the sliding of the lock, and then the opening of the door. Before seeing who it was, he began to introduce himself.

"Hi, I'm Neil," his voice quieted at the end, as he noticed it was not Marshall who opened the door. Before him stood Autumn, wearing a large sunhat, a light green sundress, and gardening gloves.

"Hi Neil, I'm Autumn. What can I do for you?" she said as she took off her gloves. She then offered him a handshake and looked down at his shirt. Autumn knew instantly he was a fan of her father; he was not the first to come and visit. She waited for his response anyway.

"I'm so sorry to intrude. Or disrupt…if you all are busy. I'm so sorry, but I am… I'm here to see Marshall. I was really hoping to speak with him about his work, *Andy Armadillo*. If he's not too busy, that is."

Autumn gave a small smile before frowning. There were many different types of fans who had come to visit her father over her life. Some of them were for his writing, some for his philosophy, but most came out of interest in his cartoon. When she was younger the number of visitors was staggering, but as he stopped working, the amount steadily dropped off. In the last few decades most of them merely wanted to take a picture of their house from the outside or to simply pay their condolences. The lovers of his cartoons were always the most passionate and excited; they matched her father's energy with their enthusiasm and silliness. She had not yet had to inform one of them of her father's passing.

"I'm sorry to info-rm you, Nii-eee-llll. I guess you may have not heard but my father's been dead for quite a while."

After the words came out of her mouth, Neil's ears shut off and suddenly he froze and entered his thoughts. He had not even contemplated the idea that Marshall might not be alive. He tried to think back on everything he had read, to see if he had simply not paid attention. His mind raced defensively, almost as if she was lying to him. His face grew flushed with embarrassment as he pulled out his phone and began to quickly search the web. He ignored Autumn as he began to mutter out loud to himself.

"I'm sorry…I didn't mean to bring up… I mean I hope I haven't. I'm sorry, I guess I didn't realize." Neil then looked up from his phone and muttered something too sincere. "I'm not sure what to say. I honestly don't know anyone who's died… I guess I still don't. Just anyone I cared about. I mean, I didn't really know him. I really wanted to."

Autumn gently interrupted him. "Don't worry, you're not the first visitor to not know," she lied. "My father would have never wanted his death to be a big deal. He was a relatively private man. Sorry to accidentally spring death on you."

"I have known of some friends of associates who have died in accidents. Some people I had played games with. I know it's a thing…just… I apologize and hope it wasn't too rude of me to arrive unannounced." Without making eye contact, Neil then nervously reached into his pocket and presented his small trinket, a small armadillo he had carved out of a small piece of red wood. "This was the last thing on my outline. I was hoping to give this to your father. I made it myself while watching his show. I'm not sure if it would be awkward, but please accept this as a memento to your father. My-my condolences."

Autumn reached out and took the toy, then shifted it around in her hand. "You know, my father would have loved this. He was always the biggest fan of cute things. I bet in the attic we have a whole collection of his old stuff like this." Autumn's frown turned back into a smile, and she looked at the stack of papers Neil held in his hands. "Obviously, I'm not my fath-hhh-eeer but perhaps I could answer a feeee-wwww of your questions about him? Would you like to come in for some coffee or tea? I was about to have a cup before lunch."

Instinctually, Neil gripped his papers close to his chest and responded "No…no…no. I couldn't impose."

"Are yo-oo-u sure?" she asked before letting out a small chuckle. "You seem to have a lot of notes. I don't normally ooo-ff-er, but you could see our living room and su-uuch. I haven't changed much since he died. I'm a person who enjoys consistency."

"Concurred," Neil responded, smiling. Something about the sincerity in Autumn's voice calmed Neil's nervousness and made him feel welcome. He nodded in excitement and began to get slightly nervous about the prospect of actually being able to come inside. He had thought he might be able to talk to Marshall at the door but the idea of getting to see his home was a dream. "I'd love to."

Autumn then led him into the house and quickly off to one side. Neil wasn't sure what to expect. He wasn't sure if Marshall would be one of those creators who surrounded himself with his work, but the entryway was very tame, whites and grays. It was only when they entered the living room that he saw anything unusual. It was like being teleported to a different world with its red couches and rug.

Autumn walked over to the couches with Neil at her heels. She pulled a throw pillow off of it and used it to quickly dust off the surface. "Sorry, I haven't dusted in quite a while. I don't actually use this room much. I usually sit at the dining room table. If you're comfortable here, I'll go get us a drink. Did you decide on what you'd like?"

"I'll have some hot water and lemon/honey, if you have."

After she exited, Autumn continued to talk and now yelled from an adjacent room. "Sure, I'll heat up some water for us and then I'll be happy to answer any questions that you have for my father. Hopefully, I can provide some insight."

Neil sat on the couch and took in his surroundings. "I'm sorry again to intrude," he said, far too softly for Autumn to hear. He then cleared his throat and yelled a bit louder. "Again, I'm sorry and I'm new to death so I'm not sure what to say, but we don't have to talk about your father if you don't want. I'm just happy to be able to see your home."

"No worries," she yelled. "Just a few minutes on the hot water. Truly, I love to talk about my father, but I don't get the opportunity much." After a bit, Autumn returned with two small cups on saucers; each was decorated with a small packet of honey and a slice of lemon. She handed one to Neil and made her way to the second couch.

"I'm surprised to see that your home is so tame, well except this room. Is the rest of the house so colorful? I would have thought your house would be more vibrant from the little I know of your father's work."

"He was actually a rather dry man. His jokes were always subtle and silly. He would buy new salt and pepper shakers and draw faces on them, then hide the old ones with a ransom note. You know, that type of stuff. This living room was some of my mother's design. She was more flamboyant and direct."

"Has your mother passed away as well? Or will she be coming home sometime?"

"I can answer both questions with a heavy 'I don't know.' She has been missing for even longer than my father has been gone."

"Missing? As in taken?"

"Nothing so sinister, that I know of. She simply walked away from our life one day."

"Oh, I'm so sorry to hear that. I know where my parents are; they just choose not to speak to me much."

"I'm sorry."

"We're just very different people." He paused. He didn't want to talk about himself anymore. "If it's not too much, could I start by asking you how he died?" He looked down at his notes the entire time and then gestured toward her with his hands. He was too uncomfortable to make eye contact. He took a sip of his drink. "This is delicious honey and lemon, thank you."

"Thank you. I grew the lemons in my garden. I-I-iii think I might try to keep some bees and make my own honey. Seems like an o-ooovvv-er-all simple and self-sufficient pet. To answer your question, we didn't put in the news much but he was very sick for a long time. He had a degenerative disorder, similar to deee-eee-mmmentia but slower developing. He was alive for a very long time but slowly lost himself, and most of the time he was only partially there."

"Is that why he stopped doing art?"

"He actually kept doing art until his final days. It was truly his favorite. We'd actually draw all the time. He'd create so many drawings of strange creatures and beautiful landscapes. He was just never there for long enough to make his show."

"It's such a deep and often dark show. What inspired him?" Neil continued to stare down at his papers.

"My father never talked much about his childhood, but I gather it was never the most supportive environment. He and my mother ran away from home together in their teens—she was preggg-ggg-nant. He always said I inspired him to create it, but it never seemed to have much to do with me. I was an infant when he started it. He was always hard to read because he used humor as his method of dealing with his trauma. I think I learned more about his past from watching the show than he ever divulged in person."

"So, you think some of what happened in the show is about him?"

"Oh yes, of course. I think it was his way of sharing it with the world. For instance, the episode where Andy has to fight against the corporate builder to save the new tree, my dad wrote about my birrrr-tttt-th. They have to dig it up and run away, but then they find a beautiful new place to live."

"That episode was so sad. I really resonated with being rejected. When I watch it, it really helped me feel not so alone."

"I think tha-aaaa-ttttt was his hope." Autumn let out a small chuckle as she wiped a few tears from the corners of her eyes.

"I'm so sorry. We don't have to talk about him anymore." Neil grew even more uncomfortable, having noticed Autumn's "extreme" emotion.

"No, no worries. It's nice to think about him before he was sick. It's been so long since he was that person to me. Talking about him kind of feels like bringing him back to life." Even though Autumn's eyes were beginning to puff up, she flashed a large smile at Neil before she sipped her tea.

The two continued to talk for an hour about their favorite scenes from the show and which of them were inspired by things Autumn had done as a child. It was then that Autumn's watch began to ring. "Oh wow, I totally lost track of time. I'm actually going to have to go get ready for work."

"I hope I didn't keep you," Neil said politely. He was growing tired, and his social battery was running out. He was secretly excited he could soon be home. The two stood up and Neil made his way toward the front door. As they walked, the small trinket he had given her rocked in Autumn's pocket.

"Oh wait," she said, putting her finger up to him. "One second." She made her way over to the fireplace mantel, which was decorated with framed pictures of her and Marshall. She then placed the small toy onto it. Autumn searched through a set of hanging folders that were on the side of the fireplace. From the small cubbyhole-like file folders, she grabbed a mangled stack of papers. "Thank yoo-oou for the gift. I'm sorry that my father wasn't here to sign something for you, but I think I have something you'll like. She began to spread open the stack to show each page. "Feeee-eee-ll free to take one. He drew them all." Each page that Autumn held was a hand-drawn piece of art, most of them variations on Andy the armadillo but a few with other creatures.

Neil's hand shook as he reached out to exam his choices. "Of course, I'll have to take an Andy original." As he looked through the drawings, he shuffled the pages past the fully drawn ones, and his eyes settled on a half-finished black and white drawing. He took the page and placed it with his notes into his pad. The two then made their way to the front door, and Autumn let Neil out.

From there, Neil walked down the block and waited patiently for the bus. As he sat on the bench alone, he caught his breath and checked his pulse. As he waited, he then looked over his drawing, his newest and most prized possession. He would admire it all the way back to his home, a small studio apartment located uptown. Neil pushed into his apartment, starved and exhausted. As the door closed behind him, he slowly lowered himself to the ground—face first. Neil started by placing his papers onto the ground before he fully lowered himself, laying down. The synthetic wood felt cool against his face, and he found the pressure of the hard ground against his body calming; something he had been doing since childhood.

Neil lay there catching his breath and settling his still-racing heart. He had not spent so much time outside of his apartment in many months. Even then, he had not talked to anyone in person in even longer. His anxiety had been screaming within him all day. Neil's anxiety had always been an innate barrier between him and the world. He took medicine for it each morning with his Rejuverron, and though he had gotten better with time, his mind always eventually convinced him that he was alone.

He reached into his pocket and pulled out his phone. With one hand he began to scroll through his food delivery apps. He searched through each without success; there was nothing that jumped out to him. He couldn't make a decision. He then clicked on *Previous Orders* and selected the top order—*tacos, chips, and guacamole*. He placed his order and returned his phone to his pocket, then he slid his body to the side slightly and turned his head. He was now cooling the other side of his face. Neil continued to lie on the ground until a knock was heard at his door; it was his food delivery. He once again pulled out his phone and applied a generous tip to the order. Once he heard the footsteps of the delivery driver leaving, he did a slow and exaggerated push-up. He used it to both stretch and raise himself from the ground. He walked back to the door and received his food.

Neil didn't need much space. His apartment was a single room with a small twin-sized bed in the corner. Its covers and pillows were immaculately made because Neil rarely slept in it. To one side of the room was a small stove and sink, both also unused. The one used item was the garbage can that sat filled with leftover fast-food containers. The majority of the room was taken over by his workstation, which he slowly meandered toward with his dinner. This was the place where he spent most of his life. Neil used his foot to press a button on the base of the large chair in front of his computer. A small side table rotated out and up from its large pod-like body. He placed his food onto it and sat in his chair; its plush foam had perfectly formed to his body. The presence of his body activated the monitors in front of him, and the light from the three fifty-two-inch screens that curved around illuminated him. Neil placed his limbs on opposite sides of his armchair with his palms straight down. As he moved his arms side to side, his computer responded to the movement and clicks of his hand. By mimicking a keyboard with each hand, he was able to type. As he leaned back, his chair began to recline. The screens moved with him, and the side table remained steady, flat, and within reach.

Neil was now plugged in. With the exception of going to the bathroom, on most nights he would not look away from these screens until he fell asleep. Neil navigated through his apps and made his way to his emails and messages. His inbox was filled with work emails and spam, both of which would be ignored. Then he made his way to his favorite discord channel. Logging in, he saw he had thirty-seven notifications. Upon further inspection, though, he found they were all group-wide messages, nothing particular to him. The server was for the fans of Neil's favorite streamer, Senior Styles the small streamer only had between one hundred and two hundred people watching at any time. He then went into his browser, opened the stream, and pulled it to one of his side monitors. *Full screen.*

Now that Neil was alone, his adrenaline had run out and his body was suddenly exhausted. Now that he sat in front of his computer, his mind raced, and he was somehow wide awake. Slow but awake. When his body was out of sync like this, and his social battery was drained, his depression kicked in especially hard. He *just* felt alone. While he found his medicine made the prospect of dealing with others on a daily basis easier, it did not remove the numbness Neil felt with the outside world. At best, they instead made him indifferent. He could ignore his disconnection. He knew how to live with it.

This evening Neil sat as he did every Saturday, and Sunday, most Mondays, every Tuesday and Wednesday, and most Fridays, lurking in the lobby of the stream. Currently, Neil watched as Senior Styles sat calmly in his chair and watched videos on the internet with his followers. He alternated between watching the local news, silly videos suggested by viewers, and Styles' favorite, cooking videos. This stream was where Neil had first learned about *Andy Armadillo*. Another viewer had brought it up. Neil watched as the crowd of a hundred people, all seemingly friends, brought up topics of video games, politics, and movies. The Discord was an extension of that as it provided the friends with a virtual home when Styles was away. Neil watched other people's messages scroll up the screen. They contained misspellings, emojis, photos, criticisms, compliments, and praise. The words flew by, and it was hard to keep track, but the constant movement of words and the voice of the streamer kept him calm. For some moments it briefly made him feel as if he was not alone.

Though Neil was always there, he never said anything. Sometimes he would write a response, a joke or opinion, but he would never send it. His finger would hover anxiously above the enter key. What if he were to say something and it was ignored? That would be mortifying. What if he were to say something just wrong? He could never speak again. He would then rationalize, *Someone already responded* or *I took too long; the moment is over*. But the truth was that he was always too afraid to join in the conversation. As someone who had watched in silence for so long, it felt strange for him to say anything, as if he was intruding on a family dinner, a second-class citizen. Instead, Neil sat there in silence and enjoyed the crowd being a family. Sometimes he would donate large sums of money to the stream anonymously. Styles would cheer and thank the internet, begging to know who it was, but again, Neil never responded. It filled him with slight joy, but he was not comfortable receiving direct praise.

Instead, he sat alone.

Instead, he fell asleep.

On these long nights, Neil fell asleep with a mind racing with depression and disconnection. When his computer screen was left on still bright and blaring, a voice would call to him through the soothing sounds of static. Normally, he would sleep through it, unaware of what was about to happen to him, but this time was different. From within the static of the screen, a face began to form. Faint ridges of eyebrows and large cheeks pushed out from it, and with it a voice traveled to Neil. The sound could not be heard; instead, Neil could feel the voice echo in his mind like his own thoughts.

"Neeeeeiiillllll," the voice began. "Welcome back, my friend. I felt your distress."

Neil's sleeping body turned toward the screen, and his eyes shot open like someone throwing open a trunk. He was still half-sleep and unable to control his body. Normally this was where Neil would black out, unaware of what was feeding on him, but instead his eye caught the photo of Andy on his table. As his body turned toward the side screen, he attempted to fight it but was unable. Now facing the screen, the essence continued to talk.

"Neil, are you awake? Why are you resisting? Who are you thinking about?" As it spoke, the light from the screen intensified and filled the room. It bounced off Neil's glasses and bathed him. A blue mist made its way from the screen and began to envelop Neil. "It's okay. Sleep. Join me. Forget about them—forget about the world." Its voice was smooth as butter.

Neil could not move his mouth to speak, but as he thought, the face could sense it. "No, who are you?" he questioned.

"What? Oh, you are really responding," the creature replied, surprised. "That's beautiful. Neil, you know me. What changed? You know, I am the only one who understands you. I'm alone just like you." The creature then took control of Neil's computer and turned on the primary screen. It moved toward the web browser and began to open tabs, each one a different stream. One after another the creature placed them in their own space, eventually showing Neil fifty images at once. "Look, look at everyone. Look at everyone having fun without you. Without me."

"What do you know about being alone?" responded Neil. The monster's words had stabbed at something deep inside that he hoped to ignore forever.

"I've watched you. You're special. You're my friend. Don't you remember? Be not afraid. We're only getting closer. Don't you want to find me?"

"I don't know you. I don't know what you are. How could I ever be your friend?"

"BECAUSE I AM ALL YOU HAVE," its voice boomed. "Where is your family?" it said in a now gentler tone. "I can be your family. We can be your family."

"You're a monster."

"From what I know, that is a very ugly word. How could you say that? Just because I am not human, does that mean I am terrible? That I deserve to be alone? I am Eensaamheid and neither of us deserve this." From the screen a thicker mist of dark blue began to flow out. As it wiggled toward Neil, it shaped into the form of a snake. Slowly it coiled around him, making its way up his body and gently constricting him. Once it had reached his face, it stared at him for only a second before striking and jumping down his throat. Within the static, the face drew back, and Neil felt himself fall into the screen. From above he watched as the creature's words turned to images, and there he saw visions of the past.

Eerste stopped and rested her knee on her walking stick; it was the third time since their trek started that day. Her old body was failing her, and each year it took longer and longer for her and her family to make their yearly pilgrimage across the continent. Now it was impossible for her. Her group was made of her sons and daughters, their mates, and many stragglers they had saved along the years. Those who were sick or old were generally left behind by their groups to die. Even Eerste's own parents left many people behind to ensure they made it safely over the mountain. Once Eerste had become the matron of the group, she refused to continue that tradition. She refused to leave anyone else behind. That is how she built the large family she had now, and why they now waited for her.

Eerste rested on her stick as pain shot through her bones. It ached most in her ankles and knees. Unable to fake it anymore, she stumbled to a nearby boulder and started to lower herself against it. She was barely able to use the stick to stabilize herself as she dusted off the rock. She haphazardly wobbled on her cane while she took a seat, leaning her back against it. She caught her breath, and her heart sank as she thought about how close to death she was. She watched as the group continued to walk away from her. She hoped they would continue to safety without her. She knew how much more difficult it was to care for someone who could not care for themselves.

It took a moment but Eerste's youngest daughter, Uthando, was the first to notice her mother's disappearance. "Hey! Everyone, wait," she shouted in a language now lost to time. She signaled to the others to stop and hastily made her way back toward her mother. The group swiftly turned around; didn't just stop, they followed.

Eerste waved at her daughter as she approached. "We're very far behind schedule. You can't keep stopping."

"You! Mother! Are the one who cannot let yourself stop. But if you do, you must tell us. Don't be stubborn. Now get up. Let us carry you if need be."

"Utha, I cannot be this much of a burden. The weather is growing worse. It's dangerous for you to all stay. You won't make it over the mountains if you stay. I promise I'll catch up. I've made it before."

"We are not going to leave you. That is ridiculous! I will not hear any more of it. You are the reason we are here. We can and will carry you. We have plenty of strong people."

"You do not understand, my child. It will be a waste of your energy." Eerste now lowered her body more, and violently let herself drop to the ground. She slid down the rock and into its shadow. She needed to use it as a respite from the heat—a small area in the shade. "I can feel it, I'm dying. No matter how you feel, you cannot carry a corpse. Even I didn't save the ashes of my parents."

"Do not be dramatic. You're as strong as I am. Now get up." Utha reached her hand out to Eerste to try and help her up. "I promise you. You can die elsewhere." Eerste failed to respond; her face became paler. Uthando noticed the stark difference in her mother's face. There was something growingly absent about her. "She's getting overheated, again. We'll need to stop."

"Here, help me with this this," one of her sons said while motioning to the others. Three younger people helped him to move a large portion of tree branch off the ground and against the rock. The leaves now fluttered in the wind and provided a sparkling and cooling shade over Eerste's body.

"This is wonderful," thanked Eerste with forced breath. "Thank you so much. Now you really must be going. My children, my vision is fading. Don't worry for me."

Uthando ran her hand across Eerste's head and felt a fever. *Not hot, cold—cold and clammy.* "I'll be right back, Mother," she whispered before kissing her cheek. Uthando stood up and went to go talk to the group. She needed to inform them of Eerste's condition and the plan of their trip. After a few minutes of discussion, Uthando, with the family close behind, returned to her mother's side.

"We don't know what to do. We don't want to leave you," Uthando said, grasping Eerste's hand in hers. "We could not think of a word to properly explain what we mean. How intensely we felt. So, we have created a word simply for you. What we have said is: We *love* you."

"*Love?*"

"It's the word we made to describe the feeling you give all of us. It's a feeling of peace, comfort, trust, and pride. You do so much for us."

"Then I *love* you too. I *love* you all. That is why I know you must go. From what I see, *love* makes you fools." Eerste forcefully chuckled.

"Don't worry," someone shouted from the group.

"We've discussed it," continued Uthando. "If we leave you, you'll die. I won't have you left for some predator. If we take you with us. You'll die. The mountains are too cold for you. I won't have you a frozen monument. But if we stay here, we think we can take care of you. We'll be able to keep you alive and comfortable." Uthando signaled with one hand, and someone brought Eerste some water and poured it into her mouth.

"You'll starve in the winter."

"We're going to stay with you. We'll figure it out because we have to. I think that is part of the love you provide; you give us hope. Look, try this. Athar made you this. Do you like it?" Eerste reached out for the food and pulled it close to her face. She attempted to rip a small piece, but the tough jerky was too difficult for her to chew.

"We'll break it up for you," Uthando said while taking it back. "It is meat from the deer we killed weeks before. It has stayed good for a very long time. We think if we can hunt for the remainder of the season and store food for the coming winter, we can stockpile enough to stay here for a while. We won't have to leave you."

"That's madness."

"These lands are actually quite beautiful, Mother. You seem to have chosen a good land to stop in."

"We cannot let you die alone. We won't," echoed people in the crowd.

"There is nothing I can do to stop your stubbornness, is there?" Eerste then signaled to be helped up. It took three people to lift and stabilize her. "If you are going to stay, you cannot stay here in the elements. You'll need shelter. You cannot stay here." Eerste slowly led the group down the side of a hill and directed them toward a cave whose mouth opened toward the sea. She signaled to have them place her down by the entrance and off to the side. "I will not come in and curse your new home. Leave me here."

They did as she wished and then began to break into groups. Two sons carried large fallen trees on their backs and ripped off branches to begin construction. They started by jamming pruned branches into defects in the rockface. Their simple half-circle provided plenty of shade. Others traveled to the nearby fields and began to harvest straw and leaves to make beds. With the resources of nature around them, in a few hours they built Eerste her own room, a hut around her, protecting her from elements. Uthando stuffed straw under Eerste's body and head, attempting to make her comfortable. From it, Eerste could hear the echoes of her children in the nearby cave. For a few days she listened. "The stone here is soft. We can dig to make more space. Smaller rooms could keep it warmer." They then started to build what would eventually grow to be an underground city, carved into the land.

Neil watched as a week passed in an instant. In the darkness of the night of the seventh day, Eerste had a visitor. Through the straw- and mud-covered door pushed a small humanoid with the body of a man and the head of a bird. Though he looked different than the last time she saw it, Eerste knew this was the beast that had attacked her in her childhood. The Being approached her slowly, cooing and clicking in unnatural tones.

"You're too late. I am barely here. My family has moved on. So, take your meal and leave. Here, it'll be your last." The Being sensed something new in Eerste, a new flavor in her fear. He could feel it within the lights that dazzled within his body. This was not only the love and fear she had felt for her parents. No, this love was stringy and thick. He could feel it flowing from Eerste and into the cave. Like threads he saw the connections between her and everyone within it. The Being walked over to her, and stood above her, sniffing the air. She was not afraid for herself. She was afraid of what the Being might do to them once she was no longer there. He placed his hand over her and began to feed; to draw the heat and life out of her.

Excited at the new taste, he fed with reckless abandon. As he drew in her fear, he felt a pullback from her connection to the others. The Being could feel the strings of love tying each person within the city to the heart of Eerste. All of their fear fed into her and then into the Being. This time Eerste would not survive. Her frame was too frail and her heart was too weak; it put up no resistance. As heat pulled from her body, it aged and decayed in an instant—skin, then bone, then dust.

"And there I was born, a creature of pure love and connection. Left alone, dejected and neglected," Eensaamheid's voice echoed in Neil's head. "I still felt the pull of Eerste's connections, but they were weak, hollow, and desiccated. In a way I was born numb, craving the love I truly deserved. I know somewhere deep inside me, Eerste calls for it."

The Being walked away from the corpse, satisfied with its meal, and made its way out of the small hut. Behind it a small blue snake uncoiled from the soot. It shook off the dust on its body and made it way toward the Being. It hastily caught up and spiraled its way up the Being's body, finally resting on his arm.

"He looked at me and rejected me. Rejected by my parent. Sound familiar?" The Being looked at Eensaamheid. Without any fear in the newborn creature, it had zero interest. Love was a flavor, not something the Being felt. It flicked Eensaamheid off with his hand and the snake smashed against the wall of the hut. His small body slammed to the ground. The Being exited the hut, satisfied with its meal. It stepped off the edge of the cliff, and large blue owl wings sprouted from his back; then he sailed into the fog.

"When I traveled into the cave to meet her family, *my* family, I was met with similar disdain. I hissed and called out to them, but they failed to trust me. No one could understand my cries. They attacked me with spears and threw rocks. I could not enter safely. I had to flee. I had to live in the hut, alone. When they came into my birthplace to find her, they found a sea of flowers growing from her ashes, my ashes. Instead of honoring me for my magic, they chased me further away, into the hills. They stole my home and my birthday place. They didn't love me like they loved her.

Even though they rejected me, I felt compelled to make them love me. From a distance, I watched them, and I learned their language. I learned their words. At night, I whispered to them, but that was not enough. Only a few, the ones who also felt the disconnect, even heard me. They tried to come to me, but others would stop them. Like I didn't even exist. I never belonged with anyone, just like *you*."

Below him, Neil watched as grass and flowers began to sprout from the mouth of the hut. It quickly traveled and blanketed the surrounding area in beautiful life. At night within the tall grasses the snake of mist flowed, traveling along the mouth of the cave. There he sat calling to those still awake. His whispers echoed into the cave, beckoning them to join him, to help him, to be with him. Most within the cave spread ghost stories about the mysterious friend of the mountain. "I eventually found a better way to convince some to join me, a way to make a deeper connection."

Neil watched as the small group grew into a colony, into society, into a city—all connected. Neil watched as they built a graveyard within their cave and brought flowers from Eerste's hut to them. He watched as they all cried together in remembrance—without Eensaamheid. He watched as society evolved and time passed. As the things people used to stay connected changed, so did the monster's ability to connect to them.

"With all the other lost souls. You don't have to be alone anymore, Neil. You could join us." Then the world started to become static, and throughout the speckling Neil could once again see Eensaamheid as a snake. He swam through the internet. His body was infinitely long and disappeared into the static of the electricity. His scales were bright with an iridescent sheen in all shades of blue, from the brightest day to the deepest night.

"Join us," he spoke once again. Then scales on his body shined and glistened in beautiful iridescent blue. Below the snake drifted mist that condensed into the ghostly shape of a man, as if wearing the snake as a hood. It then slowly and unconvincingly walked toward him. From the snake's back, its scales began to float off and enlarge—they remained tethered to his body by a phantom chain. Each scale had two long hollow divots, and the sparkling of the light gave them the appearance of tortured faces. As they floated further from his body, they grew larger. From the mask-like scales seeped blue light that eventually formed human bodies. The scales were now their masks. They repeated in unison, "We're not alone. Not here."

Neil could see that through the internet, through Eensaamheid, he was connected to others, also being fed on, lied to, and pulling them toward him. He was not alone, nor special. Each of them connected to their phone, or computer, or TV through a snake appendage, unaware. As they watched, Eensaamheid spoke to their subconscious and helped to stoke the sadness and loneliness in their world. Neil even saw himself as he was fed on throughout the years, but then he began to black out. As the world faded, Neil could feel that no amount of connection was enough to satisfy Eensaamheid. Nothing was enough to make him feel not alone, and he would collect forever.

Neil awoke the next morning still in his chair. The mornings following the feedings were when Neil felt the most alone, and now he knew the cause. During these mornings an especially heavy weight sat on his heart. A feeling of self-disgust would wash over him, though he did nothing wrong. He never did anything. The computer monitor had turned itself off from lack of use, and his chair was still slouched back in its reclining position. As he stretched and his morning fog began to go away, the memories of the creature he had seen, and the history he watched, came flooding back. Without sitting up, his arm instinctually reached to turn back on the computer screen. He began to push the button before his instincts kicked in. Neil was now scared, and he held the button down for far too long for it to respond, staying off. He stared up at the machine, afraid that the creature could still be on the receiving end.

"Hello?" he whispered to the machine, hoping it wouldn't respond. Neil took a calming breath. He felt alone, emotionally and physically. "It was connected to me through the internet, right? How am I supposed to avoid him. How am I supposed to find out how to stop him." Neil did a nice full-body stretch in his chair and rubbed his eyes.

"What am I going to do?" Neil rose from his chair and made his way over to the small kitchen nook and opened the miniature freezer that hung from the ceiling. He fiddled with some buttons, then the shelves rotated and revealed some energy drinks. He pulled one out and began to drink it. The pop of the tab felt like an explosion compared to the silence of the room. Usually he had a stream playing by now. Neil pressed a few more buttons on the fridge and pulled out a small cup of instant oatmeal. He added some water and started to eat. He stood leaning against the small kitchen counter, enjoying his breakfast.

Where can I get information? Besides the internet, he thought while he played with his spoon in his mouth. Neil walked over to his window and opened it to let in the morning sun. Usually, the curtain would remain closed as he spent his morning still on the computer, and he hated the glare. Neil wandered around the room, laying on surface after surface, pondering. It took until late in the afternoon but then it hit him, and he felt rather embarrassed.

Library.

He could go back out into the world two days in a row and go to a library. Instead of through the internet, through electronic means, he could instead use books. He needed to figure out what was going on, and desperate times called for desperate measures. As Neil prepared to leave his house, he felt his normal strain of anxiousness mixed with something new, a small rage. Something had been stirred in him, and he felt a new knot of discomfort with even the idea of talking to others. Neil exited his apartment, body rigid, with his hood over his face and large headphones over his ears. He would take the bus downtown.

The entire time he rode he listened to music and ignored everything around him. He felt like he was floating through life. Normally, his anxiousness would make him hyper-aware of everyone. This time, he failed to notice anyone. His body was numb and it spread to his mind, controlling how he felt with the world. He awoke when he stepped out of the bus and looked up at the many stairs that led to the large public library. It took him a few minutes to slowly walk up, but eventually he entered through the large doors and walked under a blunderbuss; the library was built to mimic the classical design of a castle but with a few minor updates. The entrance was decorated with columns, and the windows were large stained glass images.

He walked through the large arches, and on both sides of the hallway large stacks of books rose to the ceiling. After passing several rows of them, the building opened up to a large room. A beautiful dark wood semi-circular desk stood there to welcome guests, and directly next to it, Neil noticed an atlas on the wall to the right. He lowered his head, hiding his face, and approached it. He then read over the layout as he contemplated where to start.

"Can I help you find anything?" a woman's voice called from behind. The sound of Neil's music drowned her out. She watched as he continued to stare at the wall, overwhelmed by the options.

Ancient history? Mythology? Religion? Fiction? Where? Neil was startled out of his thoughts by the feeling of a hand touching him. He spun around and threw the hand off his shoulder violently as he turned to face it. There he saw the librarian, who was still trying to get his attention. The short, stout redhead was looking up at him with a smile.

"Would you like some help finding something, sir? The building is six floors, and so the map can be really confusing at times." Neil jumped back. He had almost forgotten that other people existed. In his mind, the room would be empty and nothing but books would exist. Like a web browser in real life.

He also recoiled because he had not felt anyone else's touch in months. Neil had never been comfortable with physical contact. As a child he was yelled at for refusing to hug relatives; it was one of the many things his parents misinterpreted about him. Though normally contact would almost make his skin crawl, her hand and her pleasant smile crumbled some of the knot of the loneliness the monster had placed in his heart. He slowly removed his headphones.

"I was... I was looking for information on umm... A monster. Do you know where I would find that?"

"I'm Gwen. It's a pleasure to meet you." She reached her hand out to shake his but only grasped the tips of his fingers while doing it—a very soft handshake. "That's a great question. I guess that depends on what kind of monster you're looking for. Are you looking to learn from the people who write about monsters because they think it's fun? Or the people who think it's for real?"

"I think I'm looking for the serious people. Is that weird?"

"Oh, no. I was just messing with you. Of course not. Religion might be one of our largest sections." Neil smiled knowing now it was a joke. One he enjoyed. "I will warn you, though, we have thousands upon thousands of books in our religion section. I would suggest you use that terminal there to look up anything specific."

"What if I don't know what I should be looking for, exactly? Also, what if I'm trying not to use the internet?"

"Huh…weird and old school. Very cool. In that case, you'll be happy to know that the terminal is not connected to the internet. It's an internal registration and search system. There was a time it was connected but we removed that."

"Why?"

"From what I was told, you'd be surprised how many people get bored enough to want to hack into the library index and change book titles to inappropriate things." Gwen then led him to the nearest terminal and gestured to it with her hand like a fancy waiter. She began to walk away but Neil turned back toward her.

"What if I don't know what to search?"

"Uhh, you'll need to think of some keywords. Like do you know anything about it?"

Neil shrugged. "It's kind of like a snake?"

"Just vague enough to work. Uhm, I think I know someone who might be able to help you." She walked back toward the desk and shouted at someone he couldn't see. "Weirdo!" Then she turned back toward Neil, embarrassed. "Not you. My friend who works here. Weirdo! Come out!"

From behind the rows of stacks, Neil saw the bounce of a large afro. A Hispanic gentleman came out from behind it carrying books. "What?! What do you want? You know you are yelling in a library? A library you work at, I might add." He stopped, embarrassed at how loudly he was speaking. "Great, now you have me yelling." He was wearing suspenders, a tie, and large fishbowl glasses. His shirt was light plaid and striped, half red and half blue.

"Someone needs your help, nerd."

"You're one to talk, *Creye0Pheonix*." Weirdo placed the books he was reshelving onto the table and made his way with Gwen toward Neil. He extended his hand and provided a much stronger handshake than Gwen had.

"Weirdo?" Neil questioned.

"My name is Eddie but my gamer tag is Weirdo. Gwen likes to abuse friendship and inside information. How can I help you?"

"Should I call you Eddie or…?"

"Weirdo is fine."

"Well, I'm trying to find out information about this monster I heard about. All I know is that it's a snake spirit-like thing. It has scales that might also be people. It was confused, honestly."

"People scales, huh? Sounds dope. Well, you said it's like a snake spirit? So more misty and less corporeal? That doesn't sound like one of the major religions. Their snakes are usually literal and demonic. It's an interesting line they toe. No, it sounds like one of the more in tune with the earth religions."

"Like…"

"You might want to search 'snake spirit' and then add like 'indigenous.' Many of them had many spirits central to their religions…. You could also search Shintoism—the Japanese thought everything had a spirit. I'm sure that included their snakes."

"Spirit snakes? Doesn't that sound like your ancestors too, Ed?" Gwen questioned.

"*Yeah*, that's a good point. Thanks, Gwen," he said sarcastically. "She's annoying but right. You could also look up Santeria and any of the other Creole religions." He then smiled. "You have a fascination with the afterlife?"

"No, I just…" Neil looked down to the ground. "I had a really weird dream last night, and it's left a really heavy weight on me. I'm trying to figure out what's wrong." It was easy for both of them to see the sadness in Neil's eyes, a vulnerability he couldn't hide.

"Hey, don't worry, Neil. We're both weird. We all got our problems. Do you know anything else from your dream?" That little comment made Neil feel not so distant.

"I saw dozens of people yawning. As they breathed out, these clouds of snakes flew out and drifted on the wind like pollen. They would be sucked into people as they yawned in response. It was like some social disease."

"Woah, that's really fucking cool. I've never heard of anything like that. If you're still here in a few hours when my shift ends, I'll totally help you look that up. That sounds metal," said Gwen as she played with her fairy necklace.

"That's awesome. Well, I think you should go start looking with those religions—there will be many 'primary' and secondary texts for you." Weirdo looked over to Gwen, who was smiling and gesturing toward Neil. "How about when we get off of work? We'll both help you. I'd like to learn some more too."

"If you go to the northeastern wing, you'll find another terminal and you can find specific books. Most of what you're looking for should be in that sector." The two pointed Neil to the hallway he needed, and the elevator to the upper stacks. Once he got there, Neil became lost in the sea of books. He spent several hours traveling between the terminal and the stacks as he pulled book upon book. Some books he pulled and read immediately; others were too big and needed to be brought back to a table. He grabbed books from every religion that mentioned spirits, snakes, or loneliness. After a few hours Gwen and Weirdo joined him. They searched together, showing each other interesting entries. At first, nothing was exactly like his description.

"Ugh, I hate to be a downer but if we're going to keep doing this, I'm going to need to eat," complained Gwen, slowly flipping through an old book.

"Are we allowed to eat in here? Around the books?"

"As long as you're with us, you have librarian privileges. Plus, the library is open twenty-four hours. Do they expect the nerds to starve in the stacks? Some people pretty much live here." The group ordered food and continued to search. This was the first time Neil had eaten dinner outside of his house in a long time and especially with friends. He really couldn't remember when the last time was.

Eventually, Weirdo emerged from the stacks with an old book filled with academic papers. "Hey, Neil, check this out. The scholar in this paper is talking about how he believes that there are a series of spirits and monsters lost to time. He thinks that several of them were partially adopted by many religions, but they are all bits and pieces of the larger story." He then dropped the book onto the table in front of Neil. "Does this sound right?"

Neil then read out loud, "The monster I describe below I have named **Eensaamheid**, giving credit to the regions where the first accounts were made. The serpent of loneliness spreads his influence throughout the community, infecting the hearts of his victims. Those who fall prey wander off into the woods, never to be seen again…. Those who are lucky enough to hear from the monster have said it speaks eloquently and aggressively to his victims…. Most are otherwise recruited through his infection. A disease that translates most directly to 'the hermit's yawn'…. Seers have attested they have seen a blue mist as some people yawn. It is said they spread through the air, winding like a snake. Symptoms include loneliness, delusion, extreme depression, isolation, and emotional detachment…. Those who wander away seem detached from the world as a whole." Neil's voice trembled at the end and the blood rushed from his face.

"That's what happened to me. I've seen the snake."

The two saw the fear behind Neil's eyes and gently put their arms on his shoulders. "Don't worry, we'll keep looking for something we can do to help. This thing came in your dream?" Weirdo asked.

"No…no, I think it actually came to me through the internet."

"Ah, that's why you're being a baby about the network. I get it now," commented Gwen. "Well, are you online a lot? You could just hide. You know, like, forever."

"I work online. I live online."

"Yeah, I'm just giving you a hard time. I'd go crazy without my computer." She paused and started to play with her watch. "Actually, you need to give us your gamer tag. I can find something calm and easy to play if you'd like. We love to play Friendship Putt-Putt. Weirdo *loves* it. Don't you."

Neil could feel a connection to these two souls. Their care traveled into his body through their contact like pulses pumped by their hearts. That and their words of encouragement seemed to dissolve the knot inside of him. Neil became less tense and scared. He agreed and they exchanged information, then they called it a night. When home, he hesitated before putting on the computer, but after a half hour of pacing, he did. As he turned it on, he immediately lowered the brightness. His eyes darted around the screen and scanned for any trace of the monster.

After entering their information into his console, Neil soon received friendship confirmations from both Gwen and Weirdo. Then their joyful messages popped up.

"It was great meeting you today. That was really weird and fun. Sorry If I come off a bit strong. You'll get used to it," she said.

"If you're right about it living in the internet, I'll see if I can program something to track it down. Perhaps we can stop it next time it appears. I'm kind of a computer programmer in my spare time," Weirdo said.

It wouldn't be for several months that Neil would be attacked again. "Neil, are you cool to hang out next week? Are you capable of looking at people yet? I haven't seen you in what feels like a month. I'm asking *HOW'S THE BATTERY?*" Gwen said over her microphone.

"You act like you don't talk to him almost every day," harassed Weirdo.

"It's different!!!!"

"Maybe for you," responded Neil. "Yeah, of course. I'll see y'all at dinner soon."

"Sick. Well, have a good night then."

"Yeah, I'm heading out too. I gotta work an early shift tomorrow."

Neil disconnected from his friends and navigated to a new tab and once again pulled up a stream to watch. He nuzzled into his chair and attempted to get comfortable. He had not begun to go outside more than usual in the last couple of months, but knowing he had friends somewhere out there helped him feel connected to the world. He was still disconnected but it was different now; the world was large, but he had a small community in it. His newfound comfort wouldn't stop **Eensaamheid** from trying to reach him, though. That night as he tried to sleep, the screen turned to static once again. The static formed into **Eensaamheid**'s face and leaked blue mist.

"Neil, I've been gone a long time. Have you had time to reflect? I left you alone, like them."

"I'm not alone," shouted Neil's mind at the monster.

"You're still awake? You can see me, yet again? What a strong mind you have. You really would be such a great guest, Neil. You could even be family. We could reach so many people with your intelligence."

"No, I mean even now I'm not alone." Neil then used his left hand to input a command into his computer terminal. His computer opened several programs and sent signals to his friends. Elsewhere in the city, Gwen and Weirdo were woken up by loud emergency alarms, a recording of Neil yelling "GET AWAY" and "the imperial march," respectively. They jumped out of bed and onto their computers. They had practiced this. They both logged onto the group chat, and within it they could see Neil's computer camera was successfully turned on. They could see Neil enveloped in a bright light but failed to see the blue mist that actually consumed him. His body was completely still, and though he was talking to the monster his voice was unheard by his friends.

"Guys, he's here. What do you see? Are you ready?" Neil's mind raced. He felt like he was shouting. He was pushing so hard, trying to project, but the lack of response said otherwise. Through the chat he could hear them talk, but he could not respond. It was in their hands.

"Neil, are you okay? This isn't one of your silly test drills, is it?"

"Yeah, I'm exhausted, dude. I just fell sleep."

"Why isn't he responding?" questioned Weirdo.

"Oh, shit! Maybe he can't? Is this for real?" panicked Gwen.

"You're right, the book said people were put into a trance. From what I read, I don't think he should even have been able to contact us. What should we do?"

"Do we just go straight aggro?"

"What does that even mean in this context?" asked Weirdo, frustrated.

"What even was the plan? We practiced this, didn't we? Aren't you supposed do something?"

"The idea was to confirm and record it. But we can't see anything. We're just recording a weird internet reel."

"He would be so embarrassed. Could we?"

"You're annoying when you're nervous. He gave me access to his computer. Maybe I can find something. I…guess. What am I looking for?" Eddie took control of Neil's mouse.

"Who are these people? You can't know them too well. They are going to abandon you. Didn't you hate it when I did it like everyone else. I've seen it a million times before. Look at all the beautiful people grace my body as scales. We are all a family. Together forever."

From the screen, the hermit's yawn continued to leak as the snake smashed against Neil's face and tried to enter it. They watched as Neil's body trashed and fought something invisible. His mouth was pulled open, the light shined into it, and after the snake entered it, light shined out.

"Can you destroy it? I HATE NOT BEING ABLE TO HELP. DO SOMETHING! I'M NOT TRYING TO WATCH MY FRIEND DIE! Can't you just delete him or something? Isn't that how viruses work?" panicked Gwen.

"No, it isn't. Even if it was, I couldn't build a program to do that so fast, and I don't think he's a virus. But, maybe I can find the connection and close it." As the two talked, Eddie navigated to the computer settings and looked at the network connections. "Look! Do you see what I'm seeing?" groaned Eddie.

"No, as I said. I can't see shit," said Gwen.

"The monster is coming through the internet, so he's registered through the computer hardware. He's drawing a lot of bandwidth."

"Thiccc boiii," Gwen joked.

"The monster even has an IP address. Let me see if I can close the connection," said Weirdo excitedly. When Weirdo deleted the connection from the computer, the screen went blank. The light went off and Neil's body stopped moving. Neil tried to respond but his body was still paralyzed.

"You did something. Hell yeah!" cheered Gwen.

"Now let's add it to the firewall. Hopefully this will fully block the connection from now on. We have an IP address so we can block it."

Gwen and Weirdo let out a sigh of relief. But then Neil's other two computer screens turned on. Each flicked erratically before becoming static, one followed by the other. Then they became loud and blared static through their headphones. The light from the screen grew even brighter and they could no longer see Neil at all. Neil watched as from the screen emerged even more snakes. Hundreds of tiny snakes wiggled out from the screen, and as one exited the screen another began to crawl out. They flowed like water and wrapped around him.

"Why would you try to throw me away, Neil? How did you do that?" The snakes flowed over his body and crawled into his eyes and his mouth.

"I thought you stopped it!" What's happening to him?"

As Weirdo looked at Neil's screen, he could see new connections, dozens per second attaching. "The signal is now coming from at least fifty different places. He's flooding the computer with connections. I can't possibly close all of them fast enough. I even shut off his Wi-Fi card; he just turned it back on. I'm trying to track where they are coming from, but it doesn't look like it's coming from anywhere in particular. It looks like it's coming from everywhere. He's not just somewhere on the internet. He's omnipresent. He could come from anywhere. Let me share my screen. This is what I'm dealing with." Weirdo showed the flashing screen of alerts. The sound of the new connections pinged so quickly that it sounded like a single tone.

"If he's everywhere, why can't we track his body?" Then Gwen started to bounce to the sound of the notifications. "Man, if this wasn't so overwhelming the beeping could be a great beat."

"Wait, a beat. Exactly."

"What? Did I help? Weirdo, what are you doing."

"You're right. His essence is coming through as a distinct signal. No matter where he comes from, he can't hide it. It's like a heartbeat. That's why the alerts all ping in unison. There are far more than even the beeps are suggesting." Eddie continued his search through the computer and pulled up his own music program. He recorded the signal and could see it was a strange sinusoidal connection. "I followed it—I found his signal," he announced. With this many connections he could be feeding on **thousands if not** millions of people at the same time, on the same night. If he's like music, I might be able to filter him out?" Weirdo began frantically typing. "We can't destroy him but if we sense his heartbeat, we'll shut him out." With a stroke of a key all of the connections were instantly detached. The screens surrounding Neil shut off and the snakes began to vanish into puffs of smoke. For a moment the screens continued to flicker, as the snack attempted to reconnect. The screens danced and flashed back and forth, left and right but each time the connection was killed. Eventually, it grew tired.

Neil heard the voice of the beast one last time as the last connection faded. "I'm not angry at you, Neil. I understand how they could have tricked you. I'll find you again, one day. You'll need me. We have forever."

Neil was finally able to talk to his friends and simply ignored the voice. "Guys! Guys! Are you two there? Are you okay?"

"We're fine, dude. Are *you* okay?"

"I am now. Thanks to you two."

"What do we do if it comes back? Could it come after us next?" asked Gwen, excited and nervous. "What a rush."

"I think I can attach this to a private VPN. That way we can install it on any computer and filter his connection, remove his influence. We could even spread it to help people."

"Sell it? You think someone would believe us? People are going to think we're insane or trying to trick them into some trash."

"I was gonna give it away, but I would be missing some shifts at the library to program it. But I guess we can only help those who ask us. There have to be millions of people being attacked every night. Some will believe us."

"Thank you for saving me, guys. I mean it. In general, thank you in more ways than one. I love you, guys," Neil said with bated breath. He then closed his eyes and placed his hand on his chest.

"Neil, are we still up for dinner?" interrupted Gwen.

"You're *already* asking about next week again?" asked Weirdo as he shook his head in disappointment.

"I figured this might have drained Neil's battery. Just trying to plan."

"Good question. I'll let you know."

Dancing for the King

Dancing for the King

For the fifth time this week Camilla found herself unable to sleep. Something deep inside her told her to go for a walk, and she felt compelled to scour the city for some sense of comfort—though she had no idea what form that would come in. The first night she only walked for a few minutes, but then her walks began to take hours, almost all of which she failed to remember. Though her ankle was still sprained, and the muscle in her calf was still bulging, she somehow felt no pain as she forced herself to explore the city. Even though it was late at night, and she was alone and young, only 24, she felt safe. She had grown up in the city, one that was rough but nevertheless safe and there was nowhere she didn't feel comfortable roaming. Her mother told her it was because she was a fool, but Camilla loved the city, even if that feeling had been fleeting in recent months; nothing bad had ever truly happened to her.

The streetlights flickered above her and illuminated her face as she wandered into unfamiliar alleys and neighborhoods, directionless. She had a dark complexion, a long face, a strong chin, high cheekbones, and a nose that jutted out with a long slope that fed into her mouth in just the loveliest way, a stone face but soft and bright. The warm summer air was comforting as she marched forward in her bright pink pajamas and gray hoodie. Her comfortable clothing was in stark contrast to her immaculate hair, which blew with the light breeze beneath her hoodie. Her hair was a mixture of weave and wig that aimed to cover up a large scar on the back of her head. She had suffered an accident as a child that left her with a large patch of hair that refused to grow and a scar that she was always self-conscious about. That is why, even in her most tired and delusional states, it was always perfect.

When she was younger Camilla's father, very into traditional gender roles, had always made her shave her head down to match his. In her late teens, when she felt comfortable enough to finally tell the sweet but stoic man who she really was, he allowed her to partake in her mother's fashion. It was then that Camilla learned she could not only hide her scar but could also make it something beautiful. Whatever she wanted. Her family was completely accepting of her identity. At school, everyone was so different that she didn't even make waves; most importantly her friends already knew.

Before then she would steal her mother's clothes and hide them under her father's suggested uniform; her white button-down shirt and black tie concealed bright fabric. Once she got to school, she would proceed to change, unknown to her parents. As she grew older and bolder, she would sneak into the girls' bathroom with her best friend Jolene, who would happily help her apply matching makeup before first period. The two were more like sisters than their own blood. They had met during dance classes, hip-hop inspired fusion, and had stayed close ever since. Now they were twenty-four and on the eve of starting to take Rejuverron.

Though the two worked together, Camilla hadn't seen Jolene since she sprained her ankle a few months back. In fact, Camilla had not seen anyone since then. After she hurt her leg, she felt embarrassed; she was too young to be hurting herself already. No matter who you are, dancing is demanding on your body. Even those who took Rejuverron for years could suffer from body-constricting illness and muscle fatigue from earlier in their careers. If she wanted to be perfect, to stay healthy forever, she would need to make sure she was as healthy as possible before her twenty-fifth birthday. When she was made to stay home to recover, she felt rejected and worried about her body and dance future. After a while she stopped responding to anyone, and they seemed to stop reaching out to her.

As luck would have it, this evening Camilla happened to wander down a street of popular bars. As she passed by Ray's Pub, she heard loud music coming through the large, open garage doors that led inside. From below, she looked up at the concrete patio and saw familiar faces. Among the crowds of young people drinking and talking, Camilla saw Jolene and their *supposed* friends. Jolene was wearing a long, neon-red dress with matching accessories in her hair and eyeshadow. The three friends, one fair and blonde and two vastly different shades of black, were Brittany, Ade, and Jeff, respectively. Each of them was dressed similarly to Jolene, in that they were each in only one color. Brittany wore a yellow dress and matching headband, Ade a bright and sparkling blue dashiki, and Jeff an orange crop top with matching skirt and heels.

Camilla peered at them through her hoodie but kept walking forward at a steady pace. Her leg was throbbing, but it didn't hurt. Her attempts to be stealthy failed as Jolene spotted her out of the corner of her eye. "Camilla! Is that you girl?" she shouted. "We thought you were dead." Jolene, who was holding Brittany's hand, let go of it to run toward Camilla. She then slowed down as she began to descend a small set of stairs; in one hand was a drink and the other was used to stabilize her drunk heels. Camilla had stopped but barely turned back. She continued to peer through her hoodie.

"What are you doing? Come over here—you know I can't have this drink on the street. Come inside—we're having a rainbow party night. We missin' colors. I tried to let you know we need our green girl."

"I hate green," Camilla responded a bit too seriously. Her voice was feminine but strong with a touch of vocal fry.

"Well, you were last to pick. You snooze you lose. Anyway, we haven't seen you. Did you get my message? Is your ankle better?" Jolene scanned Camilla's outfit.

"Does it look like I got your message?"

"Well no, but dogs see gray rainbows, I suppose. Fits the theme." Jolene laughed. "You should join us. Want a shot?" she asked as she started to turn away, beckoning Camilla with her hand. Camilla only took a few steps toward the stairs before stopping again. At the top of the stairs appeared Jeff to help Jolene make her way back up.

"Camilla gurl, what are you doing out here so late? I thought your ankle was still busted," said Jeff, helping to stabilize Jolene. Then the other brightly colored friends joined in.

"Heyyy! I thought you were hurt. Did you come out to drink with us?" Ade smiled as she placed her beard onto Jolene's shoulder and started to fall asleep.

"Off of me, giant. Hold your own ass up," Jolene said while laughing and taking a sip of her drink. "Besides, Camilla, where you headed looking all comfy? You look like you could use a shot."

"If I take another, I'm going to throw up. We'll get that green you wanted," said Brittany before making a fake throw-up noise.

"I don't really feel like drinking with y'all just because I happen to find you. Seems pretty fake. I haven't heard from any of you. I'm not feeling very party ready."

"What do you mean, you haven't heard from me? I've reached out to you nearly every day. You don't respond. We've also been trying to get in touch with you about your classes.

We've needed to get another instructor, and Ade has been picking up some of your hip-hop and ballet classes," Jolene ranted.

"It doesn't seem like it was that difficult for you to replace me. That seems fine. I didn't reach out since everyone only seemed interested in getting me to work again."

"We all work together, so obviously we are gonna talk about needing to fill in for you. What are you on about? You really have been a *bitch* since you hurt your ankle," commented Jeff.

"Y'all could have come and visited me."

"You're right, I could have but clearly you can walk just fine, so maybe you should have seen me? Anyway, are we the drunk ones or you? Can we just say we're sorry and have fun?" Jolene joked. "Let's…take…a shot." She reached out for Camilla's hand.

"Maybe I don't want to drink with you."

"What is wrong with you? I'm sorry I never came to see you. I'll come by tomorrow and we'll all go to brunch. Come on. Anyway, we've been waiting for you to return to work. We thought your injury wasn't supposed to take that long. Were you staying off of it? Anyway, if you can work, bring your lazy ass back to the studio." Jolene continued to joke, failing to properly gauge Camilla's annoyance.

Camilla was especially defensive because she had not stayed off of it, prolonging her injury. She didn't know who she was if she was not dancing around her room and apartment; her movements were instinctually fluid, and she forgot about her ankle often. Even more, she tried to test it too early. In her mind she insisted that she was young and strong, and her body would be able to perform. She might have tried too many physical therapy exercises, too soon. It still hurt, but at this moment something was giving her the energy to move. "Nice to know you think I'm lazy *and* stupid. My injury takes as long as it does…maybe I just really hurt myself. Obviously, dancing is much harder than walking around. You should know. Just because I can go for a walk doesn't mean to can lead dance classes. But thank you for letting me know how much of a burden I've been." Camilla then began to walk away.

"Is that all you got from what I was saying?" Jolene called out, but she was met with no response.

"Hey, where is Milla going?" asked Ade.

"I don't know. Don't worry. Something's up with her. Maybe she'll actually respond to us tomorrow."

From there, Camilla's body brought her out from under the streetlights and into the large park at the center of the city. Her path was a large and scenic method of returning home, adding over an hour to her trip. The park was filled with a diversity of trees and this late into summer they were all green. In the park there were small shrubs and long grasses, the occasional pond, and many paved paths broken by the flow of one large river. The miracle river flowed through the park, but on each side it ended and continued underground.

As Camilla wandered through the park, she could not stop arguing with her sister in her head. In the moment, she was so taken aback she didn't have time to truly form her thoughts. Everything was weighing heavily on her mind, and now she had so much more she wanted to say. As she argued with Jolene in her head, Jolene's hypothetical responses felt as if she was shouting directly in Camilla's ear, as if she was really there. The sensation made Camilla even more angry. In her rage, she lost direction of where she was in the park. The voices grew until she could not take it anymore. She grew so annoyed she had to stop and shout at herself, "SHUT UP." Her mind was running amok.

Camilla lowered her hoodie and looked around herself to make sure she was alone. The air was silent except for the faint sound of crickets. She was alone; no one had seen her outburst. She searched around for a trail sign or monument to orient herself. Nothing. She began to walk again, heading toward the distant streetlights that guaranteed civilization. It wasn't very long before she felt a voice in her ear again. This time it was different, though—deeper. At first it began as a whisper, but as Camilla continued to walk it grew louder. Louder, louder, louder until it was a scream. She could no longer think or hear her own thoughts. It repeated, "You're almost there. You're so close. I'm so excited to meet you." With each repeat, it sped up until it was only shrieking white noise.

She was lost and wandering; her body took her deeper into the park and away from the city. When she finally got enough strength to think, Camilla stopped once again and shook her head before she screamed, "Who are you?" That plea was the only thing her body could focus on. By the time she had been able to break free, she was deeply lost. At least, for a moment it was silent.

"Turn here," the voice whispered. This time Camilla felt her head pushed down and to the right. She now realized she was standing in the middle of a small stone bridge. Down its side, she could see a small and densely packed trail surrounded by patches of beautiful flowers. Their petals were a bright white, bordering on purple, and others were shades of yellow and orange. Her body pulled her to follow the path down to the riverbank below. The heavy rains of the spring and the hot summer left the path dense. As necessary, Camilla weaved her way between the path and the flowers, trying carefully not to damage them too much. They did not give her the same courtesy; the thorns of the flowers ripped into her pants and sweatshirt as she struggled down.

The entire time the voice had directed her, it came from over her shoulder. That changed when she finally made her way to the river's edge. Instead, the voice now came from a large sewer pipe that was built into the body of the bridge. The arch of the bridge made the pipe look like the entrance to a damp temple. A tiny stream of clean water flowed out from the rusted sewer system; it joined the larger river that continued out of the park as several smaller tributaries.

From a distance, Camilla searched the darkness of the pipe for the source of the voice. "Come on in," it hissed. The sound echoed out from somewhere deep in the pipe. When the words were spoken, long, thin, serpent-like eyes and the large ghastly blue smile of Eensaamheid appeared. Once again, the voice called out to her and the echo grew, shaking the pipe. As it did, air billowed from behind the barely visible and misty face.

Camilla began to walk toward it; she felt deeply compelled by something. The shore quickly ended, and she was forced to make her way unsteadily across wet rocks. She stepped from rock to rock as the water flowed around her. It was after a small jump that her ankle began to rock, and she slipped into the cold water. It rushed through her thin shoe and filled her sock. She pressed her foot down into the squishy discomfort, and the sensation broke her out of her trance.

"What am I doing?" she thought as she looked around herself and shivered. Her rage was gone and replaced with only sadness. She looked back up at the entrance to the sewer.

Eensaamheid was still waiting, his smile unfazed. The two stood in silence, staring at one another before Camilla grew the strength to turn and run. She sprinted across the submerged and slippery rocks. Her ankles rocked and her leg throbbed. She only slipped two times before she made it to the shore.

"Wait! Come back!" shouted the voice. It no longer seemed to follow her, but it was loud and commanding in the distance. At the hill, Camilla couldn't find the path she had taken down from the bridge, and so she had no choice but to run into the foliage. She charged through her own path and attempted to rush up the hill as fast as she could. Soon she found herself on all fours climbing through the plants. Her legs were tangled in branches and vines, and she stomped through the flowers as she fell into the thick bushes. Camilla pulled her body from the thorns that cut her and ripped up her clothes. She never looked back; she was afraid something could be following her. She escaped the plants and rolled her way onto the paved path that fed to the bridge. She quickly pushed herself up and ran along the only path she saw. She ran toward the streetlights in the distance, and still, she never looked back.

It was a blur, and she didn't remember how long it took, but after a few moments she was out of the park, through the first exit she could find. As she looked around the unfamiliar streets, she pulled out her phone and attempted to find her way home. The sun was beginning to rise, and she now realized she had been wandering all night; the streets were already filled with people starting their day and on their way to work. Camilla stopped at the first bus stop she could find and scanned its code to pull up its route map. On her phone popped up the interactive map, and she looked at the options of all the connected subways and buses. She saw this stop could eventually take her home, if she transferred a few times, and that was all she needed. Her leg was steadily swelling, and she didn't want to walk anymore.

Within a few minutes, Camilla was surrounded by more people; a crowd had gathered for the bus. She ignored everyone around her, preferring to hide in her sweater and made her way to the middle. She sat by the first open window seat and pulled down her hoodie even further and began to use her hand to inspect her hair under it. As she ran her fingers along the strands of the wig, she could feel the crunch of leaves and petals in her hair. Her fingers began to tense as she tried to catch her reflection in the window.

"Your hair looks so cool and creative. I love the design. What inspired it, if you don't mind me asking?" commented a voice from in front of Camilla. She turned to see a woman, Autumn, seated a few rows ahead. She wore purple scrubs, her hair pulled back in a ponytail.

Camilla continued to inspect her own hair; she couldn't see herself in the bright shine of the morning sun. "What?" she asked, as she turned on her phone and used the camera to inspect her reflection.

"The flowers in your hair. I love them. I figure you put them in on purpose."

"Why on earth would I do that?" Camilla snidely responded. She realized her hair was displaced. She was mortified. She continued to frantically adjust it.

"Oh, I've just been reading this biography here." Autumn held up a small book with a bright blue bookmark. "It's about Marsha P. Johnson. She lived around a hundred and fifty years ago. She used to make these intricate headdresses but was poor, so she loved to do it with simple flowers. You just reminded me of it." Autumn leaned forward to show Camilla a picture of one such headdress. Marsha's large smile took up half the photo, and though it was old and had a large glare across it, Camilla could see the cute patterns of flowers in Marsha's hair.

While she analyzed the photo, Camilla stopped pulling out the flowers in her hair and instead began to gently touch them. "No, I've never heard of her. But she looks fierce. Thank you for the compliment." Camilla smiled as she ran her finger over the photo in the book. "I'm just a mess." Camilla let out a little laugh that almost brought tears with it.

"Well, you seem to be doing great not trying. So, I'm sure if you tried, you'd look even better. A natural." Camilla continued to look over the photo and for the first time in months, she felt connected to something. She wasn't sure why, but she just needed to look up more about this woman. Autumn turned back and returned to reading, while Camilla peered out the window as she ran her fingers over her hair and stared out at the busy city. The morning had just started by the time Camilla got home, and though she was exhausted she still sat at her computer anyway and booted up the antique laptop. The small fan emitted a loud grind as it chugged away and tried its hardest to navigate her to the internet.

For the next few hours, Camilla was transfixed to her screen as she searched through the life and history of Marsha P. Johnson. She felt like she had found one of her ancestors, a friend. As Camilla read about her accomplishments, she realized that Marsha was one of the two women who had started the Stonewall riots, one of the many events that led to the society of acceptance she now lived in; struggles that Camilla was too young to have learned. She had grown up with support always by her side. Those darker, less tolerant times were not history taught in schools anymore.

She read about the struggles her people once faced for healthcare and housing. How Marsha and Sylvia Rivera had started the Street Transvestite Action Revolutionaries, and how they helped to save the community from the spread of an ancient disease known as AIDS. She found videos of Marsha from interviews saying, "I was no one, nobody from nobody-ville, until I became a drag queen. That is what made me into the world." Camilla then followed links to more videos, interviews, and shows. Marsha's laugh and voice resonated in her mind. "As long as one person has to walk for gay rights, we all need to walk for gay rights."

As Camilla jumped from link to link, she was directed to old drag performances of Marsha's, done in illegal underground clubs. With every subsequent video she learned how truly terrible of a singer Marsha was, but Camilla could not help but watch more; some performances were songs and others dance. In each video Marsha performed with a new crown of flowers, a huge smile on her face, and her friends by her side. Their movements were unrefined, but their feelings came through their motions and Camilla could easily see the passion. These were stories about their lives in song and dance, done in secret with their friends because they were looked down upon.

Then Camilla began to notice something distinct about all the women she was seeing. With every video she saw the passage of time, how some people came and went from videos; how the community honored those they lost. She noticed it most on the face of Marsha, whose constant use of a smile led to lines around her mouth. As these women struggled for freedom they also aged; they lost time. Their work, losses, and triumphs were shown on their faces as wrinkles. Something that Camilla rarely saw anymore.

Camilla found it so beautiful. The swinking around the eyes from laughing. The forehead wrinkles that come from years of love and concern for friends. In her current world, they were unique and rare. Camilla felt a ball of guilt in her heart for never having known about these women and wondered how she could make up for it. She wanted to embody those souls for all of time. How could she live her life as a tribute to the great ones who came before?

As she began to fall asleep, Camilla finally looked up to the fates of Marsha and Sylvia, hoping to find out they had made it to the invention of Rejuverron and were still alive somewhere. She was disheartened to find that not only were either of them alive, but they had both died prematurely; only living around fifty years each. *What a short time*, she thought. It was barely twice Camilla's life. Sylvia was robbed of life by cancer and even worse, Marsha was found murdered and her killer was never caught. Though they had fought for rights, the real victories wouldn't come until much after their deaths.

The weight in Camilla's chest became even heavier when she realized Marsha was never honored in the way she deserved. Her stomach ached at the thought that they were only appreciated by a small number of people. She felt part of the problem; she could not even claim she had known about them. In a matter of hours, the joy of her new heroes was taken away. Her heart was broken and the small connection she had regained to society that evening was crushed. That's when Eensaamheid's powers took hold again.

As Camilla fell asleep that night, her face down on her keyboard, blue mist flowed from the depths of her computer screen. The thick cloud leaked over her and filled the room. As the mist covered her body, each text message and missed phone call was deleted. A blank and lonely screen was left. As she slept, Camilla breathed in the smog deeply. Her body was still and while she rested, she could hear his voice in her head once again.

"The world mistreated her, and it mistreats you. Can't you see cycles are eternal? Look at how deeply she was dishonored, and further dishonored by not having her story told. If you feel so accepted, then why do you still feel so alone? I can help you feel together. Just join our family. I know plenty of lost souls who were searching for comfort and instead found peace. Why were you so afraid of me? I'm still waiting for you, Camilla. We love you. We're still here."

Camilla woke up that evening as the sun was setting. She had slept all day on her keyboard; a deep outline of each key was embedded on her forearms. She leaned back and stretched, then checked her phone. Nothing. As she let out a yawn, she finally felt how dirty she still was from the night before. Her clothes were bloody and torn, and her hair was still filled with leaves. She was still even wearing her shoes. She needed a shower.

As she turned on the water and got in, everything seemed fine. The scalding hot water felt great against her neck and back. She stood in the comforting stream and disassociated. It wasn't until she began to wash her hair and ran her hand over her scar that she could hear him again. His voice brought her mind back to what she had read the night before. She was filled with isolation and grief. "Together we have the gift of perfection. We can help to heal your scars together. Our bodies are all perfect. Your ankle, your scalp, all perfect. No one ever ages. We all love each other. There is no difference here." Camilla awoke walking in the streets. She had apparently finished showering and gotten dressed. She was wearing a bright blue dress. With every step she felt her body guiding her back toward the park. It was as if no matter how hard she tried to resist she was on a tether slowly pulling her toward it. Before long she found herself once again in the park, standing on the stone bridge.

This time his voice was not calling to her from the pipe but instead came from somewhere deep inside her mind. As his words beckoned her down the side of the hill, her body moved with no resistance. There was a morbid curiosity deep inside of her. Once again, the vines scrapped at her bare legs, but her ankle was strong, and she easily made her way down to the river. His face did not meet her at the entrance this time. Instead, she followed the whispers in her mind. At the riverbed she removed her shoes and followed its call to crawl into the pipe.

Then she followed the water upstream. At his direction she walked through various sewer pipes and made her way throughout the city underground.

Here

Left

Right, left

Down

Climb up

His words did nothing to warm her wet body, but she followed its directions anyway. The old service tunnels were filled with water; leaks from pipes traveled down the walls and made their way into larger sewer pipes. Their mangled bodies intersected and stretched out in all directions, down every hallway. Camilla climbed out of the water and made her way to a much larger set of hallways. Here, the pipes fed into concrete and steel corridors; mold laced everything in the old passages. Mystery liquids dripped from them onto the floor in front of her.

In certain areas she could see light from the city above; the sound of cars and people on the streets fell in quietly. Someplace in the back of her mind lived her sanity, which told her to leave. By the time its screams got loud enough that she could have listened to it, she was too lost to turn around. She realized she had no idea where she was. Then as if he were trying to calm her nerves he spoke to her again.

Almost there

At the end of a series of small corridors, she climbed up a ladder attached to a weak metal scaffolding and found herself in a large room whose floor was a large metal grating littered with large pieces of machinery. Camilla looked down and saw that they were suspended above pipes and pits of running water. She knew now she stood on a shaky balcony; the dangling room sat above a sewer abyss. Periodically, large brick pillars shot through it and continued a hundred feet into the air where they held up the city.

She stood in some deep internal system for the city barely anyone had ever seen. It looked like a retired service area for some grand project she couldn't fully imagine. Along the walls were small side rooms separated by bars. Everything in the room was rusted and wet. In the center, one shattered pillar sat like a throne among the rubble. Over the seat was draped a large neon blue snakeskin. Its head hung down and its scales shined iridescently in the sunlight that came through the sewer grates above. She heard him speak again but the voice was no longer coming from within her head, but from the chair.

Closer

As Camilla moved toward it, the snakeskin lifted up as if someone was sliding under it. It floated above the seat and below it shined light that formed into the body of a man. The open mouth of the snake rested over his head like a cap; a king sitting on his throne. The eyes of the snake opened and lit up and as he spoke, and the mouth of the snake moved while the man sat stoic. Behind the throne, the snakeskin extended far into the darkness and continued down another pipe even deeper into the sewer.

"Thank you so much for coming to find me. Camilla, you really are special."

"Where is everyone else? You said there was a family waiting for me. You seem…alone."

"We are a family, Camilla. Didn't want to overwhelm you. You're such an excited girl. You wanna meet everyone? Then of course." The scales that coated his body began to float off and separate, revealing his impossibly black skin beneath; light failed to escape it. As the scales floated off, they enlarged showing their strange and unique shapes. They spun in the air and began to float above the ground. Like the body of light that existed under the snake, for each scale a body began to form from it and the scales acted as their faces. They were engraved with long and hollow marks that appeared like eyes; each one was unique. They lined up by the hundreds behind the throne; each moved and waved at her from a distance but none of them made any sound. Then a lone scale landed close by his side. The mask was stout and covered in scars. The body that emerged from it was, in contrast, long, thin, and bony.

"This is my assistant—well…our assistant, Art. I think the two of you would have a lot in common. Art will prepare you to become one of us."

"What do you mean become one of you?" Camilla took a small step back.

"To connect you, to me… to us. We have to be one to be a family. Isn't that what you are missing? Everyone abandons you and everyone leaves you. You thought you had a family, your friends…but they left you. You thought you had a society, but it's been a hollow lie. People forget and move on. Once you are part of us, then that will never happen again. No one is honored anymore but with us you will be for eternity. Here, you will be honored as part of us. I even have a mask for you already."

Another scale detached from the beast's body and slowly floated down to her. Like all the rest, a phantom chain joined it to Eensaamheid's long body. It came into her hands, and as she looked at it, she could see her image reflected in beautiful blue. As she pulled it closer to her face, she could see the image of her sister, her family, her dance students, and her friends. She could see all of their faces but for only an instant. Then each of their faces became full of anger.

Silent shouts of disappointment radiated into Camilla's chest. Her heart sank as she reached out and pulled in the mask. Right before the mask touched her skin, she saw one final face, Marsha. Her voice played in Camilla's head: *"We're all dying, dying, dying, but I'm not dead yet."* Camilla pulled the mask away from herself.

"What makes you any better than them?" Camilla said while a tear ran down her cheek. Her heart was filled with resentment she had never felt before. Something about his presence was corrupting her further.

"I've never abandoned you, and I never would. I've always been there to check in on you. Even before you noticed me, I saw you. Even after you rejected us yesterday, here I am for you. Where are *they*?"

Camilla reached into the pocket of her dress and pulled out her phone. The screen still showed no new notifications. "They are just busy, and I was kind of a bitch," she whispered to herself while putting her phone back in her pocket.

"No such thing, my dear. We make time for the things we care about." The scale was thrust toward her face. The crowd behind him was active once again; they cheered and threw their hands into the air. Camilla grabbed the scale and stepped forward into a small area of sunlight. In her scale Camilla saw Jolene smiling, and in that moment her phone rang. The deep bass of the upbeat song was a special ringtone for only Jolene. Camilla went into her pocket to answer it, but as she pulled it out, it flung from her hand. She looked up to see Eensaamheid's hand extended toward her. He wiggled his finger and mist flew from him and covered the phone. The phone was silenced, and the notifications erased again.

"You went through my phone?" Camilla questioned. She now knew he had been deleting her messages. "I need to go. I've made a terrible mistake." Camilla let go of the scale, which dropped slightly before it began to float back to Eensaamheid.

"You were so close. I am so deeply disappointed. No matter." The snake then turned toward Art. "Retrieve her for assimilation—use one of the side rooms. I have others I must attend to." The once humanoid Art started to shift, and as he stumbled toward Camilla, his body pulsated and throbbed randomly. Each limb grew larger and smaller, and his mask grew in size as his head beat. Before she could turn and run, he had grabbed her arms with his skinny and bony hands. His long fingers laced up her forearms. Then his old bones creaked as his arms began to stretch and wrapped around hers. It slowly rode up her body multiple times, fully constricting her. Once she was tied up, Art proceeded to walk her back to Eensaamheid.

"What was it you wanted me to do with her? Assimilation?"

"You're smarter than that, Art. You know what I meant—we'll give her some time to change her mind but first." The snake's head turned toward Camilla. "Why did you decide to fight? I thought we understood each other?"

"The fact society is doing so well now shows their deaths were not in vain. We may have forgotten them, but we can still honor them. It's not too late. Jolene and my friends love me, even if I've been isolated and rude. I miss them and you've been lying to me. You've been making me feel alone."

"Listen to her spout nonsense," complained Art. "Why is she important? Why does she deserve to join?"

"She was so close to joining, Art. If I knowingly abandon her, at these hardest times, am I any better than anyone else? We have to save her, and you will help. We have to make our families sometimes. Don't you want to help your family, Art? Did we forget our lessons?"

"Sometimes we do not know what's best for ourselves," Art said before he dropped his head down, as if he suddenly remembered something.

"That's right, Art. That's exactly right. You know what to do." The figure of the man on the throne vanished and the snakeskin dropped onto it. It dangled on the throne for only a moment before it quickly shot off, rolling itself up as it disappeared into the darkness. Art was left alone with Camilla, and he dragged her off to one of the partially built cells. Once inside his arm fell off, dropping Camilla to the ground. As he walked away from her and exited the cell his arm grew back. Art then focused on the small, open doorway and began to wrap it shut with his arm as he did to her. His arm stretched and wrapped around the frame over a hundred times until it made a strong and sturdy structure. Once it was complete, he looked down at Camilla, who was still tied up, and nodded. The arm around her vanished and she was left lying on the ground. Art curled into a ball and sat on the ground outside her cage in silence.

It wasn't more than a few minutes before Camilla was compelled to stand, and as she did, she talked. She was not going to stay here. "How is sitting here gonna to change my mind?"

"You will realize your shortcomings and the peace we offer and change your mind. Sometimes you just need more time to realize what the right thing to do is. What is best for you."

Camilla tried to ask why, how, and what, but each time she was met with the same response. "What is best, yes, what is best." Art was a broken record. She quickly realized that her attempts to trick him or to get information would be in vain.

As she thought of what to do next, she felt tense and began to stretch; she needed to move. In the chill of the sewer her ankle didn't hurt, and she felt she might be recovered somehow. She began to do her dance stretches and warmups using the bars as support. She smiled as she could finally comfortably balance on one foot. The stretch felt like she was releasing months of tension. Her brief joy was ruined by the gravity of her situation.

Soon the room was filled with only faint moonlight, and though Camilla's eyes fought to adjust, it was still very very dark. She shivered as she was still wet, her cell too cold for her to dry. To comfort herself, she tried once again to talk to Art.

"So, your name is Art?" she asked in an overly polite tone. She then lowered herself and sat on the floor, facing him. "That is interesting. Why did he say that we would get along?"

"You should not be talking. You should be contemplating. I am here to merely facilitate."

"But we're family—are we not supposed to get to know each other?"

"True. But that can happen later."

"Art, my brother. Please?"

He sighed and turned toward her. "Well, I don't remember my real name. Art is the name our father gave to me. I'm not sure when but it's been a long time."

"Is there a reason he chose it?"

"Oh yes, of course!" Art laughed a long, dry, and exasperated laugh. "It is because of the paintings I used to do. Art. See." He gestured toward the moon with one arm. "I used to love to make oil and charcoal pieces. My studio was once filled with large tapestries. My hands were always dirty. My clothes, too."

"That sounds wonderful. I would love to see them. Do you have any still?"

"Oh, no, no, no, no. I haven't done *that* in a long time. No painting for me. No art for Art." He released another hollow and forced laugh. Camilla felt like he truly meant it.

"Don't you want to paint? Does *he* stop you?"

"No, no, no. He would never. And *I* would never. I haven't painted in such a long time. I can't even remember how I would start. What I would make. I haven't wanted to paint in so long. Once I became part of the family, that need was gone. Slowly, I didn't need to paint anymore." He smiled below his mask as he finished, "I am content."

"But didn't you live for your art?" Camilla asked in disbelief. She could not understand the idea. In both her deepest sadness and happiest moments, dance was all she felt and how she interacted with the world. She could not imagine a life that felt so out of touch, one where she couldn't find a purpose to dance and create movement.

"It comes with peace. When you don't have to worry, you don't need to create. You'll be so happy one day that you don't have to dance."

"I can't image that." Camilla knew now more than ever that she needed to escape. There was no hope here. She scanned the room while she started to dance back and forth around the small cell again. She subtly tapped on the barrier made of flesh to test for its strength. It was sturdy but squishy. She knew she couldn't break through it, and she really didn't want to touch it again if she didn't have to. Camilla's mind raced with thoughts of how to escape. It took several hours, but eventually she had a plan. A simple one. She knew what she needed to do. She needed to flatter Eensaamheid.

He returned the next morning when Camilla's stomach was heavy and empty. Even worse, she had not been able to sleep much. She could hear the streets above them grow loud and small rays of light came through the grates above. The snake entered the room as he had left, appearing out of the darkness and draping himself over the throne. The large celestial body emerged below it again and Eensaamheid began to talk.

"It's nice to see you are up and so active. You seem to be in much better spirits than yesterday. Have you come to your senses? Art, has she accepted us?"

"I'm not sure—I'm sorry. She kept trying to talk to me about dance and art. So, I started to ignore her."

"What he means to say is that I have truly come to understand the beauty of your family." Camilla reached her hand through the bars of her cage toward Eensaamheid. "I was inspired by the peace you've been able to give to Art. That and your strong leadership, and respect you have of your family."

"So, you are ready to take your place with us?" The snake smiled, gestured toward her, and he looked at Art. "Bring her out for the ceremony. Her mask is waiting."

Camilla stepped away from the bars and toward him. She put her arms behind her back, and she stretched and talked. "But first if you may…*Father.*" He was pleased to hear her call him that. "I have choreographed a piece for you. I was up all night doing so. I'd love to perform it…in your honor, of course."

"That won't be necessary, but if you wish, once you join us, you can teach everyone to dance." He gestured with his arm again, hurrying Art to release her.

"I have no want to dance but thank you," Art responded. He walked toward the barrier of flesh and raised his arm in the air. As he waved it back and forth, it disintegrated.

"*Father*," Camilla repeated in a growling voice. "You *must* let me show you some of it. I believe it really captures your elegance and strength."

"Fine…," Eensaamheid said, unable to turn down something in his honor. "I would never want to stifle my children. Please, *honor* me."

Camilla stepped out from her prison and moved in front of the large throne. Her feet were raw from hours of being wet and from the rusty grating she stood on. She began her movements with a plié, and she shuffled from side to side. Her dance was a soft ballet, but she mimicked the distorted bodies of the masked creatures she saw. As if possessed, she shifted between different heights and shapes. Between each form she flowed in a sidewinding manner. With each move, she contorted and slowly moved away from the monster. After only a few moments she was interrupted.

"Thank you, my dear," he shouted. "That was beautiful. I *really* am honored. The way you captured Art and me in those moments. Inspired. *Now* it's my honor to bring you as one of the family." The same beautiful blue scale floated off his body and toward Camilla.

"I wasn't finished. I still have a lot I could show you." Camilla began to dance once again, backing slowly away from the scale. Her movements this time were smoother.

"STOP," he shouted. His voice echoed in the chamber and silenced the city above. His body began to shake with anger; the light of his body pulsated. "Stop," he repeated as she continued to move, not listening. "Stop moving. Don't belittle yourself by dancing anymore,

darling," he attempted to say calmly. "You don't need to do anything *but* worship me."
Eensaamheid once again moved the scale toward her and placed it in her hands.

As Camilla lifted it up to her face, he hoped she had gotten far enough away from him. She looked at her reflection and then with one swoop, she swung the scale down. At the same time, she kicked up with all her strength. The scale shattered against her foot and fragments shot all around her. Art covered his face, and she began to sprint away. She failed to feel the cosmic shards that were embedded in her skin. They glowed as her skin absorbed them.

Eensaamheid let out a feral scream. "How dare you! I have plenty more scales for you. Don't you worry. You'll be alone without us. They'll leave you and you'll be alone, and I will still be here," he shouted in annoyance. Camilla made her way down the ladder and made her way back into the sewer corridors. She didn't need to know where she was going. She just needed to find a way out. Back at the throne, the scales on Eensaamheid's back began to fly off by the dozen. Though he appeared calm, each person who formed beneath the masks came out rabid. Though they were still connected by the phantom tether, they all sprinted forward, some upright, others on all fours. They pushed over each other as they chased down the ladder. As more and more made their way through the corridors, they pressed against each other and filled it like water. They began to flow over each other as they all fought to get to her.

Behind her, the mass moved swiftly, filling each hallway and pipe at each junction, unsure of which way she went. She could hear the crack of bones and the scrap of skin against the walls coming from behind her. Camilla sprinted and chose each direction with instinct. She never stopped to assess her location; that might take too long. She merely attempted to make her way through the sewer paths to anywhere. She could not remember any of the trip there and though it was only the night before, it was all a blur. "Just keep moving," she told herself.

Before long, Camilla made her way into another large chasm of a room. She stood on a grating with nothing but a railing surrounding her and a drop below. Water from pipes on the walls leaked into an abyss below her. She listened for the sound of a splash but the flowing water seemed to disappear. The drop could be forever. Behind her, she could still hear the noise of the twisted bodies advancing. She had one option, the rickety pipes that hung in front of her. She hoisted herself onto the railing and stood up. As she balanced, she attempted to grab a set of pipes jutting out of the wall. In front of them were smaller pipes she hoped would hold her weight. Across the room she could see another railing and another balcony.

She began to make her way across the small, wet pipes and used the ones within reach to help support her. When she had made it over a single pipe, behind her she could see the creatures finally begin to pour down the long hallway. She continued to make her way across the pipes to the best of her ability, now floating halfway to safety. Camilla's hand slipped as she shifted her arm from one pipe to another. She rubbed the slime on her dress and moved forward. Slowly, her hands and feet were being covered in slim and gunk, and she fought to maintain her grip. Behind her, the bodies of the monsters began to flood into the room. It stopped at the grating and looked around, as if it was one creature. The wall of masks turned toward her and let out a screech. Then it charged over the balcony. Some of them fell into the darkness but slowly the falling bodies began to grab onto each other. Like ants forming a bridge, they started to rise out of the darkness and toward her. As she scurried across the pathway, they built their own passage. As the arms of the monsters reached out for her, she finally made her way onto the other platform.

A grasp at her bare ankle dropped her to the ground, where she scraped her knee. Still, she stood up quickly and began to run away. The mass was almost over the gap and ready to follow her. Camilla sprinted down a hallway to find another ladder at the top of a set of stairs.

Above her was her salvation—a manhole. She raced to the top of the stairs and climbed up the ladder. With all her might, she pushed her shoulder into the manhole and tried to lift it. It felt like twenty minutes before she was able to push it up and out. As she brought her face into the warm morning air, she saw a car coming straight for her. She ducked back down into the sewer to see the mass of monsters still making their way toward her. She breathed heavily and looked back up through the opening. She listened and once she could not hear a car, she jumped out.

Camilla rolled off to the side as cars began to reenter the intersection. Behind her the arms and limbs of the monsters pushed through the hole. She used her legs to push the manhole back into place, and with all her weight she laid on top of it. Traffic had now built up. Cars stopped at the intersection and began to honk at her. She then dragged herself off to the side of the road. She stared up at the trees and breathed heavily, then she realized she was still somewhere along the length of the park. Her body was tired and sticky, but she lifted herself and made her way down the street. After a while she found a public phone, and typed in the only number she knew by heart. It was Jolene's. The phone rang a single time before she picked up. "Who on earth is this?" she questioned.

"It's Camilla. I'm sorry I missed your call. I miss you."

"Girl, I'm happy you called me back, but what happened to your number? You know I don't like random numbers."

"It's a long story—I'll have to explain later," answered Camilla.

"Great, I'd love some tea. Also, I don't know exactly what I said the other night but I'm sure I was drunk and a little out of line. I hoped after we fought I would have heard from you yesterday, but since you didn't, I'm reaching out. I'm trying to be better about calling but can we talk in person? We miss you."

"Yeah, we can talk. I'm a bit exhausted at the moment, but are you and the girls going for brunch today?"

"Hell, if you want, we can make that happen. I don't have any classes I couldn't teach a little more *fluid*."

"I need a nap but call the gang together for a late brunch. Also. tell them I'm sorry."

"Not necessary, booboo."

Camilla went home and showered once again before falling asleep on her couch. The whole while her mind was calm. The voice was nowhere to be found. After a short nap, she got ready for her brunch date with her friends with a new passion. She donned her favorite sparkling purple shirt; brunch was for bright colors and mimosas. Instead of throwing on her normal wig, Camilla grabbed a strip of cloth from her drawer. She wove the cloth through her hair, leaving space over her scar. She then snuck downstairs and discreetly stole some flowers from a neighbor's garden. She returned to her room and placed them in her hair. She used her scar as a highlight of a ring of yellow and red petals. Once she was ready, she made her way to their favorite brunch spot, fashionably late as always, where her friends already had mimosas.

"Damn, look at your head. Fancy, but did you forget your hair this morning?" joked Brittany.

"I thought I looked cute and wanted to spruce it up. Thought I was having a good scar day," responded Camilla confidently with a big smile.

"Don't let her talk shit to you. You look great. I love the flowers. You stole them from Mitch's garden, didn't you?" Jolene said while she poured Camilla a drink.

"No comment, but I have big news."

"You're coming back to work finally?" asked Ade. She broke off a small piece of bread and slathered it in butter.

"Well, yes, that is part of it but not all of it. You know how Jolene and I are turning twenty-five in a few months?" questioned Camilla.

"Yeah, and it's going to be a party. I already have my Rejuverron dress picked out," cheered Jolene.

"It's going to be a celebration for one." Camilla paused. "I'm going to be there of course but I'm not going…to take mine. At least for now. I'm going to wait to take my Rejuverron. For how long, I'm not exactly sure."

"Oh no, Milla, you didn't join one of those cults, did you? You haven't been out of the loop that long, have you? How many Gods are there?" questioned Ade, still chewing on bread.

"No… This is my own decision. I do it with a sound body and mind and not under religious duress of any kind. Just, before you judge, do me a favor and look at these pictures. I think you'll understand." Camilla flipped through photos she had saved on her phone of Marsha.

"Wow, those clothes are retro. When are these photos from? Is your phone broken or are they really that blurry? Who are these ladies? I can see you copied your flower crown from one of them," Jolene said, squinting at the phone.

"These are some of the women who gave us the rights we have today. Look at how beautiful they are. This was way before Rejuverron was invented."

"Oh, so they're like really old then. What do they have to do with you?" asked Brittany, pouring herself another drink.

"I think these women are beautiful. Look at their distinct faces. Look at their wrinkles. Look at their smile lines. I want to be like them. I think the best way I can honor them is by also letting myself age. At least a little. Solidarity."

"Letting yourself age for fashion?" scoffed Jeff.

"Not for fashion, to honor those who came before us. It just so happens that drag's pretty cool and already in my clothing wheelhouse."

"You do realize you won't just get wrinkles, right? You're going to *get* old. Don't you know how dangerous that could be?" scolded Jolene.

"Yeah, I thought you wanted to be a dancer forever. Old bones are gonna creak during the shows," joked Jeff.

"I didn't know you were into shows like that. You never mentioned it before," commented Ade, a little behind in the conversation.

"Well, I didn't know what I was missing. We'll all have to go to a show sometime soon. I hear some of them do mimosas."

"Of course, you know I'll be in," Ade said, taking a sip. "I love someone who can sing."

"You're not going to be able to move the same way you do now. You think your ankle is bad now. Wait till you ain't got no cartilage," Jeff said while starting to eat a parfait that was brought to the table. "I'm not trying to be mean. I'm just trying to take care of you."

"You're right. Thank you for caring. I love you, Jeff. I won't be able to move the same, but I'll still be able to move. In some way, what will be my new way, I'll figure it out. I'll adapt. There are plenty of people without perfectly functioning bodies, some who even took Rejuverron later in life. I'm sure some of those people would love to pay for a dance class with me. I know I'm never not going to want to dance, so I'll make it work. I can have both."

Jolene's face looked very concerned, and she said, "You're going to get sick more easily, and…" Camilla then interrupted her.

"Which happens to everyone…so don't worry. And even if it did, you're going to be there to help me."

"Yeah, yeah, of course I will," Jolene said as she reached for her mimosa and raised it to the sky. "Let's cheer to having our little psycho back in the group. May her old, wrinkly butt keep us looking young and beautiful in comparison." The group cheered and laughed as they clinked their glasses.

"Oh, don't worry. I'll still be hot. You four will be running around looking like preschoolers. I'll be a real woman."

There's a Rock in the Room

There's a Rock in the Room

"Hooooonnnnney…there's a rock in the room!" Paulson Peterson shouted upstairs to his wife, his voice was nasally and gruff. He was standing at the bottom of the basement stairs with a shovel in his hands. His gray t-shirt and work gloves were covered in dirt, and his auburn beard was filled with sweat. His hair was short and flat on top, cleanly shaped in a tight military cut. He trimmed his own hair once a week, on Saturdays.

Julie Rose Peterson appeared at the top of the stairs wearing a yellow plastic jumpsuit and carrying a microfiber duster in her hand. The suit was tucked into matching yellow boots and extended into a hood that was presently over her head. She removed the lightweight gas mask that covered her face and called down to Paulson. "Not to be rude, dear, but you've been digging for a couple hours. I would hope there are many rocks down there. Some real big ones but hopefully a lot of little ones too. Are you trying to say you just started?"

"No, smartass. Obviously, I've broken up most of the sheetrock and stuff. What I'm trying to do is… I'm trying to get your attention. Why don't you come down here and see? I think you'll find it interesting. I found this weird rock." Paulson banged his shovel on the stairs and gestured toward her.

"Is it really worth it? I'm kinda in a groove up here."

"Yes, I'm telling you, come here. Also, do you really have to wear that suit?" Rose placed her duster at the top of the stairs and made her way toward her husband.

"Yes, I do. There is dust built up all over the house. The chandeliers are raining skin flakes down on us. There is paint chips on the molding I'm touching up, and…" Rose's words picked up speed with each subsequent one. She then began to place her gas mask back on until Paulson cut her off.

"Okay, I'm sorry, you're right, but you don't have to wear that mask down here. It's totally safe." Paulson put out his hand and lowered the mask to her side. "I have to comply with construction safety regulations every day at work. I promise you, these are not hazardous work conditions."

"I don't know why you're so loose with these rules. Sure, it's just a little rock dust here and a little insulation there, but it will build up. Do you want to have lung cancer in seventy-five years? Will that be worth your carelessness?" Rose raised her mask again but this time to point and scold him. Paulson smiled and pushed it down again. Then he leaned in and gave her a little kiss. "I'm not going to wear it—for a minute, *but* I will not stay down here long. There are not enough fans in here."

"There are six! Two are industrial, you loon." Paulson led Rose down a small hallway and around a corner. In the outskirts, Paulson was beginning to renovate; he had already ripped down all the drywall from the large basement, leaving only wood planks and exposed cement. A construction worker by trade, he refused to allow anyone else to work on his home. Between his busy work schedule and time with his family, the process was slow. He was excited that this week he finally had a small break in his schedule.

Rose attempted to ask more safety questions as the two entered the back room, but the sound of the fans made it impossible. Along the walls were all the fans that he had promised. Paulson went to a generator and turned them off. He then stood by a mess of broken ground and gravel. "So, isn't it cool?" He smirked and leaned on his shovel.

"What? Are you trying to do an impersonation of our son right now? What are you talking about? Do you mean the pit of death you started building into our ground?"

"Well, we *need* to redo the floor to make sure it's properly level, but really? You don't see it? You're so supposed to be so on top of things…so observant. Well…" He paused annoyingly. "Check this out." Paulson walked to the edge of the room near the biggest hole he had created. He used his shovel to move away some of the larger pieces of ground to reveal a small, blue-white crystal sticking up from the rubble. "See, look at that color! Isn't it beautiful?"

"What? That tiny thing?" Rose walked deeper into the room and got down on all fours. "You expected me to see this? After you covered it? It's gotta be two inches high…tops. That's what's so amazing? I'm going back upstairs. Let me know when you finish the room. Then I'll be impressed with how many rocks you moved." Rose began to turn away, but Paulson grabbed her hand.

"Boy, you're just *go go go* when you start getting things organized. No, stand right here, and look down." Paulson positioned Rose so she had the sun to her back and directed her to look straight down. As she peered at the stone, light shined through it and scattered below—like a kaleidoscope made up of only beautiful shades of turquoise, white, and navy. The way the light shined it was clear the crystal was much larger than was currently visible, like an iceberg. The lights bounced and their beams showed Rose the dancing of a young girl with a look of dread on her face. Rose felt the image dance around her until the girl was hiding behind her. She stood silent and a rock built up in her chest, then a strong pull. She felt that she wanted to protect the girl.

No. That wasn't it.

Her heart ached for *her* child.

After a moment, Paulson shook Rose back to her senses. "It's something, isn't it? I think it goes deeper. I actually tried to chip it with my shovel but it didn't crack at all. It just bent the tip. I probably can't return this one to work anymore. But perks of being the boss, I guess." He lifted his shovel to show his wife his proof.

Rose slowly responded, turning her body toward Paulson but keeping her eyes transfixed on the small fractal. "Wow, that was…that was something." She was having a hard time getting her words out. "Did you, did you get a kind of…kind of feeling…of cold." She finally turned her head toward Paulson. "Like a draft down here." Then she snapped out of it completely. "Is that going to be a problem? Are we going to have to do something about the temperature down here? Oh, also that reminds me." She pointed a gloved finger at Paulson's face. "Are you coming with us to the picnic tomorrow?"

Paulson began to take off his gloves and shook his head. "You know I have to go in to work tomorrow. I already took off a few days for this basement. The crew needs me. Also, if you want me to finish this this century, I'm going to have to skip dinner tonight."

"Yes, yes, yes… I figured, but you can't blame me for trying. Okay, fine—I'll leave something in the microwave for you whenever you're done. While you're at it, do something about this cold and make it clean for Lillard." Rose began to walk out of the room. She was acting calm, but she missed her son.

"You know, you really don't need to let him down here…if you think it's so dangerous. Though, I still think it's fine if he gets some dirt on him." The two were now yelling at each other to make up for the distance.

"He isn't supposed to come down here, but obviously that isn't going to stop him from *possibly* coming down here. So…just…in…case."

"Okay, okay, yes. I'll make it clean!" He was now calmly screaming, something he hated doing. In the distance he could hear the sound of Rose's feet stomping up the stairs. She had a habit of jumping from side to side as she ran up steps, especially in her large rubber boots. The noise echoed in the basement and Paulson thought of where he could add soundproofing. He reached into his pocket and pulled out a small Chapstick-sized tube. He twisted it to slide out a small, gold-colored disc. The small box once contained a few hundred discs but was halfway empty. He used the tip of his finger to transfer it onto his temple. The small disposable Bluetooth device immediately connected to his watch, which switched to audio mode.

Paulson searched through his playlists, and he looked for something to entertain him during the next few hours of groundbreaking. His concentration was broken again by the ringing of the doorbell. Paulson selected a song quickly at random to drown out the buzzing. Then he continued to search for something more pleasant, but the sound of the doorbell continued—its beat between lulls in his music became impossible to ignore. Then he received a text message on his watch. It obscured his possible music selections further. Paulson's shoulders were starting to get tight. *"Could you get that, please? I'm up here with Lillard. He got dirt all over his shirt."*

Paulson let out an exasperated sigh. He wished he could finish this project; it was going to take forever. Once he had started something, he liked to finish it, and he barely had been able to start this. He turned off his music and began his journey to the front door, throwing his gloves to the side of the room. The doorbell continued to ring, and with each one his pace picked up. By the time he reached the door he was at a small run.

In front of Paulson stood a man in all black. His outfit consisted of flared suit pants over boots with a large, wedged heel. His dress shirt was yellow and unbuttoned at the top. His coat was long and ran to his knees. The sleeves were immaculately cuffed, and his shirt peered out from under, just a little. At the tip of his head, he wore a large tricorn hat that tapered to a point and was ordained with a yellow ribbon that matched his shirt. Paulson scanned the man. He was patiently waiting with a large grin and held a small briefcase in his hand; the gold buckle was engraved with the initials *SR*. He then checked his watch, this time to verify the date.

"Ah, I can't believe I forgot. It's the 14th already, Mr. Romero." He looked down at his watch again. "I'm sure you have a whole pitch ready as usual, but I don't really have time today. Either way, our answer is going to be the same as it always is: *No*."

"I always tell you to call me Sidney—no need to be so formal… But yes, it is I, Mr. Peterson. It is so nice to see you again." He bowed slightly before he continued to talk. "Yes, of course. It's August 14th. Same time, same date every year. I am nothing if not very persistent, and this year I think I got you. I assure you…" He paused to open his briefcase, then pulled out a yellow folder and attempted to hand it to Paulson. "The offer I have managed to get this year is much better than last. You should at the very least take a look at it."

Paulson reluctantly took the folder without looking at Mr. Romero and opened it. He scanned through the paragraphs of technical jargon to the offer at the bottom of the page. His eyes widened as he read the number. It was significantly more than they had ever been offered. Somehow the large value actually made Paulson a bit angry, as if he was being teased—being told he could be bought. His voice rattled as he tried to be civil, "Wow…that *is* a lot. *BUT* we really don't want to move. Can't you buy any of the other houses in the area? I've checked with our neighbors; you haven't approached anyone else. Why is our home so important to you…specifically?"

"I don't make the rules, Mr. Peterson. My employer is quite particular about placement. I can attest that your house has the perfect balance of nature, neighborhood, lighting, and plant coverage. It's simply a mini oasis. *And* before you say no again, I want to point out something new this year." Sidney placed his hand in between the pages still in Paulson's hands and flipped one up toward Paulson's face (he did not appreciate that). "I saw that you were starting construction, and that means you already are doing some of the work for us. Your house is lovely, but really we are interested in the location. So, at the bottom of page two, there is a second offer under these circumstances that is much better. A little bonus for your time."

"That is *also* a very generous amount of money, but again…we have a child. We have a life here. We really don't want to be moving. We don't need the money and we'd really just like to continue making *this* place our home." Paulson began to close the door, but Sidney placed his briefcase in the doorway to jam it. "Maybe next year."

"Please, Mr. Peterson, please just have an honest look at our offer. Your life could be much easier and it could be even better for your family." That comment was the final straw and Paulson could no longer hide his anger. He opened the door again and pushed the briefcase back into Sidney's chest. He walked forward and forced Sidney back. Sidney noticed the anger in Paulson's eyes and began to use his briefcase as a shield. Paulson was much smaller than him but much angrier.

"Don't you dare come to my home *unwanted* and talk about my family…*especially* my wife and child. Get off my property now, right now! I said no, and I will always say no. You cannot buy us. Now kindly fuck off." Paulson signaled with one arm that he should leave, and Mr. Romero walked away backward, defeated. He made his way back into the house and slammed the door shut.

He began to walk down to the basement, and while doing so he started to look over the offer again. What began as anger sank into self-loathing as he realized truly how much money it was. Paulson and his wife were well off, but this was an amount of money they could never have thought of. He came from a long line of hard-working civil servants and blue-collar workers. With Rejuverron he had been making an honest living as a construction worker using a forever young and strong body. He never questioned how he worked every day and never thought about it. He just assumed he would be doing it forever. The prospect never crossed his mind; it seemed like the easy way out, too easy.

Paulson made his way back into the basement and started his ritual of choosing his work music. Another message interrupted his watch. *"We're going to have dinner now. Thank you for dealing with the door. Who was it? We'll be here if you want to eat."* Paulson spoke into his watch to text his wife back.

"It's the same weirdo that comes every year trying to buy our house. I sent him off. But he ate up some time, so I'll need to keep digging here if I want to make it to work tomorrow. I love you both, see you soon." Paulson finally found a band he wanted to listen to and pressed play—a soothing melody for his burning muscles. He put back on his work gloves, grabbed his dented shovel, and once again dug into the earth. It wasn't long before he lost track of time.

The sun rose.

Paulson was still digging when Rose woke up. His watch had died overnight, and the music had stopped playing, but still he continued to dig. His concentration was broken by Rose stomping into the room. That day she wore a bright orange dress with white flowers, and her hair was in two small buns on top of her head. Under her dress she wore her yellow boots. The basement was much too dirty for her good shoes. When she entered, Paulson was deep in the ground; everything below his nose was hidden. Over half of the floor had been removed, mostly around stone. It was nearly exhumed and clearly visible on most sides—at present it stood nearly five feet tall. Rose tapped him on the top of the head as he threw dirt over his shoulder and into a huge pile in the corner. Her touch sent a shock through his body, and he jumped.

"What time did you wake up this morning? Or, don't tell me you've been working all night? I thought you were supposed to leave early for the site?"

"Oh…" Paulson looked at his watch and noticed it was dead. He fumbled taking out his phone to check the time. He was already two hours late. "No, yes… I was supposed to, but I figured I would get a little more done here before I go in. I uhm…figured Derrel could handle set-up and deployment for another day," he lied. His face then turned toward the window and light shined through the large, half-opened stone. "Look, look. Come on down here. I've uncovered part of the rock. It's a lot bigger than I expected. I wasn't sure what direction it extended into, so I dug out all sides. Still a little left, though."

"The floor is ruined! Isn't this going to take a lot longer now?" Rose turned her nose up, disgusted. "I am not getting in that hole. It's filthy and I have a bomb dress on right now." She began to walk around the hole to find a good vantage point.

"No, no, no, no. I'll fill it all in and fix it. It'll be better than before. Eh, if you stand over there it should be good enough, but look at it. It's not actually a rock…well, it is not only one rock. Look at it: There is a darker, deeper blue stone inside, and this clear blue crystal is like surrounding it. It's like two rocks. A rock in a rock."

"I truly can't see anything. It's so shiny." Rose covered her face with one hand; it was as if the sun was directly in her face. This time the stone obscured its structure from her. "I'll have to take your word for it. Will we be able to get rid of it? Is it too heavy to move?"

"I still can't break it at all, but why would we get rid of it? It's gotta be worth a fortune. Doesn't your sister deal with all this BS?" Rose looked at him confused. "The stones, the candles? All that spiritual shit. Doesn't she feel energies and things? Think she would want to help us sell this."

Rose's face became sour, and she stuck her tongue out at Paulson playfully. "Oh! Yes, you're right. She does sell gems and such, but she's not really an appraiser. She more thinks they are pretty, and she's a little crazy, but *you treat her* with respect. Her hokey-ness seems to be playing to your advantage now, huh? I'll ask her if she wants to see your rock. No promises, though." Rose stood up and began to walk away. "Actually, since you're not going into work…that means you have time to come with us to the picnic after all?"

Paulson felt an itch on his brain at the thought of the question. All he could think of was finishing his dig. He needed to reveal the stone. "No…umm no, I can't. I said I was not going to be starting the day, but I did tell them that I would be back later. So…sorry," he lied again. "Let me clean up and say goodbye, though," he said to soften the blow.

"No, don't worry about it. Lillard is all dressed and ready to go. We need to leave before my platter gets cold." Rose blew a kiss to her husband and continued to walk away. "Oh, also I feel like there is smell down here now. Did you hit something?"

"Nope, there are no pipes down here. Just stone and other stone…and other stone. You probably smell the old, wet concrete and wood. I'll replace it." At the top of the stairs stood Lillard in his dark blue shorts and short-sleeved button-up shirt. His hair was combed forward into a little twist, and he had brown shoes that would be horrible for running in; he would not be winning any picnic games. As he stood at the top of the stairs he noticed a faint yellow mist, as if sand were flying around the room.

"What is that dust?" he shouted to his parents before he began to make his way down the stairs. With each step he grew groggier and groggier and he began to choke on the thick air. Before he made it down three stairs, he lost his balance and began to fall. Luckily, he caught himself with one arm, but his momentum swung his body forward and slammed him into the bottom of the railing. Just then Rose came around the corner to see her son disoriented and *sitting on dirt!*

Rose helped her son up and began to swat at his pants to get the dust and cement particles off. She continued to do so as she led him up the stairs by his hand. In his fog he tried to speak but was too slow to respond to his mom's constant barrage of comments, questions, and critiques. In the kitchen, Rose used a damp cloth to clean off a few new stains on her son before handing him a basket of goods to bring with them. They would be taking the tram car today.

Outside the house, the two began to make their way down the road. They had only made it a short distance before they were stopped by Mr. Romero out on a stroll. "Good morning, Mrs.

Peterson, what a beautiful day we are having today, isn't it? And don't you look like a peach in that dress!" He tipped his hat to reveal a large bald spot between his ring of fluffy brown hair.

"It really is a nice day, and it's nice to see you again, Sidney. I hope Paulson didn't give you too much of a problem while rejecting your offer this year. I had my hands full with Lillard here." Sidney leaned down and patted Lillard on the head.

"He was firm as he always is, but I truly did think our price would make a difference this year. He didn't seem to pay it much mind." Rose realized she had not known what the offer was.

"How much larger?" she wondered out loud but then caught herself. "Well, we will have to be going. Don't want to miss the tram. Going to a little picnic celebration, but you have a great day, Sidney." Rose turned and began to pull Lillard away, but Mr. Romero quickly opened his briefcase and removed an identical yellow envelope to the one he had given Paulson.

"Here, you can look over the offer as well. Perhaps he misplaced the copy I gave him." Rose took the envelope, but before she could respond Mr. Romero had already begun to walk down a side street—going nowhere in particular. At home, Paulson used his watch to send a message to his assistant developer; *"I will not be coming today, son sick,"* it read. He put his music back on and once again lost time.

The sun set.

When his family arrived that evening he was still in the hole, but now the rock was completely exposed. Rose and Lillard arrived with smiles on their faces and dirt on their clothes—they had taken a tumble into the mud during the three-legged race, but they won. The pair proudly wore their blue first-place ribbons, and Lillard was especially excited to show his father. The two walked by the open basement door, and the sound of silence coming from the basement made Rose nervous. She sent Lillard to shower as she crept downstairs in search of Paulson. The light from the back room was still on, but she couldn't hear the clank of Paulson's shovel.

She entered the room to find that the walls were lined with dirt and cement chunks piled up to her knees. In front of her, what started as a sizeable but understandable hole was now completely dug out; the back room had been turned into an altar-like pit. Rose then saw why there was no more noise; Paulson stood calmly but diligently rubbing the stone with a microfiber towel. The pit was now lower than the rock, so it stood triumphantly on a stone pillar. It seemed to proceed over the other stones below it. The crystal was exceptionally large and wide, almost four feet in diameter and seven feet tall. The outer white crystal was jagged in all directions, as if it were exploding from the smaller but much darker blue center. The bottom of the rock was layered with piles of small gems surrounding a larger piece that looked like feet and legs.

Around the stone were scattered dozens of tools—axes, saws, hammers, and picks Paulson had used to try and break it. When Rose entered the room and saw how much he had accomplished, she was astonished, confused, but mostly impressed. Her face then turned to a scowl when she realized he was still wearing the same clothes. *He lied! He skipped work and family time!* Rose took off her shoes and threw one at Paulson, which finally broke his trance.

"How dare you!" she shouted as she threw her second shoe. "Why didn't you go to work." In his shock, Paulson shook his head and attempted to mouth *I did* but was cut off by Rose. She then climbed into the pit and continued to shout, "How dare you not join in on family time! What happened to the *crew* needs you?" She was angry but mostly concerned about his change in behavior; she had heard that mini-strokes could cause sudden changes, and that was irrationally weighing on her mind.

"I didn't come to bed last night 'cause I was up so late and I didn't want to wake you up, but I took a nap. You know me, so much energy. So, I came back down here and have been trying to tidy up. Told Derrel to end the day for me," he lied again.

"You've been strange the last two days. Why didn't you show me the housing offer from Sidney? Why did *he* give it to me?"

"Because you told me to tell him to go away. I wasn't paying attention to the offer. What do you think?" Paulson turned his back toward Rose and continued to polish the rock.

"Don't turn away from me when I'm talking to you. What do you mean what do I think? I think we don't need it. I think something weird is happening. Why would they make it so large, and why is Mr. Romero still hanging around? He usually leaves the neighborhood immediately after we reject him. Also, you're being weird. What did you say to him?" Rose approached Paulson and pulled on his shoulder.

"I didn't say anything. I did what you asked, and I told him to leave. Okay…I lied about not seeing the offer, but I didn't bring it up because I know you wouldn't go for it, but did you seriously not see the magnitude of this money? And the second part about doing work on our own for extra. This could change our lives." Paul was thinking on his feet and beginning to mutter.

"I'm sorry that our life isn't good enough for you, but I thought we didn't want to sell. This is our home and I'm proud of it. You don't want to live here anymore? You want to uproot your child? You've worked so hard to make this home a customized paradise." Rose raised her hands to gesture to the whole house, but her enthusiasm was muffled by the realization that she stood in a dirty pit.

"We could buy any other house on the block; we wouldn't even need to go far. It's a ridiculous amount of money. We could even foreclose on that snooty Nanette Manoir's house and kick her out of the HOA committee." Rose didn't appreciate Paulson's attempt to deflect her annoyance onto someone else.

"Since when have you been so obsessed with money? How could you be so selfish?"

"Selfish? How is it selfish to want a better life for you two. I am never selfish. Even when I try to be it's all for you and for him. There is nothing I can do that isn't for you guys. I *try* to be a little selfish, just to make a little money. So I can quit this stupid job and do something better. But apparently even when I'm willing to work for it, I can't have it. I'm being selfish. You know, it would better his life too."

"Him? You mean your son? Does that rock have you now thinking about how much better your life could be? Why don't we try selling that first and see what it brings? I actually talked to a lady at the picnic who was very interested in it. She says she has a friend who is a geographer...I mean geologist."

"NO! Why would you tell random people about it." Paulson was angry again but not sure why. It was as if his brain itched. "I mean...why would you tell people about the rock, if we don't know how much it's worth? We could be robbed. Someone might come here and try to take it."

"What do you mean no? We're not going to keep it. You said you wanted to sell it. Since when are you so paranoid? No one who is sketchy knows where we live."

"Someone could have followed you two, easily seen where you got off the tram. I don't want to sell it." He paused again to lie. "I just want to make sure we get what's right. Besides, whatever it is, there is no way it's worth more than their offer. One's life-changing. One's nice. I have worked every day and every night, in some way, giving myself for the last eighty years. Do I not deserve some rest? Do I not deserve to end with more than I started with?"

"Again, I'm sorry your family isn't enough for you. I thought you were happy here. You have a home. A wife. A son who loves you so much. When did we become a burden?"

"I did too. You're not a burden. I just think you're being selfish. Your child is strong. He can adapt. He's not as weak as you act like he is, and he's growing up fast. You can't stifle our family because you're afraid of change. You're not used to it because we don't age, but you see it in Lillard now and you need to calm down."

That was such a sudden and personal attack that Rose didn't know what to say. Instead, she started to walk away with tears in her eyes. "We only have so much time with him before he grows up. We need to savor this time because you're right, he'll be an adult soon. We'll have him as our best friend forever and I look forward to that, but I deserve to be able to enjoy my life with my son without feeling guilty for being content." Rose used her bare feet to grip the wall and boost herself over the lip. At the top she looked back at Paulson, who didn't say anything—instead, he went back to polishing the stone. Rose went upstairs to sleep in her bed alone while Paulson polished until he fell asleep on the ground.

In the middle of the night, while his parents slept, Lillard was awoken by the sound of a woman's voice echoing through his house. At first he merely rolled in his bed, but then sat up at the realization that the voice was coming closer. Eventually, he felt the gentle whisper of the voice in his ear. "Don't worry, I'll protect you." Her voice came through clear as day. He searched his room for someone but found nothing but darkness.

"Mom?" he called out in a whisper. "Is that you?" His voice was tired and mouse-like. The whisper moved away from him and repeated the same line. Though his door was closed, he could hear the woman in the hallway.

"Don't worry, I'll protect you," she repeated again, still clear as day.

"Who are you?" called Lillard to the darkness—he was not allowed to talk to strangers. From under his door, the same yellow fog he had seen in the basement poured in and rolled under his bed. Lillard leaned over the edge and ran his hand through the mist. Like when in the basement, he felt no resistance as he moved through it. The particles simply danced in the air. He dangled his legs off the bed and kicked back and forth; his motion did nothing to disturb it, it moved on its own.

"Don't worry, I'll protect you," he heard, again coming from the hallway. He calmly jumped off his bed and made his way to the door. He opened it slowly and attempted to minimize its creaking. Lillard saw that the mist had spread throughout the entire second floor. From the stairs he could see it was rolling up, then spreading down each hallway, but for some reason avoided his parents' room. "Don't worry, I'll protect you." Lillard now knew where the voice was coming from.

He made his way down the stairs and toward the basement. While the mist was only a few inches high on the second floor, it was a few feet thick on the first. With each step he descended, Lillard was wading through deeper and deeper mist. When he reached the kitchen the basement door was slightly ajar and the mist was seeping out through the cracks. Lillard opened the door and the mist fell onto him from above. Below, it was up to the ceiling. The basement was dark except for a small, faint light that was coming from the back room. A few stray beams of light made their way through the mist and guided Lillard.

He bravely descended the stairs expecting for his head to hurt. Unlike last time, he felt fine; he was not dizzy nor was it hard to breathe. Instead, he made his way through it with ease. *This must be what it feels like to be a fish*, he thought as he swam through the mist. Lillard could hear the sound of the fans rattling in the back and used it with the stray light to guide him around the corner. When he reached the room, he realized the lights were off, but the crystal was glowing so intensely it's light filled the room—the once white part glowed turquoise, and the internal crystal became even bluer. Somehow among all the noise and the light, his father was asleep against the wall. The crystal beckoned Lillard toward it.

"I'll protect you, if you protect me," it finally clarified in a whisper. "Help me," it pleaded. Quietly, Lillard climbed down into the hole and approached the rock. He held his breath as he moved past his father, who twitched and snored with exhaustion. Lillard approached the stone cautiously, but once he was within arm's reach, he couldn't help but touch it. Inside he could see lights dancing; it was clear as day. He touched his palm to the stone and felt Navi's thoughts radiate through his body and then saw a vision of her words.

"Roshni should have lived a life of luxury and delight; not simply because she was a princess but because, like her name would imply, she was a ray of joy. In all my decades of serving the royal family, never had I ever seen someone so pure and hopeful for the world. Her love of her family and the kindness with which she treated everyone was unprecedented. She would have made a most wonderous queen—but that was not to come. While yes, for part of her life she had gold, jewels, fancy dress, and servants and that is more than most, but that was all stripped away from her. When those were gone, she was still her same self, but it was when the truly precious things were taken that she changed. Family, friends…those things that make you rich in fortune, not materials, were all also stripped away.

She was the youngest princess of five, the youngest child of ten, and she was my entire world—I was her guard. Each child had their own and their parents had dozens. I love Roshni like she was my own. With my pledge to protect her, I gave the family my heart and my soul. I joined the guard young, and with my pledge I underwent surgery to stop my ability to have children of my own. The king would not allow for the possibility of loyalty to another.

Their kingdom was a palace built in a desert oasis. In the hot season, the tall, ivory towers were abandoned, and the kingdom lived underground in the royal caverns. For each plot of land on the surface there was another owned by someone below. With the seasons, life transferred below and continued to thrive. Limited water was provided by underground streams, and the crops grew well—small holes led to termite mounds that provided circulation of air and the briefest moments of sunlight.

When the weather grew colder, it brought with it massive rains that filled the caves and we had to move above ground. The ivory towers absorbed the little sunlight and heated the rooms to a wonderfully toasty temperature. It was a nice life. Even those who were not royalty lived comfortable lives in our kingdom. Her family simply reaped the benefits of their good leadership. For many years we lived in peace in this cycle. It was paradise.

Roshni's troubles began during the floods of her ninth year. Before the seasons change the sky darkens for weeks at a time. We are never quite sure when it will begin each year. During that time, she lost her first precious thing, her best friend. While playing in the rice fields, the floods began. When they tried to escape, the soft earth held onto her friend, and I had to make a choice. I was only able to save one child and that would always be Roshni. As the waves came and flooded the room, we floated on a board through the monstrous caverns and into the main cavern.

I looked into her eyes and Roshni knew she had made her first genuine mistake, and her friend was lost—in some way it was her fault, and she couldn't let go. She realized things could be taken from her. That was when she lost her first drop of confidence and belief in the world. The child who was lost was the son of another dignitary. A lesser but powerful politician. His father took his death as a sign of favoritism among the people. Rumbles of civil unrest began to stir, but because of the floods and the desert we were forced together.

Our ivory walls became blood-soaked saunas, and our underground caverns became cages. Even so, Roshni kept her same joy in the world. She lived just as happily, to make up for the loss of her friend, but I could see that something in her had changed. After that she became, no less of herself, just different. I could see it in her eyes. I could see the pain she felt and the memories she held. What replaced her heart was anxiety, and the deep love she felt gave away to deep worry.

As we would come to learn, in times of war and in times of great death, a monster known only as the Being grows especially strong and hungry. In the beginning of the wars, he merely wandered our desert lands. Guards kept watch all night and scared away any monster or man who came to pillage. Underground we were safe, for the time. Even in the cold season, the guards watched from towers and shot arrows at the beast that hovered above the land, scouting prey.

The palace was safe until the death of her parents. The monarchs were killed as a symbol of rebellion. Roshni was close with both of her parents, so the blow was especially hard on her. Her eldest brother became the king, and life returned for the most part to normal. When men stopped being our fear, monsters did. With the loss of another one of her precious things, the love of her parents, she became a beacon of anxiety and worry—a beacon for the Being. Though he was constantly scared away, he refused to leave for long. When troubles grew between her siblings and turmoil erupted again, the monster found the strength to break through their defenses. When the second war began, he was able to hunt indiscriminately—the souls he stole were not noticed among the deaths from war. When everyone lives in fear, the Being is free to walk around and feed as he wishes.

We fled the capital not because of the war, as horrible as it was, but because of the Being. Her family remained, refusing to give up the life they grew to live with. Roshni didn't care about losing her gold, only the people she loved, but I pulled her away for her safety. She trusted me beyond everyone, and when I knew we should go, she followed. We snuck out of the palace gates one evening and took an underground route to a nearby town. Shortly after we arrived, the Being descended onto the town, and we had to flee again. We left a wake of fear and death behind us, but at every turn I protected her and moved her to safety. I still had hope that one day there would be peace for Roshni, for a day where the Being clung to someone else—but there would be no peace.

One night as we hid in a random cave on the side of a mountain, we were pinned by the Being. My sword had been destroyed in our last battle with him, and I was left with very little to defend us. Then, in my exhaustion I fell asleep. The last time I would ever sleep. My dreams were nothing but nightmares—nightmares and the faintest hope for Roshni. His form always changed, and he seemed to delight in the surprise of the monster he would take. This time he aimed to tease her, remind her of her homeland and wealth. He entered the cave as a sloth bear, ordained in gold and jewels; he had a crown on his head and bracelets along his arms. His legs and toes were studded with gold rings. In the glint of the torchlight, he appeared like a man in a morbid costume.

I awoke to her screams. Though I had fallen asleep at the cave entrance, he simply stepped over my body. He could have taken my life but chose her. Without me, there was no one to fight him off. The two others who had abandoned their post for Roshni with me had already perished. Now, it was only Roshni and me. He had backed her into a corner, his gigantic frame looming over her. Between them was a stream of the brightest and purest light I have ever seen. I could see Roshni was not looking at the beast…no, she was somewhere else. Somewhere in her mind. Her arms traveled up and down her face, deforming her mouth and her eyes. As the light left her, a darkness fell over her. I threw a spear into the back of the beast, and even though it stuck he didn't respond.

I picked up the one last spear we had and dashed to Roshni's side. I stood in the light and thrust the spear at his chest. He still didn't respond; he was impervious. When I pulled back, I finally realized I wasn't stopping him. He was merely feeding through me. I could feel all of her spirit and her light leaving her body and it stung. With one last jump I stabbed at his chest, and after it stuck I hung in the air. I then dropped to the ground and grabbed Roshni. "I love you," I shouted as I threw her behind me. Her light pulled through me once more and I crystalized. Then I felt my body fall away, and all I've felt since is longing. He then merely walked through me, and with a pawed fist he shattered me. Then he took Roshni. I have no idea where she is, but I *know* she's still out there… I have no way to find her. Will you help me?"

Instinctually, Lillard attempted to lift the rock with all his might. "Don't worry, I'll help you," he whispered. He couldn't help but try. "I'm sorry, you're too big. I don't know what to do." He struggled with all his might, but the stone would not move at all.

"Poor child, don't worry. *It's okay*. You can only do so much. Just don't forget me. Take me with you, and as long as you remember me, you'll come back to help me. I know you will. There is so much more of me, scattered somewhere. This will help you find me, and I'll bring you good luck." The stone in front of him began to flow like water, and when Lillard touched it, it shot ripples throughout. He put his hands into it and reached deep into the dark blue gem at its center. This was Navi's body and as he pulled on it, the rock came with him—it stretched like putty and then broke away like clay. When he pulled his hand out, a small blue gem surrounded by a clear and glowing coat was in his palm. The stretched blue rock inside floated within like a lava lamp for a moment before falling and settling at the bottom.

Lillard held the gem up to his eyes and he could see the image of Navi again—it was beautiful and captivating. "Why are you talking to me?" he whispered to the rock.

"You're a good boy, Lillard. I've seen how you listen to your mother. I knew talking to you, you'd help me. Children help for the sake of helping, especially sweet ones like you."

"Is my dad sweet? Is that why he's been down here with you? Is he helping you too?"

"Adults need an incentive, and your father seems to have found it on his own. Most people have something they long for. Something that they think will make their lives easier. But no, I haven't spoken to him. He wouldn't understand. Not yet." Lillard placed the gem into his pocket as the voice explained it to him, then he felt his legs give out. As his body crumbled to the ground, he passed out.

The sun rose.

Lillard was awoken the next morning by his mother hovering over him. Still in her pajamas, she was sweating and pouring water on his face. "Baby, wake up! Baby, wake up! What are you doing down here?" Lillard woke up feeling refreshed and happy. He smiled up at his mother and noticed the mist was gone. "Why are you down here? Why would you sleep down here? Explain yourself." Rose then took the remaining water in her cup and threw it at Paulson, who was sleeping next to his son.

"I thought…" He remembered what the stone had told him. His mother wouldn't help him without a reason. He couldn't think of one right now. "I just wanted to help Dad. I fell asleep trying to dig. I'm sorry," he lied—like his father.

"Paulllllllllllllll," Rose shouted as she picked up Lillard by the armpits and threw him over her shoulder. "Paulllll," she yelled again. Her husband still didn't stir. "Honey, get up here and go take a shower." Rose propped up the half-sleeping boy onto the side of the pit and shooed him away with one hand. Lillard scratched his eyes and yawned but didn't move. He let his legs dangle over the edge and sat with his hands on his thighs. Rose made her way back to Paulson and opened her metal water bottle. She poured it onto his face and made sure to hit his nose and eyes. Paulson coughed himself awake; he was suddenly afraid he was drowning. "What are you doing keeping your son down here late, especially without a safety mask on? His lungs could be filled with dust at this point."

"Well, no, I didn't know he was down here. He must have come down after I was already asleep. But also, who cares if he comes down here with me? Don't you want me to spend time with him?" Paulson was groggy and defensive.

"But something is wrong. Your *child* is coming down here…trying to do manual labor so he can help you. So he can be with you." Lillard flinched while hearing his lie being used to hurt his father's feelings. "You and your child are not sleeping well, and neither of you have ever acted this way. You're not going to work and you're not working at home tonight. We're going to heal! As a family." The doorbell rang fast and often. They both knew it was the uniquely annoying buzz of Mr. Romero. "Lillard, let's go upstairs. When I get back, we need to have a talk, Paul."

Lillard helped his mother out of the pit and the two made their way upstairs. Rose held onto her son's forearm with an authoritative grip. As usual Mr. Romero would not stop ringing the doorbell. The two were met by a constant *ding, ding, ding* as they rushed to the door. Lillard was not going to be leaving Rose's sight for now. They opened the door to find Mr. Romero in his normal attire, except this time his shirt and the matching ribbon on his hat were orange. "Good morning again, Peterson family. It's another beautiful day. I was wondering if you had a chance to rethink our offer…now that the family has hopefully…convened on the manner." His smile was so forced and his jaw so clenched that his teeth were at risk of snapping.

Though it was only the morning, Rose's patience had run out for the day. The worry over her son and her husband made her short. "No…" Rose paused, trying to calm herself; after the sound of the doorbell, she was even more tense than normal. "I mean yes, we have looked at the offer, but *no*, we will not be taking it." Mr. Romero started to speak but was cut off. "Now I noticed there was no end date on the document. So, that must mean we have some time. So please, if you wish to have any chance of getting this house in the next one thousand years, I suggest you leave my family alone. We'll report to you if we have something to report. Until then, keep it as you always do, as a no."

Sidney noticed a small yellow gleam in Lillard's eyes. "But of course, Rose. I didn't mean to be imposing or pressure you. I simply have what's best for your family at heart. I'll be sure to wait for your call." Sidney then leaned toward the two of them and spoke directly to Lillard. "We all need to take care of our friends." He tipped his hat as he always did with a little bow, and made his way down their driveway.

Down in the basement, Paulson had only moved a couple feet from where he had slept the night before. He was now sitting cross-legged with his fingertips on the stone. For the first time, Navi spoke to him. "Paulson, you're such a strong and honorable man. I would have reached out to you sooner, if I knew just how truly you were a man of ambition. Thank you for not trying to sell me. You were so right to not want to sell. I'm worth so much. I could bring so much prosperity. I'm priceless. Why settle? Why ever sell? I need your help."

When Rose returned to the basement, Paulson was still sitting in front of the crystal, in a trance; her patience was gone. "I don't know what is happening in my home but clearly we've forgotten what life is all about. *Family.*" Rose took out her phone and showed Paulson she was calling Derrel. "Yes, sorry to bother you, Derrel. I'm sad to say that I gotta come clean: My husband has been lying to you. He hasn't come to work because he's actually sick and bedridden at the moment. Yes, you're right, he hates to admit it when he's not feeling well. Right? It's like he thinks he's too strong to get sick. Yeah, so expect him to be out for a few more days. Okay? You can handle it? You were born for this? Perfect. He'll get back to you soon."

Rose hung up the phone without another word from Derrel. "Thank you, honey…," Paulson said sarcastically under his breath. Like he was her son, Rose took Paulson by the wrist with a geriatric grip and brought him back to the stairs. He stood at the base, not moving, but Rose pushed him up in front of her, like he was an antique dresser. Then for good measure she used a key to lock the basement behind her. It was the first time in two days Paulson had been out of there.

"Now shower and get dressed—we are going to be spending the next few days as a family. Starting now," Rose reiterated proudly. She hid the key in a place that only she knew (in a plastic bag inside the oversized jar of rice). For the next two days, Paulson and Lillard were coached through trips to the zoo, family board games, and getting-to-know-you ice-breaker questions. During the day their behavior seemed normal, but the whole while their minds itched in their own ways. This was not the first time Rose had sensed an issue with the family. Once when Paulson had yelled at Lillard, and he said, "I hate you," they went to the beach, aquarium, a picnic, the movies, and the zoo in just two days.

During the evenings were when Lillard and Paulson were most active, while they sleep-walked. Navi's mist seeped from the basement and awoke their bodies. Though their bodies were moving past each other all evening, they were oblivious to one another. They moved on their missions back and forth, each looking for the key—zombies trying to help Navi. Most of the time Paulson searched for the key; his body, led by closed eyes, opened drawers and walked through closets. Otherwise, Paulson's body spent the majority of the night sitting by the basement door. With his head against the wood, he tapped on the door with his finger and listened to the vibration throughout the basement. With each moment his body ached for Navi's voice. Lillard was lucky to still be able to hear her call. At night his body fumbled with her gem and passed it from hand to hand. He spent his night within the kitchen only a few feet from his father. His fingers ran across the counters, the shelves, the stove. He searched through the dressers and drawers.

By the third day, both of their behaviors had devolved. No longer were they docile and obedient. Lillard's itch made him rude. At the dinner table, Paulson's itch made him angry. That night Rose went to sleep with a heavy heart, thinking perhaps she had been a bit too forceful with her family time. She slept lightly that night and was awoken by the movement of Paulson's body. As he sat up and threw his legs over, Rose watched. She watched as he got up and walked out of the room. The light of the hallway shined on his face, and she realized that his eyes were shut.

Stealthily she slipped out of bed and followed behind her husband. Luckily for her, he left the door open behind him. As she snuck around the corner, she watched him travel downstairs. Then from behind her, she heard a door open. It was Lillard doing the same as his father, exiting his room in a trance. Rose instinctually put out her arm to stop him, but he pushed through her as if she were a saloon door. "What in the world?" Rose said to herself, half hoping her son would respond. From the top of the stairs, she saw him walk toward the kitchen and followed. She alternated between silently moving and stomping, not sure if she was more interested in seeing what they were doing or making sure they woke up safely. In the kitchen, she found her husband at the basement door. Paulson tapped his head against the wood.

Tap…

Tap…

Tap…

"Paul, what on earth are you doing?" She hurried to his side and grabbed his arm. He didn't respond. He simply continued to knock against the door—now, a little louder.

Tap…

Tap…

Tap…

Rose stared into her husband's blank eyes with shock. She slowly placed her hand between his head and the door. He simply continued to slam against her. Rose began to push Paulson in the chest, as if trying to start a fight, but still could not elicit a response. That was when she smelled something. She sniffed the air. "That is…gas." Rose looked across the room and saw Lillard standing at the stove, playing with the burners. She darted across the room toward him. "Lilli, Lilli, Lillard…*Lillard Matthew Peterson.* You stop that right now."

Lillard was moving one of his arms slowly across the knobs of the stove. He turned them one by one—never lighting them, only releasing the gas. Rose grabbed his hand and tried to stop him, but he pushed against her. She found it was easier to follow behind and simply turn off the gas after he was done. When he reached the end of the stove he started to dig through the drawers. He made no effort to be quiet as he pulled pots and pans to the floor in search of the key. Behind her Rose heard a loud thud. Paulson was growing angrier and fed up with the stability of the door. His head bumps were now replaced with slams from his fists.

Rose started to move toward her husband but then froze. She was trying to take stock, to triage the situation. *Which one of them do I need to stop first? Which one could I actually stop? What in the world is wrong with them? Should I just call the ambulance? Is this a psychotic break?* Then the decision was made for her. Paulson had reached his limit—he rushed from the room and out the back door. Rose dropped to the ground to try and speak to her son. He didn't respond to anything she said. He only whispered to himself, "I know how to help…now."

Paulson entered the kitchen in a huff, and in his hand, he carried an axe. With a yell he swung it at the basement door and began to hack it to pieces. Rose stood in shock, not sure what to do. She couldn't seem to stop either of them and the axe was sharp. Within a couple of minutes, he made a large enough hole to begin to use his bare foot to kick through the cracks. His foot began to bleed from a few large splinters. When the hole was large enough, he squeezed his body through it and went into the basement, axe in hand. Rose followed him.

Paulson walked in silence to the back room, while Rose followed safely behind. When she reached the bottom of the stairs, she flipped a switch and turned on the string of work lights tied to the generator; it was another safety precaution she insisted upon. Rose entered the back room and watched Paulson jump down into the pit and approach the stone. He smiled and touched it with his palm, then placed his forehead on it. "Don't worry," he whispered.

Paulson turned toward the pit wall and began to wail on it with the axe—it was an inefficient way of digging. Then from behind her, Rose smelled it again. "Gas," she shouted to herself—she had left Lillard alone in the kitchen. When she moved to go back upstairs the work lights shut off. She ran back and fumbled to the stairs to see Lillard at the top. From behind her, she heard the change from sound of metal on stone to metal on metal. Rose shouted to her son, who was playing with a box of matches. He lit one and threw it behind himself.

There was a small explosion and Lillard was blasted down the steps. Rose rushed to the side of her son and began to put out the small flames that were on his pajamas. "Baby, are you okay? Baby, wake up." Lillard lay in her arms unconscious. Above them a fire raged in the kitchen and billowed into the basement.

Rose grabbed Lillard under his armpits and pulled him with her into the back room. "Paulson, we have to go." She struggled to say as she dragged her son. "We have to get out of the house. There's a fire; your son has lost his mind and his consciousness." Below in the pit, Paulson was swinging his axe at a pipe he had exposed in the wall. With every swing it grew closer to shattering. "Paul, your son is unconscious. Get your head out of your ass." Rose let Lillard down gently and then began to pick up rocks and throw them at Paulson's head.

She struck him in the back several times before aiming for his head—it took two rocks before his head started to bleed. He continued to swing wildly. The room was beginning to fill with smoke. Rose gave up and began taking Lillard back out of the room. She came to the stairs and debated how to get him up. There was no other exit to their basement. To make it to safety they would have to move through the flames. Rose had no way of knowing how bad it would be upstairs. Anyway, she gripped her son by the wrists and began to drag him up the stairs with her back to the fire.

The shattering of the pipe sent a ringing through Paulson's ears. From it spewed the gas that was meant for the kitchen. As the fire approached, the room he sat in became a ticking bomb. In the other room, Rose struggled to get Lillard up the stairs. She was halfway up when the fire finally ate away at the wooden banisters and the staircase collapsed. The two of them toppled with the pile of burning wood to the floor. "Wake up, wake up," she shouted to Lillard while tapping him on the cheeks. Lillard lay covered in wood and though she was free, Rose realized she had been stabbed in the shoulder by a piece of banister. She tried to stretch her leg, but she couldn't move without a searing pain.

Lillard finally awoke and realized he couldn't move either. He let out a scream as he struggled and tried to remember how he had gotten there. He tried to push the rubble off of himself, but he couldn't. The room was filling with smoke, and he started to cough. He looked around for his mother and found her in his peripherals but within reach; the two held hands. He began to scream again, and Rose tried to comfort him. "It's going to be okay, baby—don't worry. I'll figure something out." Lillard's scream traveled into the back room, and his voice finally struck something in Paulson and he snapped back to reality.

"Lillard," he shouted as he noticed the smoke and covered his face with his shirt. "Son, where are you?" Paulson sprinted toward the pit wall and sprung up it. Navi's spirit screamed out to him, but his son's cry was too strong. As he came to the stairs, he could finally hear Rose's voice as well. He also could finally see the fire coming from upstairs. They were trapped.

Paulson attempted to lift the rubble off Lillard, but it was stuck awkwardly. Instead, he used his axe to cut away at the banister above him. Once he had done enough damage, he pulled the smaller pieces to the side and pulled his son free. Paulson prompted him up and then said, "I'm so sorry for ignoring you. Can you help me with Mom?" Lillard nodded and the two began to prop up Rose, who couldn't walk. "This way." Paulson led them into the back room and shut the door behind them, then climbed into the pit. The room was filling with gas, and it was already starting to asphyxiate them and soon it would explode.

"Where are we going?" Rose asked, confused as to how they were going to get out. "Are we just going to die by that stupid stone?" They made their way past the gem and to a small ledge below a high, tiny window. First, Paulson boosted his son up and allowed him to unlock the window latch. It slipped out of his hand and came crashing toward them, shattering from its impact with the wall. Paulson covered his face with one hand and used the other to push his son by his ass out the window.

Rose was next. "I love you, baby. I'm sorry for everything but also, this is going to hurt," he said before propping her on his shoulder and then lifting her over his head. He used all his strength to push on her good leg, acting like a jack. Her shoulder slammed into the wall. At the top, Lillard held his mother's hand and used all *his* strength to pull her to freedom. As Paulson grappled onto the wooden beams in the house, he heard the call of Navi one last time. She called him to come back and help. Instead, he climbed the wall and reached for his family's hands, and they helped him squeeze through the small frame. He lay there for a few seconds before they all realized they were still next to the gas. Paulson jumped to his feet and he and Lillard helped Rose hobble to safety. When they got to the driveway Rose reached into her pocket and handed the car keys to Paulson.

"You're always a genius, baby, two steps ahead." Paulson kissed Rose on the head and then helped load her into the passenger seat. Lillard jumped in back and Paulson threw the car into reverse. As the car peeled onto the street, the house finally erupted in an explosion. Fire shot from the basement and onto their lawn. Rose watched from the rearview mirror as it burned.

"My house. My beautiful house," Rose cried. Paulson put his hand over her shoulder and rubbed it with one hand. As they drove, the unpaved road caused their car to bounce, and in the jostling their glove box sprung open; from within another yellow folder fell out and landed in Rose's lap. She opened it and held the paper in her hands. The wind from the open window fluttered the pages until only the back page was still in her grip. At the bottom in tiny letters was another final offer for the house. The words jumped out at her. *In the event of catastrophic structural failure, by natural disaster or fire, the aforementioned client offers to pay double the initial amount for the ease of rebuilding on the land.* "I think we should sell the house," Rose finally admitted. "We can get far away from that rock, just like a new scene. Just a new view.

How does that sound, Lillard?" She pulled out her phone and dialed 911 to alert the fire department. The ringing echoed in the car and covered the sound of their engine.

Paulson let out a long breath and shook his head. "I'll work extra hard, and we'll remake the house. We'll use the money to make you the perfect replica. This time we're doing it exactly how you want." Paulson turned his attention to his son. "I'm sorry, buddy. I was being an idiot. I would never choose anything in the world over you. Let's be sure to find a house on the other side of town, so you can still go to school with your friends."

"I'll be fine as long as I'm with you," responded Lillard as he reached into his pocket and removed the small piece of Navi he still had. "See, I helped," he said to her.

"Aww, thanks, buddy. You sure did," his parents said, catching their breath.

Lillard rolled the gem in his hand; he could still hear Navi's voice. *"Thank you."*

The following night Mr. Romero made his way to the wreckage of the house. He passed by the caution signs and found his way into the soot. The rain had turned the ash to mud, and he walked until he found what were once the basement stairs. He dug into the rubble until he found a hole in the barely standing structure. He dropped into the basement with his suitcase and pulled out a headlamp. He placed it on the front of his hat but turned it off immediately as in the darkness he could see Navi shining. He approached the gem slowly and when he got close, he lowered his suitcase from the ground. From it he took out a piece of the rock like Lillard's but much larger. He moved it toward the gem, and when it came into contact, it was pulled in. The crystal once again turned into a lava lamp, and the new chunk floated down and joined the rest. "I knew you'd be here but there is even more of you than I hoped," Sidney whispered as he hugged the rock.

The Fading

The Fading

Vincente was woken up by a shred of light that came through a hole in his ceiling. It was okay though because he had not really been sleeping, more waiting. He never really slept anymore, more lost time. His energy varied from day to day, despite many attempts to create a steady schedule. When he couldn't sleep, Vincente often went for long walks or rode public transportation. His complexion was ghostly pale, but an under-glow of baby blue shone through him, like iridescent scales below his skin. His nose was larger than most with a mustache that hid a large upper lip and a beard that covered a small chin. His eyes were an iridescent green, though he would never allow you to get close enough to see them. He was a skittish man.

His current makeshift home was in the corner of an abandoned warehouse down by the city waterfront. Its *Do Not Trespass* signs were enough to keep out the majority of people who might wander too close. Not that he had anything of value to take away anyway. The building was one of the closest to where he arrived when he stowed away on one of the freight trains. Every night for the last five months he heard the sounds of the tracks in constant use. For his bed, Vincente had combined fragments of an old boxspring, cardboard boxes, and some semi-dirty blankets.

Though the windows were all shattered, luckily, they were also boarded up. The only light that entered was from the various holes in the roof. That also meant much of the inside was often wet from rain and morning dew. His sleeping corner was established as the driest part. Elsewhere in the room, the floor was barely intact; holes led to a basement littered with rusted machinery. Above his sleeping spot, Vincente propped up a tarp to protect from any rain that might dribble down. The tarp did not protect him but instead kept several maps that hung from the wall safe. Each map displayed a different city Vincente had been too. Their placement on the wall aimed to mimic their location within the state.

This was the fifth city he was slowly working his way through. Each map was meticulously documented with a different color pen for each mode of travel—green for bus routes, red for subways, blue for walking, purple for hiking paths. The pages contained various slashes of different colors; the top left of the map had a key to remind him of his own logic. He was running through each sector systematically; this way he wouldn't miss an angle. In each city he would look for anything that would spark a memory. On days when he was too weak to walk the city, he spent his time riding the subways and the buses. Every path would get done; it was just a matter of when. When he was strong enough to walk, especially at night, he would scour each street and alleyway. He glanced and stared at every building and every person he came across. Eventually, from some angle, he would remember something about *any* part of his life.

He wasn't sure how long he had been lost. Vincente remembered very little about his life before he looked the way he did. His memory and his energy would fluctuate over time. There had been seemingly months Vincente had lost, it all felt like darkness. His memory and mood swings were further exacerbated by inconsistent bodily urges. Vincente rarely ever felt the need to eat; his stomach was a silent void. However, there were times his hunger came deep from within his soul, and he had to binge. He needed to find food. Today was the beginning of one such mood. His plan for the day was to continue tracking the city by bus and then collect groceries on the way home, then track by foot.

Vincente threw on his only pair of shoes and least dirty hoodie and got ready to leave. He pulled down his map of Battery City from the wall and folded it into his hoodie pocket along with a small notebook and a four-color pen. He also grabbed a wallet that contained a series of public transportation passes. Most people used their phones or watches to pay, and so most of them didn't realize their cards were missing. Vincente didn't know how he knew how to do it, but he found it easy to pickpocket and steal someone's ID. He exited his hiding spot and walked a few blocks to catch a bus he had not been on before.

Once Vicente sat on the bus, he formed a defensive position, with a hoodie pulled over his head and a mask covering his lower face. Only his eyes were left exposed. His hands were equally hidden, tucked in his pockets. He lay perpendicularly to his seat, his legs sprawled out so that he took up the entire row. His head rested on the metal arm bar, and his feet pointed toward the world outside. His positioning served two purposes. One, to keep anyone from talking to him, and two, to conceal his skin.

He peered out of his hoodie and scanned the streets to analyze every sign, every inch of graffiti, and every person who happened to pass by. For the last several years he spent at least part of nearly every day riding the buses and the trains. So far nothing he saw in any of the major cities did anything to spark his memory. Today, he would ride on the R bus, and travel up and down the west side. According to his map he only had the west and southern areas left. Once he made it across the entire city, he would move on.

The only blips of memories he had were from when he first woke up and saw himself in the mirror. A vision took over his mind. It flooded back with pain, and afterward he was only able to remember a fraction of it. Since then, he hoped for another memory and carried his notebook with him just in case. He figured his recall would be best if he could draw what he saw. Trying to think of the right words rarely gave him the time to get his thoughts down. He'd get stuck and it would vanish. His brain felt like a spinning movie reel; the shattered and flickering images only occasionally lined up and illuminated a full thought.

He still didn't have many notes, but he looked at his journal anyway. He only had two entries, and both were about his childhood. One drawing told him he had been self-conscious as a teen and grew his facial hair as soon as he could to try and cover his baby face. It was unfortunate how only the deepest insecurities stayed with him. The second memory was tied to the gold necklace he was currently wearing. It was a simple gold chain with a small golden charm, a photo of a young girl. As he held it, he felt a deep sensation of family. He knew he had some somewhere. When he looked at the necklace he felt nothing. Still, he assumed the girl was his sister.

His phone was an antique and hardly functional. That was another reason he stuck to handwritten notes. At the moment, he was trying to use it to find a food bank or soup kitchen in the area. He didn't work, so he didn't have money; he didn't need to pay rent or ever really eat so it was rarely an issue. Vincente slammed his phone against his hand, as he tried to speed up the search connection. His broken phone was barely able to connect to the communal city Wi-Fi. The page was loading incredibly slowly. He sat up and raised his phone up to the sky while he shifted closer to the window; he had to get closer to the signal.

From behind him he heard a voice, "If you're looking for the food bank, I volunteer at one located on 3rd Avenue."

"Thank you," he responded instinctually before realizing his hand was exposed and that someone was paying attention to him. That never happened. Startled, Vincente pulled his arm into his sleeve and pulled his hoodie farther down to compensate. He pulled his phone close to his face and turned toward the window. Vincente didn't appreciate being spied on but wasn't quick to temper and his phone *would just not* work.

"3rd and what?" he asked without looking back, and for some reason disguising his voice in a low and clearly fake grumble.

"3rd and Market. It's near the fire station." Vincente pretended to know what she meant and nodded in agreement. He then went back to his phone to try to confirm the address. It still wasn't working.

"Here, I wrote it down for you," he heard before feeling a tap on his shoulder. He turned around to see Autumn leaning over two rows of seats. He grabbed the card with his sleeve and quickly turned around. "You have such beautiful eyes, by the way. What a unique green."

The compliment startled Vincente and he turned away without saying a word. He instead tucked his body into his hoodie even more. He then took out his map and scanned it for the address she had given him. He realized if he stayed on the bus for the next couple of hours, then switched to one going across the south side, he would eventually be within walking distance of the food bank. His plan was set. He once again took his defensive position, staring out the window, hoping to notice something. Even as the bus filled up, he lay there. It wasn't until the end of the line that he got up and switched to another. By the time the sun began to set Vincente felt an increase in energy. He decided to get off the bus early and make his way through the streets to the food bank on foot. He used his pen to mark the routes he took on the bus on his map before he got off.

Vincente had learned that most food banks worked on a first come, first serve system and they also rarely asked questions. By coming late, he would minimize the number of people he would have to interact with, but he would have slim pickings of food. It was a minor sacrifice, though, because he could not taste anything. There would always be plenty of leftover sardines, creamed corn, and soup. The few times a year he was hungry; it was about quantity, not quality.

The neighborhood that Vincente walked through was covered in graffiti but exceptionally clean. Murals covered the sides of each high-rise, and many incorporated the natural vegetation into their artwork. Many of the buildings used to be office spaces but were slowly abandoned as people began to work more from home. Now many of them were low-income or free housing. The food bank helped to feed those who couldn't work for one reason or another. If Vincente planned on staying longer and wasn't afraid of people, he could have had a decent place to live.

He easily found the food bank as it was located directly next to a firehouse, as advertised. It was impossible to miss with its large garage doors open to the streets. Out front the fire trucks sat parked. Within the station, dozens of tables were set up with food and supplies of many types. Fires had been so rare lately that the food bank began to use the fire station for extra storage. Vincente failed to miss the crowds, and though it was getting late, the line still extended out the door and down the street briefly. In the main building they were serving dinner as a small soup kitchen.

Vincente ignored the line for warm food and instead headed for the shorter one for canned goods. He didn't need his food to be cooked, just there. He picked up several plastic bags and hooked them onto his arms. He then started to make his way along the table, grabbing anything they had a lot of; they wouldn't care if he was greedy that way. He just had to make sure he was able to carry everything back to his hovel. He was feeling confident and pretty strong today. Especially now, he felt better than he had in a long while.

As he moved down the line, he kept his hoodie low and pretended not to be able to speak when approached. He kept his hands inside his sleeves as he picked through piles of food and put them into his bags. Across one of the tables, he noticed gloves. *Why do I not already have some?* With his bags half full, he made his way over to the winter supplies. He began to pick through the pile of winter gloves of many different colors and sizes. He didn't need to be warm; he just needed to hide his skin. As he picked through them, he found a single nice black glove and placed it on, then continued to dig through the pile for a match. His movements became so erratic he was approached by a volunteer for some help.

"Are you having trouble finding something in your size? We have many nice gloves and most fit—well, most," the volunteer said. Vincente tried to shoo away the helper without saying anything but accidentally used his ungloved hand. The shine and color of his skin caught the eye of the attendant, who gasped. "Sir, are you okay? You're extremely pale. When was the last time you were able to eat?"

"I'm fine," he grunted while trying to hide his hand.

"Please let me see your hand, sir. If you need it, we offer doctors next door. We work with some of the local hospitals." As Vincente continued to shoo the man away, the assistant walked toward one of the security guards. "He seems scaly and pale. I'm worried that perhaps he's on one of those street drugs? I hear they are extremely addictive. Could you get someone more qualified to try and talk to him?"

Finally, Vincente found the other glove and was free to search through the food. Unfortunately, it was only a minute or two before the attendant arrived with a nurse. "Sir, we're not here to scare you, but this woman would like to talk to you about the health services. Have you been taking anything that has been hurting your body?"

Vincente didn't know what to do and was cornered. When the nurse put her hand on his shoulder he panicked, and he got a headrush. He pushed her hand off of him and turned toward them but ducked his head. "No, no. Thank you, I'm fine," he panted before his adrenaline kicked in. He panicked more. He attempted to run past them, pushing them out of the way with his bags of food. They reached out to him and pulled at his hood, which flew off; his white hair and bright, scaly skin were revealed to everyone in the room. In the commotion, one of the firefighters by the door moved toward him.

"Buddy, are you okay?" he asked as he tried to get in Vincente's way. Vincente pulled on his hoodie and stared at the firefighter, plotting his move.

"Let him go," shouted the attendant, who was just trying to do something good. The firefighter moved out of the way and Vincente ran out into the street. "Everything here is free— what is he doing wrong? Let him go. I think the poor guy is a junky. Hopefully he comes back, though. We gotta try not to scare him away next time."

Vincente was now embarrassed and ran down one of the neighboring streets and cut down an alley, never looking back. The whole while he impressed himself; he could not remember the last time he had the strength to speed away that fast and for so long. Though the bags in his arms were filled with cans, they were weightless. When he felt he was safe, he was surprised to find that they were still mostly full. He had barely lost anything in the sprint. He hid in an alley, catching his breath, and then when he finally felt comfortable, he made his way out of it and back onto the main city street.

Vincente made his way to the nearest corner and looked for a street sign. He needed to check his map. To his surprise, he realized he had made it several blocks across town and was now in an entirely new neighborhood. This detour had not been in his original plan, but he should be able to walk or take the bus back home. Then Vincente's stomach started to make the rare but familiar tingle of hunger. That meant that he might be ready to eat in the next couple of hours or perhaps during the next day or two. He needed to make it home so he could shelter and binge.

The new neighborhood he walked through was bright and extravagant in a way few others in the city were. Known as the electric district, it was lined with large electronic billboards and neon signs. Even in the dead of night, their lights shined bright into the sky. The signs and lights that lined the streets all worked off of solar energy generated by the plants that topped the buildings. Though it was a weekday and late, the streets were still filled with people traveling between different parties and bars. Large multi-story arcades competed with each other for customers, while department stores and novelty antique shops hoped to entice drunken patrons.

As he passed the many department stores, Vincente looked through their window displays at the many computers, televisions, phones, and robotics they offered. He had no need for anything like that, perhaps a better phone, but something about them called to his sense of wonder. When he made his way past the television section of Laox, his eyes were drawn to three stories of TVs that lined the walls. Each was displaying the same show, each larger than the last. Like a moth he stared at the wall of light, and as a new program started he was compelled to watch it. His bags slowly slid down his arms until they were placed on the ground.

"Tonight, we are covering the thirty-fifth anniversary of one crime, one of so many that go unsolved every year," the TV host began. His hair was dark black, high on top and sharp on the sides. His dark green suit was in stark contrast to the bright blue screen behind him. The screen then cut dramatically to flashes of black and white footage from store security cameras. A disembodied voice continued, "Thirty-five years ago, one of the largest jewelry store robberies occurred in the small town of Sleepy Hollow. What makes this story interesting is not the overall turn of events, nor the method of thievery. Instead, it is the mystery of what happened to the prize. At the time, Mrs. Minerva was the largest collector of fine jewels in the area. She had built up her brand through decades of hard work. Her shop even acted as a small museum at times with displays of rare jewels from around the world. Her daughter continues that tradition today, picking up where her late mother left off. We have her in the studio tonight, for an interview. Even though she was merely a child during the incident, she remains a firm advocate for her mother's justice. Rose, tell us about your mother."

When the woman appeared on the screen, Vincente's head began to hurt again, much more than it had done earlier. It was as if a ball of stress was tightening in his mind. He looked through the tears in his eyes and analyzed Rose's face on the screen. She began to talk but as she did her words became muddled, like they were coming from a speaker underwater. Though she was older now, he recognized every curve of her face. She had deep blue eyes, a tiny nose and chin, and large rosy cheeks. Vincente grabbed his necklace and inspected it. Though she was now fully grown, he could tell that the picture of the small girl was the woman on the screen.

What did I do?

As she described what she remembered from that night, Vincente's memory came back in small chunks. "My mother was always the greatest woman, extremely kind. People often say that you need to be a monster to be in a cutthroat business like sales and to work with expensive jewels and gems, but that never seemed to faze her. Instead, my mother was such a sweet person and hard worker that people always just wanted to help her. I don't think there was anyone in my childhood I could think of who ever wanted to hurt her. That is why the incident was especially a shock to everyone."

"For our audience who may not know, despite your best attempts to make sure everyone is aware, tell us what happened on the night of October 15th."

"Well, it was a normal night by all accounts. I was with my mother at the office, and it was late, but we often stayed late doing paperwork, finalizing sales, etc. I was so young that I don't remember exactly what happened. I knew my mother was at her desk doing paperwork. I was playing with my computer and watching videos. Then it just happened, so suddenly."

"You mean to say the robbery and…your mother's subsequent murder."

"Yes, it seems that they were able to sneak in through a back door. I saw the two men come through a communal hallway that was supposed to be locked. I screamed, which alerted my mother, but by that time, one of them had a gun drawn. Needless to say, we were caught off guard. That door was *always* locked. My mom was so cautious."

"So, the two men proceed to steal all of the rare gems and rings. That included a set of raw gems from several countries. Your mother's shop was hosting precious jewels from both India and France at the time, I believe. Anything else?"

"The strangest thing is that they stole my mother's necklace. It was so confusing because it was clearly a cheap necklace and they even left some very expensive things in the cases. It was so much uglier and cheaper than many of the other pieces. That was one of the confusing things…it just seemed so personal. That is why they asked if we *knew* the robbers. The two robbers then got into an argument and at the end of it one of them shot my mother, then he took her necklace. His eyes were so mean…it really felt out of spite. Truly, I don't think those men got what they really deserved. They took my mother's life, then seemingly their own. They needed to face judgment."

"What you are referring to is the fact that their car was later found crashed offroad into a ditch. Then their bodies were found only a half mile away from their wreckage in the valley of Devil's Den. But interestingly and the source of our mystery, your mother's locket and the stolen jewels were never recovered. That begs the question: Do you think there was a third partner?"

"I don't know. I never saw anyone else, but I'd like to direct a message to the audience if I can." The host nodded. "Please let us know if you know anything about the jewelry that was stolen or if you spot my mother's necklace. Simply getting that piece back would mean the world to me."

"We have these two sketches generated from both your memory and the surveillance footage. To the audience, if you or anyone you know may have purchased anything from these men, let your local authorities know."

Then the screen shifted to hand-drawn sketches of the two men in question. One of them was Vincente, beard and all, and the other was a larger and broader man. Under them Ness and Lucas Maverick were listed, respectively. "Now these two men fled the scene in an old junker of a car and were chased briefly by the police. They lost the police on backroads, but the wreckage of their car was found the following morning."

The image of Lucas made Vincente's head hurt even more. Bits and pieces of that evening began to come back to him. Vincente reached into his pocket and tried to draw what he was seeing, but his head hurt too much. He was unable to keep himself writing. He stumbled away from the wall of TVs and almost abandoned his bags. He forced himself back and lifted them with ease. All the while he tried to hold his hands at the sides of his head and apply pressure against his temples. He was having so many memories come back, more than ever before. It was flooding his mind and it hurt so intensely bad.

Finally, Vincente could remember his brother in perfect detail. Lucas was younger but larger, taller than Vincente by half a foot. He was a wide man whose slight fat hid large muscles. Then he could hear the scream of a woman and the explosion of a gunshot. He could see glimpses of the robbery, the fear in the little girl's eyes, and their escape into their car. Vincente saw himself driving and his brother, Lucas, heckling him from the passenger side. He remembered something startled him, and he crashed into the trees.

Vincente could still hear the TV show. "Devil's Den has been known as a unique place by many different cultures. Across human civilization there have been many accounts of strange activities. What happened there that evening is one of those many strange events lost to time. You probably know it as the location of one of the most famous battles during the American Civil War, but the myths venture all the way back to even the natives, who considered it a ghostly and evil place. The name actually comes from them, who seemed to know it would have a long and bloody history. There is where the authority found the two bodies of the suspects badly injured from their crash, and with none of the money they took."

Vincente's most intense memories took place in Devil's Den; everything before the crash was a blur. When he woke up, upside down in his car, Lucas was gone. Vincente unbuckled his seat belt and crawled out from the wreckage. His leg was in intense pain. He looked down and noticed a bit of bone was sticking through it. In the distance he could hear the sound of someone moving, and he called out for Lucas. At first he was loud, but then he remembered they were being followed. His screaming became loud whispers; both were met with no response. With his one good leg, he hopped toward the noise, hoping to find his brother. Along his path, he saw patches of blood scattered on the dirt and bloody handprints on trees.

A small ways away and through a clearing he found his brother with his back pressed against a tree. In their crash, a branch had broken off of a tree and Lucas' ribs had been impaled by it. He was afraid to pull it out. When Vincente approached, Lucas noticed him and began to get up. Then he started to crawl away. Vincente chased as fast as he could and shouted for Lucas to wait for him. Before long, he had lost too much blood and began to crawl as well. The brothers made their way into a clearing of grass on all fours.

The memory ended and Vincente found himself still at the display of TVs. The program was now over, and they were all off. The billboards still shined bright, blocking the stars in the night sky from showing. He had no idea how long he had been standing there attempting to scribble in his notebook, but it was still in his hands—only nonsense. In the distance, he could see the bus that he needed to take home coming down the street. He picked up his bags and rushed to the bus stop.

He once again covered his body as he got onto the bus and made his way toward the back; it was mostly empty. He sat and stared at his illegible scribbles in his notebook and looked to see if he could distinguish anything he had written. *Nothing new.* Instead, his eye was pulled two seats in front of him where a young Asian woman sat. She wore a long green coat over an entirely black outfit, pants and shirt, and was wearing large red headphones. She sat rocking back and forth to her music while reading a small book, not so dissimilar to his own notebook. After a few stops he looked up again to see she was exiting the bus. As she picked up her bag, the book she had been reading fell out and onto the floor.

To his surprise, no one seemed to notice except for him. She was nearly off the bus by the time Vicente stood up and picked up the book. Instinctually, he called out to her, but she was already gone; he was not going to chase her. In his fingers, the plain pages began to glow purple and sparkle. He made his way back to his seat and began to flip through it. He then noticed something strange; at first the pages were fresh and blank, but then the edges started to glow purple. As the glow spread along it, purple handwritten words appeared. It seemed only the pages he looked at would contain material; the magic vanished as he flipped to the next one. Each page was filled with drawings of creatures and monsters and had lines of information written under them like a textbook. Somehow the book seemed damaged. Several pages failed to ignite, and the book appeared to be missing sections. In particular, he found himself drawn to one of the pages in the middle. At the top he ran his fingers along the words that sat under the title: *The Fading.*

We create ghosts in our mind, haunting ourselves with our own fears. As this fear spreads, the collective unconscious brings these beings into existence. As our fear and our collective mind move on from the tragedy the ghosts change and fade away. There is a reason you never see a ghost story of something contemporary. Ghosts are relics of our past that haunt us. Some of these ghosts are people.

The Fading are fragments of people who have been fed upon by The Being. Tragedy keeps their souls bound to this plane and they are destined to walk the world until they are forgotten. The memory of them keeps them tethered to this world and so they wander, tired and hungry, their energy determined by the minds of those who remember them. Without energy, memory, or life, these creatures wander the earth as figments of our past and their lives. Not much is known about their life cycle and their condition seems to vary greatly. Like the tides and the moon, their strength and humanness vary with time and something else. Somewhere on their

body they have a scar from their death, a branding of black flesh. Each appears unique.

That was when the most intense memory started. As Vincente and his brother both lay in the grass dying, there came a creature from the darkness. Blue lights floated from the distance and as they approached, they condensed into a man. Through its skin, Vincente could still see the light beneath the surface; it shined out of his false eyes like headlights. As he got closer, the shape of the man got more specific and, in his hand, appeared an old military rifle equipped with a ghostly bayonet. He approached them in silence—his presence was overwhelming enough. The Being stood before them as the ghost of a Civil War soldier. He sensed they were dying, so he took his time looking them over, breathing in their fear.

Vincente was too afraid to move but Lucas attempted to crawl. He pushed himself backward on his hands away from the monster. The Being did not like that. He slowly walked over to Lucas and caught up in a second. With one quick stab, he used his weapon to pin Lucas to the ground. Straight through his stomach. Vincente sat awaiting his fate and watched in horror. By the time the Being had found them they were already damaged and dying. It could sense that they were not fully alive anymore—so many of their cells were dead. Their brains were only partially functioning. Their fear and adrenaline kept them barely alive.

The Being was too good to eat rotten meat; he had been spoiled over the years. Instead, the Being ate around the fragments of dead mind and body. He nibbled on the pieces of brain, memory, and psyche that were still active. As the Being drained them for their fear, the trauma they experienced made their souls heavy and tied to the earth. The trauma they caused connected them to the minds of others in the world. As their minds faded and their bodies passed on, their souls became tethered beyond their control. Hours later, the small scraps of their souls awoke and rose from their bodies. When Vincente woke up, his body was below him and he felt groggy and confused. His body shined with a new glow. Only a few feet away he saw the dead body of his brother and, scared, he ran off into the woods. Before long Vincente found himself in a city, unable to remember anything—and that's where he still was. At least now he had a lead.

Vincente made his way back to his warehouse, where he sat in the clean corner and gorged himself—he ate everything he could before he fell asleep. When he woke up, whenever that was, he would search for his brother. Maybe, if Vincente hadn't truly died, neither did Lucas.

From then on, Vincente spent less time in each city. He was no longer looking for memories but for a specific man. A man he assumed would be as pale and scaly as he was. He could use that information to try and track him. Once he entered a city, he would find the community of locals on the streets, those who might see those not hoping to be found. Like when he entered the port city of Highland Square. Luckily, he arrived on a late-night train. He learned that night was the best time to find the encampments of other people like him. He used to use that information to avoid people, but now he had to use it to find them. The train was surrounded by abandoned industrial buildings as were most of the stations Vincente chose to exit on.

The surrounding area was rather rural, and the stars were bright in the sky. Vincente climbed to the top of the train car and looked into the distance. He searched up and down the line. The landscape was flat with some evergreen fir trees. In the distance he could see a large bridge the train would have to continue over in the morning. He assumed that would be the best spot for the camp to be and walked toward it.

As he approached the underpass, he could see the lights from fires under the bridge. Below, there was music and noise. The lights were coming from several setups, and a few fire pits had been built into the ground and were being used for warmth. The encampment looked less like the poor and more like a set of stalls, tents, and canopies. These people did not live in squaller, merely simplicity. He caught the eye of several men and women drinking by the entrance. With the incorporation of universal health care, and access to food, many people found it easy to live outside of the system, as long as they were willing to live simply. In these camps you could find both the smartest scholars and the craziest prophets.

Vincente covered himself in his hoodie as he always did and skulked around the fires and vendors. The first couple of people looked to him like they might be thugs. He didn't want to risk talking to them. He searched for someone who might have a reason to talk to his brother, someone who was untrustworthy enough to admit it. As Vincente looked around, he searched for a friendly face. *Who might have he talked to? Someone who might be selling*, he thought. He would need to talk to a vendor, or someone drunk and charismatic. He passed by a setup that clearly doubled as a home, with tarps pinned up on posts. The front of the store had many small trinkets, and cheap jewelry. The man behind the desk sat drinking and singing to himself. His eyes were closed and he was using one hand to conduct an invisible orchestra. Vincente might have found both.

"Hey," Vincente said quietly, trying to interrupt the man's singing but not draw any more attention to himself.

"Oh hey, welcome to the shop. Are you trying to sing or are you interested in one of my rings? One hundred percent thirty-two carat. All antique."

"They are antique, you say. How much are they?"

"That depends on what you have to trade. I give a discount for alcohol or drugs. But I love something surprising. You trying to trade that necklace?"

Vincente grabbed his necklace with one hand. "No, I was actually looking for some gems, some uncut ones. Any idea where I could find some? Or perhaps you've gotten some?"

"Oh, no. I'm definitely not the man for that. I just set up this shop because I found some rings."

"Well then, perhaps you can help me with something else. I'm interested in actually some information more than anything. I was wondering if you had in your time run into any men who look like this?" Vincente held up his notebook, where he had an extremely accurate drawing of Lucas he had made from memory. It was much more detailed than the one that had aired on TV. "If it helps, and this should be the distinguishing feature, he should be pale as a cloud and have deep green eyes, almost like the gem in this ring here." Vincente picked up a ring and handed it to the man, who was about to start singing again. "Deep emerald green."

"Well, that sounds like a beautiful prince you have painted for yourself, but there are a lot of pale people out here. Druggies, Gingers, Albinos, the Scandanavians. I meet a lot of people. How am I supposed to know what you mean? That could be so many."

Vicente sighed before pulling down his hood and presenting his face to the man. "He should look like me."

"Oh, holy shit, man, you are pale. Nah, you are actually kind of shiny. Interesting. No, I've never seen anyone like you, but I'll keep an eye out for you. Do you have some type of disease I should be worried about?" he asked while he cleaned off the ring with his shirt.

"No, I'm not contagious. I'm just…a little different." Vincente had grown used to having to show himself, to explain what he meant, but it never became more comfortable for him.

That is what would happen to Vincente in nearly every city he went to. He would search through the camps, then look through the cities briefly. He assumed he would not find his brother walking on the streets. Quickly going through the cities, Vincente would search and hope to find a lead as to his brother's location. It wouldn't be for another year, in another city, that Vincente would find him. Well, Lucas would find Vincente. One morning Vincente awoke to the sound of someone rummaging through his things. This time he was staying in a small wooden building that used to be a ticket station. It sat as one of many buildings at the abandoned train station. The shattered window Vincente had used to enter and then boarded up was busted in again.

He jumped to his feet and shouted, "Hey, there is only one hobo allowed to be here right now. I think you should go. Put down my stuff." He grabbed a piece of wood that he propped up by his bed.

The person stood up and turned around to reveal that he too had pale white skin and white hair. It was Lucas. His eyes were dark green just like Vincente's and his skin shined like scales. Vincente recognized him in an instant. "Lucas, is that you? How did you find me?"

"Hey, bud," he said as he walked toward him, playing with some of Vincente's maps that were on the table. "I'm happy you weren't trying to hide from me. There is no way you could leave more clues."

"What do you mean? Were you hiding? I tried hard to find you."

"Exactly. I found you because you were looking for me. You made a trail, man; you know how easy it is to track the ghostly white guy looking for another ghostly white guy? Obviously, people would ask about my skin, but eventually I got to a town where someone said you were looking for me. Then I just followed where they said you would go. You love that train."

"How did you find me here?"

"Oh, that was completely by accident, I've been traveling up and down the train lines. Just so happened to come across you."

"Well, at least we finally did it. It's great to see you."

"It is," Lucas said while putting the maps down and continuing to walk toward Vincente.

"Lucas, do you remember what happened to us?"

"Not exactly, but I do know there is something clearly wrong with us. I haven't gone to the bathroom in years." Lucas continued to look through Vincente's things. "I woke up wandering through a field and I've been trying to find you since." Lucas eventually picked up the magical book and started to read through it.

"Well, I guess it's good you started reading that book. Turn to the middle. Look up *The Fading*." Vincente swallowed loudly. "I think we're dead."

"What? That's ridiculous. Look at me. Look at us. We're messed up but we're not dead. I've actually never felt better in my life. Plus, people aren't as racist as you might think. No one's ever judged my skin. I just pretend I have a condition but maybe it's just because I'm white now."

"Just read. See if it brings anything back." Vincente signed for Lucas to read through the passage, which he did.

"So that nightmare I always have about the creepy drill sergeant doesn't have some weird other meaning. Thank God."

"This is serious. Did you read the part about a scar?" Vincente removed his shirt and showed his back to Lucas. "I never noticed it before but here you can see where the monster stabbed me." In one location only, the scales on his back were black. They were in the shape of a tree with clouds swirling around it.

"Oh, that explains this." Lucas lifted his shirt to show a similar marking on his stomach, off to one side.

"We did something bad, and we got punished for it by some monster. These are our brands."

"We? I didn't do anything. You're the one who shot that lady," Lucas said with a sudden cold calmness.

"I thought you said you didn't remember," questioned Vincente.

"I said *everything*. I know you clearly don't remember *anything*."

"I don't but no, wait. I would remember if I killed her." Vincente tried desperately to remember. Nothing more came back.

"It doesn't matter, man, we're family. I forgive you. It was so long ago; you really do seem like a new man. I'm sure you've grown so much since then."

"Don't belittle me. Did you read that passage about memories? What do you think it means?"

"What? Which one?"

"The part about memories tying us to this earth. Tied by trauma. What do you think that means? Is it our trauma or the trauma we caused?" continued Vincente.

"This book is cool, but it seems pretty nutso. I don't know if you should be taking it so literally."

"What if it is trauma? What if we can atone? Maybe we'd be healed?"

"Maybe we'd fade away into nothing?" said Lucas, concerned.

"Isn't that what we deserve?" Vincente said softly.

"I think if you need to cleanse your soul then you should come to grips with yourself. I've atoned, I've said sorry. Look at me. I clearly have been changed by it. Either way, how could we ever atone for that? A woman is dead, but we got to move on." Lucas stepped back away from Vincente, annoyed.

"We could apologize, we could give peace to her daughter. She's still alive—maybe it's her trauma that keeps us tied here."

"Tied here? Listen to yourself—you sound so down in the dumps. Have you not enjoyed any of this time you've had on earth? I've been having a blast." Lucas smiled and threw his arms in the air. In response, Vincente dropped his head.

"I was looking for you, hoping that I would find you and you could fill in the gaps in my memory. To make me feel like I wasn't a bad person. I hoped you'd want to do the right thing together." Vincente stepped close to Lucas and looked him deep in the eyes. "I have a plan. Please come with me. If we can talk to her, apologize. Then either we will be healed or at least I'll feel better. As my brother, could you help me with that?"

"I have an idea," Lucas said while smacking the magic book in his hands. He then smiled the biggest smile he had since he got there. "I think that's a great idea. If it makes you feel better, we could visit the little girl you traumatized all those years ago. Then you can say sorry, and maybe she'll forgive you. Then either way you can move on, and we can get on with this gift we've been given. I think it'll make us all stronger…people."

"We made a mistake. We fucked up. We shouldn't be here and now we are being punished. How can you be so calm about this?"

"Because I'm blameless." Lucas threw the book at Vincente's feet. "But I'm here to help quell your soul. Lead the way. You always were the boss."

It took them three days but the two made their way to the neighboring city of Iwatodai, where Rose had followed in her mother's footsteps and continued a jewelry business. It was very easy for them to find; a simple search about the incident on the internet revealed the new location. On the trip Vincente was happy to not be alone for the first time in a long time. Even while he searched for Lucas, meeting many people on the streets, Vincente refused to get close to anyone, to make any friends. His mind was always on his task of finding his brother. He hoped once they got together, he would remember more. Something, hopefully everything, would flash back, but nothing more came. It seemed that they would just have to work through it together. As they traveled, they joked and even had some beers. Neither of them could taste it and it didn't seem to get them drunk, but the sensation and the atmosphere were what Vincente missed.

They arrived at Iwatodai station early in the morning, which gave them time to make their way to Rose's Boutique and scope out how busy it was. They wouldn't be able to have their conversation with too many people around. The large pink and gold building was decorated in large cursive letters built into the façade. It was still the busy season; the anniversary of the incident often brought more visitors to the store. It was clear the news was also used to advertise the business. The store would be closed at 9 pm and they would wait until then and make a late-night visit. Until then, the two enjoyed the sun.

That evening when they entered the store there were no other customers. Rose stood behind the counter and a security guard sat on a stool in the corner. Vincente immediately walked toward her. Lucas made a sour face and then nodded at Vincente before making his way into the back of the store near the security guard, who was reading something on his phone.

As he approached the counter Vincente was clearly nervous. When he tried to speak to Rose, who stood smiling but watching the clock, his voice cracked. "I am here…uhh to umm…buy a present for my wife." He wasn't sure how upfront he should be and at this point lying was comforting to him.

"Well, I can gladly help you pick something out for her. Do you know what type of metals she likes to wear? Or perhaps a type of jewelry? Are you looking for a necklace, ring, bracelet?" Vincente began to pace back and forth before turning back to her.

"Sorry, just a little nervous. Making decisions can be so hard." Rose followed Vincente as he traveled down the cases, pretending to look at the merchandise. He stopped at a small case of engagement rings and paused.

"Oh, we're making the big decision. Well, I'd be nervous too," Rose laughed in a cute but cackling tone. "Did you have a gem size in mind?" Vincente finally made eye contact with Rose and started to speak.

"I, uhh, am thinking something small?" Vincente watched as the color began to fade from Rose's face. As they made eye contact, she finally had a chance to study his face. She finally recognized him. Even through his skin, Rose knew who he was. She backed away from the case and attempted to shout to the security guard, but her voice was trembling.

As the guard stood up and placed his phone in his pocket, Lucas came up behind him and swung his large fist into the side of his head. With a large crash the officer fell to the ground and Lucas began to search him for handcuffs. Then Lucas bound the guard's hands behind his back, made his way to lock the front door, and flipped the open sign to close. Rose finally screamed, and instinctually Vincente reached over the counter and grabbed her. As he pulled her in closer, he covered her mouth. "Shhh, shhh, shh…I'm sorry. Please stop. We're not here to hurt you. We're only here to talk."

"Now, my brother is just trying to do something nice. So let him get it over with," Lucas shouted from the front of the store. "Clearly, you know who we are." Vincente released Rose's mouth.

"Of course. Your skin is different, but I remember that face." Rose then spit into Vincent's eye.

"Woah, woah, woah…now calm down," Lucas said as he made his way back to the officer and tightened the handcuffs. Then Lucas took off his belt as he walked over to Rose and began to tie her up. Vincente backed away and put his hand over his mouth as he proceeded to pace for a moment. He walked over to a camera and covered his face, but it was too late. It had already been seen. Vincente took off his shoe and used it to smash the camera. He then made his way back to Lucas.

"No, no, stop. Don't put her hands behind her back—that looks terrible. Do it in front. We're just trying to keep her calm. She's not our hostage," pleaded Vincente. Lucas rolled his eyes in response and changed his knot. He then sat her down and walked away.

"Now talk to her so we can leave," he demanded. Vincente walked up to Rose.

"Hey, look at me. I'm sorry." He reached into his shirt and took out the necklace. He then handed it to Rose, who was tearing out of frustration. "We are going to let you go in just a moment. We are not here to hurt you," he said to Rose. "I'm sorry we tied you both up," he shouted to include the security guard. "I know we did something terrible a long time ago. I know I killed your mother. I hope to God it was an accident, but I'm sorry."

"Thank you for my necklace back finally." Rose paused, trying to remain calm. "But wouldn't it be better if you just turned yourselves in?" Rose looked up at him. "I don't know how you faked your own death, or what you did to yourself, but I'm never going to forgive you. So just turn yourselves in."

"I'm sorry I hurt your mother. I hope we haven't caused any more trauma here tonight. That is all I wanted to say. Please, just forget us. We won't ever bother or hurt you again. We are just going to go live empty lives. Let that be our punishment."

"I'm sorry, you're going to have to live knowing I still want justice and my mother will not be avenged until that happens. You deserve suffering for your punishment, but him, he deserves worse."

"Why?"

"Because it wasn't you who shot my mother. It was that bastard over there," Rose screamed while spitting across the room.

"What?" Vincente then felt a heavy, chill inducing smack against his head. He had been hit with a gun and knocked to the ground. He rolled onto his back and saw Lucas standing above him. Out of his pocket Lucas pulled out zip ties and proceeded to restrain Vincente. He then added a few more to Rose as well. Lucas ran to the front door and made sure it was locked. He then closed the shutters and made his way to the back room. He shut off all the lights except for the ones used for cabinet display. Lucas then dragged all three people to the back of the room, one by one, and pushed them against one of the display cases.

"What the fuck are you doing? Where did you get a gun? And why did you make me believe that I killed that lady? Have you been pretending to not remember?" Vincente said as he struggled with his bindings.

"It's absolutely pathetic how easy it was to trick you. For such a smart college guy, you really are an idiot. Do *you* really not remember anything that happened? Or anything from when we were kids."

"When did you remember?" shouted Vincente as he struggled.

"I never forgot."

"Lucas, what are you doing? We were going to apologize."

"No, you were going to apologize. Which for your information, will not work. You're reading the passage wrong. While I technically pulled the trigger, this entire thing was your fault to begin with anyway. Why were we robbing? Your fault. The crash?"

"My fault?"

"Do you really not remember why we crashed in the first place? I wanted to keep that stupid ass chain and you got all weak-hearted on me and decided it was too personal to take. I just wanted to put *our father's* picture in it. I tried to take it from you, and you crashed like a big baby. So upset about someone you didn't know."

"Why did you have to kill that lady in the first place? We were supposed to get in and get out."

"Because she saw our faces. She wasn't supposed to still be there, but she was, and she could identify us. Just like this one can identify us now. She would have been dead then as a little girl too if you didn't get soft on me." Lucas put his gun to Rose's head.

"Leave her alone. What are you hoping to accomplish? You can't blame me for your decisions."

"My decisions. Our decisions are because of *YOU*. Do you not even remember why we needed to rob that place in the first place? That was your fault too." Some memories began to flood back to Vincente's mind.

"I had just come back from college for the semester. You told me that we needed to do something."

"College…ding ding ding. You came back. You came back to nothing. We didn't have anything anymore. We lost that. Because of you."

"It's not my fault the banks took the house. That…Dad got sick." Vincente was starting to remember the house where they grew up and the grizzled and hard worker that was their father.

"That's just it. You could have helped. You could have stayed and worked, like I did. You could have tried to protect the house. You left us alone and did nothing. Built more debt. I was forced to take care of everything. The least you could do was help me with a job."

"Dad sent me away. I had to be there. I needed to be there to help make money in the future. Dad knew that it was a waste of time for me to circle the drain in that town. The store went belly-up. The land was bad."

"You ruined our family. No matter your excuse, you left us. That's what we fought about. That's why she died. You cared more about her life than protecting us, your family. So, I did what needed to be done. Like I always have. I wasn't lucky enough to have a brother who was big and strong. You crashed the car, and I left you. You fucked up everything and then crashed. I left you to die. It's a gift that monster gave us and again you're wasting it being a sad-sack."

"So, you know where the jewels are?"

"Of course I do. I took them off your body when I came too. I knew enough to do that." Lucas then pulled out a purse from the pocket of his coat. "I've had them the whole time. I knew you didn't remember anything about me when you asked how I had money. I haven't worked a job maybe ever. I've just gotten by selling gems when I needed a little. I still have plenty, but this seemed like a great time for a re-up."

"It's not too late, Lucas. You can still be a good man. We can atone and get out of here. No one else needs to get hurt."

"Did you not read the same book that I did? We cannot atone. This is not about our souls or how good we are. This is about being remembered. This is about power. Your book got me thinking. Our only option is to live forever. We can do that strong or weak." Lucas began to pace. "You're an idiot. Think about it, we used the internet to find this place because of an article. One that thousands of people have read. We're going to be remembered by all of them. We're going to live on, on the internet. We will never be able to disappear. We can either live weakly or we can live powerfully. Our faces and our crime are on the internet and will exist forever. As long as the world exists, and these people keep taking their medicine, we will exist forever. It says memories. As long as she knows us. As long as the world knows us. We'll stay alive and strong." Lucas walked over to Vincente and now brandished the gun at him. "This mystery has kept us alive. Didn't you notice the night that our story aired? That our faces were placed on TV? That is when we were the strongest, and we've been riding that high ever since. If that can help, then we can be reignited. We only need to be remembered."

"I'm sorry that you didn't get what you wanted out of life. I'm sorry that I stood in the way. But you don't need to ruin more lives. What does that accomplish? You just said it yourself." Vincente continued to argue while trying to break out of his cuffs. Both his legs and arms were stuck and beginning to dig into his skin.

"By killing this little lady here, we continue the cycle. This cop will see us. They'll put our faces everywhere again." He then paused. "Actually, we already have the cameras. Maybe we don't need this cop after all." Lucas then walked over to the man and pointed his gun at him, turning it side to side. "No one will believe it's actually us. We're dead but we'll haunt people's minds with a big what-if. Leaving a witness would make it too believable that we are really still alive. I'd like to not have to look over my shoulder every thirty seconds." Lucas cocked his gun.

"Then what happens when people move on from your momentary blaze of glory? You're shortsighted. You're just going to get weak again."

"No, you are. As long as we kill someone every now and then we can haunt the world. People who remember will look us up. We will be stronger. And we're never able to be punished or caught. We'll be ghosts. Gods."

"You can't just kill people."

"Why not? We owe these people nothing. Look at this woman. We probably made her life. She got to be famous her whole life. If anything, we did something great."

"IT'S NOT WORTH IT TO KILL," shouted Vincente.

"Says you. WHO CARES if we kill? Someone has to be the dominant predator and I am asking for so little," Lucas said in a mocking tone, turning his bottom lip down and out in an exaggerated manner. "It's only a few people. Consider it dividends for what we never got in life."

"I won't let you hurt anyone."

"What are you going to do tied up?" Lucas laughed. "Actually, I have a question. Ness, have you tried to hurt yourself since you woke up? I noticed something very interesting when I cut myself. If you're not going to join me, we'll just have to use you as a guinea pig." Lucas then picked up Vincente and propped him up on a display case. With a smile Lucas took aim and at point-blank range shot Vincente in the chest, while saying, "Let's see if we can die…again."

Vincente was blasted backward over the counter and slammed onto the floor behind the display cases. As he fell over it, he shattered the glass. "Are you okay? Can you talk?" Lucas called over the partition. On the other side he could see Vincente lying on the ground. White glistening blood slowly dripped out of his wound and some white smoke accompanied it.

Lucas turned his attention to the cases of jewelry. He started to make his way through them, using his gun to shatter the glass. He began to fill his pockets with rings, necklaces, and watches. On the ground, Vincente was still conscious; apparently, one shot to the chest was not enough to knock him out. As he breathed deeply, smoke puffed out of his lungs. A small pain shot through his body; he could feel a sting travel through his nerves, but that was all. With his hands still tied behind him, Vincente used them to pull a shard of glass out of his back. He then used the glass to saw away at his bindings. His hands slowly bled white blood, and smoke continued to float from his wounds, but he felt minimal pain. After a few moments he cut his hands free. Then he began to free his legs.

Vincente glanced through the cabinet glass and tried to watch where Lucas was going. Then Vincente crouched and started to shuffle behind the counters. The sound of glass beneath his feet alerted Lucas that he was up. Lucas ran back to see that Vincente's body was gone. "Wow, well, it's great to know I can survive a gunshot to the chest. See, Ness. How can you really not think we are gods? How can you not view this as a gift? If anything, we were rewarded for our sins. Call it whatever you want but it's awesome." Lucas shot one of the cabinets at random, shattering it. Somewhere in the room Vincente ducked and looked over his shoulder. Lucas had shot at the opposite end of the room. Vincente had to try and get toward his brother.

"I know what to do. If you're going to hide. I'm just gonna keep doing what I do best. For instance, do you think the security guard was wearing a vest? We'll have to check." Lucas made his way over to the officer and started to fire into him. "Look at that, no blood. Good day to be equipped. I bet that still hurt like a bitch, though, didn't it?" The pain had finally woken up the security guard, who simply nodded while he gasped for air.

"Stop!" screamed Vincente, while he continued to scurry behind the cabinets. Lucas tracked where his voice was and shot where he had been. Vincente was making his way toward Rose, a shard of glass still in his hand. If he could free the hostages, he could fight his brother. Vincente made his way around the left side of the room and hid behind a large display cabinet. There was no way to get close enough without being seen. Lucas made his way back over to Rose. The security guard passed out again.

Lucas pointed the gun at her head. "You'll need to come out right now, Ness. Or she's dead. I mean it. RIGHT NOW!" Vincente stepped out from behind a cabinet with his hands up.

"You have the gun. You have all the power. All I'm saying is that you don't need to kill anyone. This is more than enough to make sure people remember you. She'll remember you forever. Why does someone have to die?"

"We die and she becomes rich and famous off of us? That's…not…fair." Lucas pointed the gun back at Rose. "Because it cannot just end with her. I can't take the chance she won't fuck up and die early. She needs to be the beginning of something greater."

"I worked for everything I have. How dare you say you made me. You did nothing but take away a long and beautiful life," Rose shouted, showing no fear.

"I knew you were a brat," laughed Lucas. Vincente used his fist to shatter the glass of a cabinet near him. Lucas turned his attention back to his brother. "What do you think you're doing?" Vincente began to grab some large crystal statues and began throwing them at Lucas. He struck him in the hand and then the face. "Are you kidding me?" Lucas shouted as he ducked and started to fire at Vincente. Another shot hit him in the leg. Vincente sprinted toward Lucas and dove for the gun. The two wrestled for the weapon and fell to the ground. The gun proceeded to fire three more times. If any of them hit him, Vincente didn't notice.

The two struggled until Vincente was on top. With his elbow he held down Lucas' hand holding the gun. "You always were fat," Lucas mocked him while he struggled against Vincente's weight. Vincente stared down into his brother's eyes and with his free hand, he stabbed Lucas with the glass shard and he released the gun. Vincente then knocked it away and used the shard of glass to stab Lucas in his other hand.

"Stop fighting me!" Vincente shouted, holding the shard of glass into the air.

"Fuck you!" Lucas responded and started to fight back even harder.

"I'm sorry," Vincente said as he brought down the glass shard down into Lucas's face and continued to stab until Lucas stopped moving. With each stab it became easier, and Lucas's face gave less resistance. Vincente did not feel bone, instead only air, as if he was stabbing nothing. He looked at his brother's face. It was spattered with white blood and smoking like a small bonfire. As it puffed into the air, the smoke vanished.

Vincente caught his breath as he made his way into Lucas' jacket pocket to look for more zip ties. Instead, he found the pouch. When he touched it his head began to hurt again. Through the pain he poured out the mass of gems into his palm. It was only a fraction of the ones they had stolen years before. He put them back into the pouch and turned toward Rose. "I hope we can call this even. I'm sorry I wasn't able to help your mother. I know it's not everything." That was when Vincente realized that Rose had been shot. She was bleeding from the head.

He rushed over to her and checked her pulse. She was still alive, but barely breathing. She had not been directly shot. Her scalp had been nicked and she was unconscious, like the security guard to her side. He needed to call the ambulance, but he needed to get out first. Vincente reached into his shirt and pulled out the necklace he was still wearing. "We never should have taken this from you. I am so sorry." He said as he placed the necklace on Rose. "I hope you don't remember any of this. The best thing for everyone is if your injury makes you forget," he whispered to himself as if it was a little prayer.

Vincente turned his attention back to Lucas. The areas of his face that had been shattered started to return. The blood that was splattered on his face was slowly being pulled back into him. Vincente knew he hadn't killed Lucas; he probably never could. He would be awake, eventually. Vicente went back into Lucas' pockets and searched for the zip ties. With them, he bound his brother and thought about his next move. He checked the pockets of the security guard and collected his keys. In the back of the store, he made his way to the security desk and accessed the cameras. Then Vincente deleted all of the security footage from the computer.

Vincente dragged his brother to the back door and placed him on a small sheet. He had only one choice. He picked up the phone and dialed 911, then placed it down onto the table without saying anything. As Vincente threw the carpet over his shoulders and started to slowly drag him through the alley, the emergency technician shouted, "Hello! Hello! What is the nature of your emergency? We'll be dispatching someone to your area."

Several months later, Vincente awoke at his home in Midgar. The abandoned warehouse was not one of his classic hiding spots. It was not along the railway but instead deep in the woods. Vincente had fled the city and made his way to one of the many still rural areas of the country. The abandoned mill factory was rumored by the locals to be haunted, providing Vincente with privacy, except for the occasional curious teenager. He would wander into town for gas or supplies but mostly stuck to himself. All he did now was people watch.

From day to day, his strength still fluctuated. He knew from the news that Rose was still alive. She remembered nothing of the break-in, but she was emotional at having found her mother's necklace; the gems were a happy bonus. The security guard did not know enough to identify them but was hailed as a hero. Another mystery had been established. So once again, from day to day Vincente's strength fluctuated. Each year he felt the anniversary approaching as he got stronger and more unable to rest. Now he continued to search, but only this time in books and on the internet. He looked to learn more about himself and what he was. If there was some way to break the curse. The magic book seemed to have run out of energy and no longer glowed or displayed its textbook of knowledge. He was on his own.

Today, Vincente was going into town to pick up more books. He had ordered some through the only tiny bookstore there was. As he began to crawl over a box and out the window he used to get in and out, he heard metal rattle. In the corner of the room, behind a large wall of books, Lucas sat in a cage. The small thing was only large enough for him to sit up in and narrow enough that it would take effort and time for him to comfortably spin.

"Let me out!" Lucas shouted. "Every day we're going to fade. We are going to get a little sicker and a little weaker every day. How dare you do this to your brother? To your only family? Just like you abandoned Dad."

"You're not my brother. You're my curse. Father would be ashamed at what you've done. He was a hardworking and sweet man. I will stop you from being evil for the rest of eternity if I have to…if that's what I have to do to repent. I will. I'm just sorry I didn't stop you when I should have."

"You would have never been able to overpower me in that store the first time. You're too weak. A shot to the chest would have stopped you then."

"No, I mean before we even got in the car. Before I let you guilt-trip me into going to that store. You're right, I was weak, but I won't make that mistake again."

Vincente crawled out of the second-story window and onto a garbage bin. He jumped down and then used his shoulder to push it out of the way. Vincente threw up his hood, put his hands in his pockets, and started toward town.

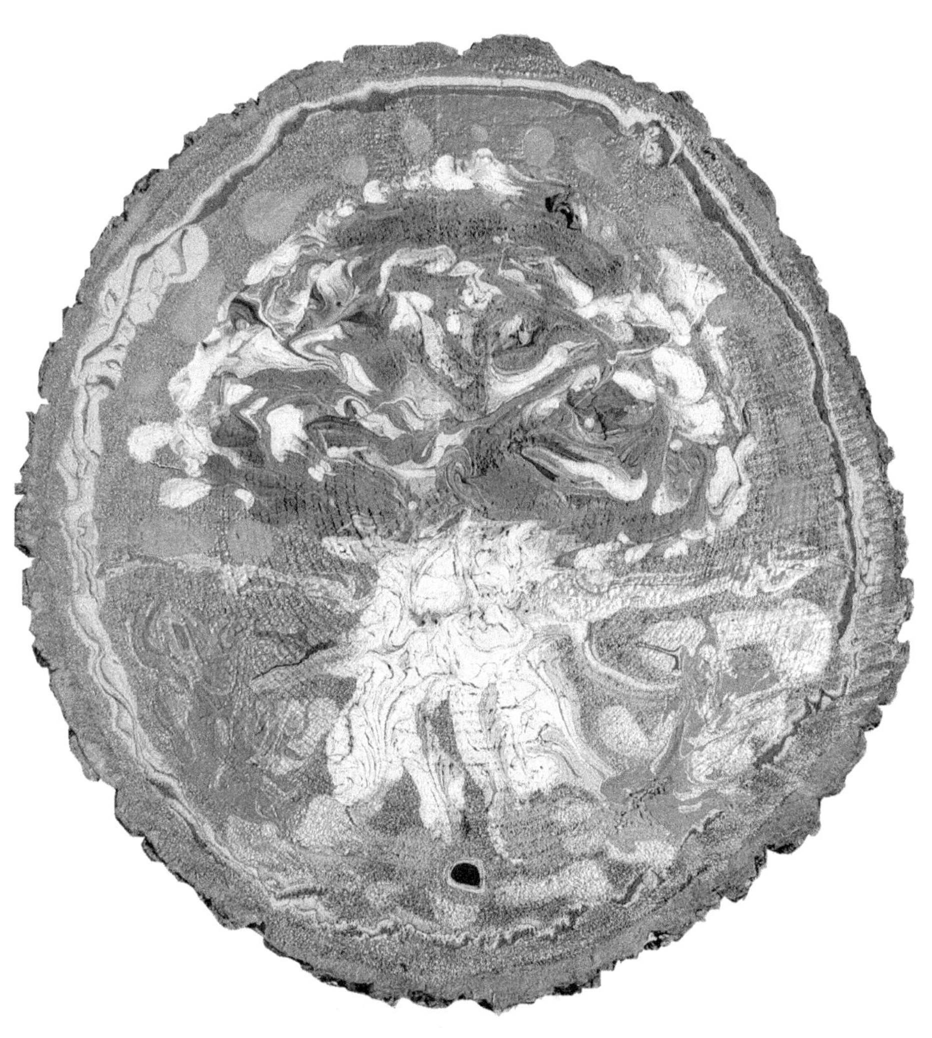

The Tower in Town

The Tower in Town

"What's in the tower in town?" asked Robin for the 315th time this week and the twelfth time this morning. They had recently turned the ripe old age of ten. Robin was small, barely four feet in height, and their legs swung off the chair they sat in, unable to touch the ground. Their hair was thin, long, straight, and white as snow. At present, it was unkemptly atop their head in an askew bun. Robin's mother, Lark, had found it easier to let the hair settle and take care of it as was necessary instead of washing it every day; Robin's adventures often ruined her hard work. Robin's skin matched their hair; both were a faint white that slightly shimmered as if ash was buried inside. Lark, the person she was presently pestering, had skin that glistened much brighter, and seemed to radiate. Lark's hair was equally snow colored but much thicker; she wore it down to her shoulders. Robin's left arm and right leg were covered in dark black birthmarks they had inherited from their parents. Lark shared the series of wires and concentric circles that covered Robin's leg, and her husband, Enu, shared the series of vine-like markings that covered Robin's forearm. Their pasts were embedded deep in their skin, even if they couldn't remember it. The trauma acted like DNA that was passed to the next generation as tattoos.

Robin sat at the rarely used dinner table; it was a decoration used to fake that they lived in civilization. It was like many things in town were, done to fake a life that none of the inhabitants could truly remember or relate to. Even so, many of them found it calming in a way they could not describe. Their town, Olmec, was built on instinct and for comfort. Robin insisted that they were hungry, in protest to Lark's reminder that Robin had eaten just last month. Now Robin sat, playing with their small bowl of oatmeal. They were still getting used to the small bursts of energy, hunger, and emotion that came with being a *Fading*.

There were very few children in town. It made it lonely and confusing for kids like Robin, who needed constant stimulation. The *Fading* were not capable of procreating by choice. It was simply a miracle that occurred from time to time. Each child was born with gray ash-like skin, and as they grew their skin began to crystallize, becoming white and shiny. Robin had ten years or so before they would look like their mother. Each child also bore the tattoos of their family, like a branded coat of arms. The amount of tattoos Robin had was unusual; both her parents were part of a long line of forgotten souls. Each one was the sum of everyone before them. Who Robin was would come in time. Some *Fading* only lived for a few decades, but others seemed to have been alive since the beginning of time.

As Robin continued to play with their food, they felt no hunger, only boredom. "Mama, what is in the tower in the center of town?" they asked again, staring down into their oatmeal and chasing the bubbles and clumps with their spoon.

"You know what's in it, darling," answered Lark in an overly positive tone to try and appease her child. Even though she rarely slept, Lark always made sure that she made coffee in the morning. When the clock in her kitchen read 8 a.m. she began her morning ritual. The coffee didn't give her any energy, nor could she taste it, but there was something in the ritual that she found so calming. It resonated with something in her soul; someone in one of her lost lives had definitely loved coffee. She began the process of preparing her coffee using a French press. When finished she poured herself a cup and closed the top hatch of their wood-burning stove.

"Mama, tell me again," Robin pleaded, while finally putting some of their breakfast into their mouth. Robin had not forgotten what their mother had said; instead they hoped to catch her in a lie. Robin always found the answer Lark provided to be too clean, and too simple; the Tower was just too large, and too important.

"The tower is a cemetery, Robin, you know that. It's where we put those from the village who have died. Is that not enough for you?" Lark pleaded. "Now finish your breakfast. I have errands to run," her voice now a little more coy and playful. Robin knew that meant they were going into town, but that could also be boring.

"What errands? Where?" asked Robin, trying not to get too excited. They began to play a game where they attempted to flip the spoon quickly before putting it in their mouth and allowed gravity to take the falling oatmeal to their tongue.

"Oh, you know, going to get some groceries…and…talking to the *Mayor*."

Robin's eyes lit up, and their ears perked like a dog's. "Where?" they whispered.

"Her home, the church of course!" Lark said, patronizing the child.

"OH, OH, OH!" Robin muttered while shoveling food into their mouth. Then all of a sudden, the meal was gone. Robin was excited because they knew the mayor's house, the church of the town, was located against the side of the mountain, and located directly next to the tower. They finished up their meal, rushed to the sink, and put their plate into its soapy water. Robin then ran toward the front door and plopped to the ground. They began throwing on their shoes.

Cough, cough…

Robin heard the noise come from behind them. They turned to see Lark standing, waiting, with her arms crossed and a smile on her face. Robin jumped up and ran back toward the sink and leapt onto a small box. They reached under the metal bason that hung from the wall and turned on the water. The counter was made of alternating colors of marble, fragments that had been found over the years. There were limited supplies in the town, but many people were excellent craftsmen; each of them remembered seemingly random skills from their past lives. Robin hung their body over the mouth of the sink and dangled into the soapy water. Then cleaned their dishes.

After they finished, Robin rushed back across the room and grabbed their thin, light brown hoodie. Robin threw it on and began to adjust the long, yellow pull strings that dangled on both sides. They leaned their head back and closed one eye as they made sure they were perfectly symmetrical. *Just right.* Robin then rushed over to their mother's side and grabbed her hand. "Let's go!"

The two walked out through their front door, an old but fancy piece—hand carved and once stunningly beautiful. The unique carvings of a unicorn and snake were worn and well loved. The wood was nearly broken in some parts, having been sanded and refurbished many times. Of the many skills the town's inhabitants had, the artistic wood carver was no longer one of them. Since he passed, and no one with his skill or passion had come to town, Lark held onto her door as a sign of tradition and of beauty. At this point, its architecture was different from each of the other doors in town, all of which had been replaced.

Outside, the series of small homes were all connected by dirt roads. There was no rhyme or reason as to their placement. It was made sure that everyone had a home, but still no one owned any of the land. It was all communal, and any separations were decorative, even the fences. The pair walked by beautiful homes, carefully made, and like their kitchen counter constructed of many different materials. Each house was a unique hodgepodge of supplies made from what was available at the time; they were constructed when someone grew up and needed their own space or, more often, when someone wandered into town from the surrounding woods. Somehow many *Fading* found their way there by instinct when lost and weak.

Each person on the street and in each house shared the same milky glow to their skin that Lark and Robin did. Each person's glow and hew shifted over time, like a town of fireflies. Though it was hot and humid, no one within the town seemed to sweat. The clothes that they wore were dirty but dry. Most simply wore their favorite outfits whenever they wanted. There was no money and so there was no need to put on airs. In fact, outfits only seemed to fill a kind of subconscious need to be clothed each of them felt; they were worn out of instinct and comfort more than for warmth or protection.

Further down, the street turned to cobblestone; it was an ongoing project slowly expanded when possible. The clean stones radiated out from the city center for only a few blocks in each direction. Robin and Lark followed the road, which led toward the center of the town where the mountainside sat. The road would eventually lead them to the church and then the tower. The town center was marked by a beautiful, large, and sparkling vein of blood-red rock that zigzagged up the rockface. At the tip of the mountain hung a hulking tree resembling a weeping willow, its branches hung hundreds of feet to touch the cobblestone below. It was distinct from all of the evergreen pine trees that surrounded the town in the other directions. Its wood was a stark and nearly black color. Its leaves were large, plumbed fans, a deep emerald green. The folding of the leaves caused them to glisten, iridizing like a mermaid between green and purple as you walked by. The town center shimmered with an unnatural beauty.

Most inhabitants of the town found the presence of the tree had an invigorating effect; it might have been what called them to the area. The tree itself was dwarfed by a large ring of mountains that rose even higher and surrounded the majority of the town. The numbers varied between a few hundred to a few thousand over the course of its history. Though the only way into the valley was a long trail through the woods and over the mountains, nearly every person had found themselves accidentally there. Once they arrived, there was never a reason to leave. Its remote location made it so it was only found by those who were truly lost.

"Let's hope the grocery is open this morning," Lark said to Robin as they walked by the tree to one of the side streets. The grocery store, like everything else in the town, worked on its own schedule. The parishioner of each could be gone, sleeping, or too weak to work at any point; you simply came back later. It wasn't that most people had to eat; instead, the grocery store was merely a collection of the surplus dried rations and building materials. Any new equipment and paint that was collected was simply added to the small warehouse. With the exception of children like Robin, the majority of the town only ate on average once or twice a year.

Whether the grocer was unavailable or not, everything was merely taken in good faith. The job was currently held by one of the oldest and physically brightest of the village members, a man who by his very nature was quite absentminded. That along with the fact that people didn't come by very often made him jump when he noticed Lark and Robin in his shop. Albeit it took him several minutes. At a counter in the back sat Artemis, an older-looking gentleman. His noteworthy feature was that his marking was on his lower face. The entirety of his head and shoulder were covered in a finely detailed black tattoo. If that was not distinct enough, and though he was always indoors, he still always wore a hat. Most of the time he sat and stared out the window behind him at the small lake. Its sight was especially calming to him. The lake would vary in size depending on the season's rain, and he enjoyed any time it existed.

"Hi, Lark." Artemis' deep voice squeaked out of a microphone that hadn't been used in quite a while. In the small and empty room, they could hear his voice come out of his mouth as clearly as the speaker overhead; he clearly got a small amusement from getting to use it. "What are we getting today?"

"Oh, you know. We were just here because our normal full year's supply is already gone. Robin is eating everything, and by eating, I mean playing with, then wasting. Can't wait until they finish growing," answered Lark as she moved along the food aisling. She sorted through many different brown bags with handwritten labels detailing their prep method (most often add water). The products were all mildly organized into large barrels. Each held a different dried ration made by one of the villagers, one season or another. A large farm was established by one of the citizens, which was now planted with rotating crops each season and provided an outlet for those with too much energy.

"Artemis, do you remember what your tattoo is?" asked Robin, while they shuffled through a basket of candies at the front desk. Individual chocolate truffles sat covered in colorful aluminum foil. "Why are these separate?"

"Robin! We talked about that. You do not bother people about their tattoos. It's not polite," Lark scolded.

"It's okay, Lark. I'm not one of those sensitive people." Artemis continued to talk over the microphone. "Those are chocolates—some people have a special attachment to them. I assume it's a texture thing. To answer your other question, I had a dream once that I was an eagle. So, I think it has something to do with nature. Yeah, I was probably a forest ranger or something."

Robin looked up and noticed Artemis was still looking out the window. "But there is an eagle outside right now," they said and pointed at it.

"Oh, yes, so that is. That must be a sign. If not then, uhhh, then I guess I don't remember," he said as he yawned. He chuckled and then leaned back and pulled his hat down across his face. "Let me know if you need anything."

"You know it's rude to bother someone about their tattoos. A lot of people are like us, Robin. They don't remember anything about themselves or it," whispered Lark.

"Exactly, I don't remember either. I don't care," Robin said naively.

"Some people, Robin, care that they don't."

"But they don't know what they are missing." Robin's lack of consistent emotions gave them little experience in empathizing with others.

"Exactly, and for some, it's better if they don't think about it," scolded Lark. "No one knows how much time any of us have and everyone is on their own journey. You don't need to remind people of their trauma. We talked about this; for many, it's hard."

"I didn't mean that I don't care. I care a lot. I just think they are beautiful, and I want to know the story behind it," Robin responded sadly and hurt. They didn't mean to cause a fuss and really did admire Artemis' face tattoo. Lark picked up a sack each of flour, oats, and coffee. That was all they needed for now. They said goodbye to Artemis and exited the shop.

They continued their walk around the open semicircle of cobblestone that constituted the center square and traveled down a hill toward the edge of town. The whole while they followed alongside the mountains and the further they got from the town center the fewer houses there were. It wasn't more than a few minutes before the cobblestones were gone and they were once again walking on a dirt road. Their path took them deeper into the valley, where the trees changed from evergreen pines to palm trees. The area itself was warmer and more humid, not that anyone could tell. A small pond sat at the bottom near the house of the elder; a mansion carved into the mountain as a permanent structure. The elder had been there long before anyone else in town and was one of the few people whose energy never seemed to dip. Near the house sat the tower that reached to the sky, the object of Robin's fascination. The morning sun was at their backs as they approached. Robin covered their eyes with their free hand to block the glare from the sun hitting the tower in the distance.

The tower stood out among everything else within the village, even more so than the deep black tree at its center. Even though the tower began low in the valley, it rose higher than anything else in town, again even the tree. It was only dwarfed by the mountain it was built alongside of. The tower stood as a monolith. Its shiny exterior was smooth and crafted of bricks made from a swirl of lavender and dark gray stone. The cylindrical body got smaller as it rose, until it reached a sharp golden point at the top. The exceptions were certain floors where the design periodically fanned out, creating a larger donut shape. Robin wondered what was special about those. Every couple floors were also covered in many stained glass windows made of combinations of seemingly random colored shapes. The gleam of the tower had an otherworldly shine, giving off light. On moonless and dark evenings, the tower could even glow. The ground beneath it shined too with a crystalline gleam that radiated out like roots. The front of the tower had two large doors that stood two stories tall, composed of a combination of precious metals, gold, silver, and platinum, and was littered with gems. It shined too but not nearly as much as the surrounding stone. The doors themselves had no visible handles or locks. Robin could not spot any way to open it, no matter how much they examined it.

Their destination was the much smaller but beautifully decorated church that stood next to the tower. The two-story building was made of gray and brown stone, the same as the mountain, but was smooth and clean. The second story was full of stained-glass windows and held up by giant columns. On the porch leaning on a stone banister stood the mayor, who was also the elder.

"Hello, Elder, how are you doing this morning?" Lark shouted while using her free hand to cover her eyes, then to wave. Aria was the oldest within the village and became the mayor out of sheer perseverance. Through many generations of *Fading* and the building and rebuilding of the town, something in the elder's bloodline kept them consistently strong. She was both the oldest and by far the largest collection of souls. Unlike everyone else in the town, the elder's skin was almost completely black. Her skin was a collection of hundreds, if not thousands, of tattoos. Only small freckles of shiny white skin remained, which looked like speckling along her body. It made an optical illusion, so that she shimmered like a diamond in the sun and when she moved. The markings overlapped and covered her body so dramatically that no one story, or image, could be made out.

"Good morning, Lark! Thank you for coming and bringing your beautiful child here today. How are you two?" shouted the elder with a huge smile on her face. She waved with one arm and leaned from a stone banister on the second floor. She wore a long pink and gold sherwani, a proper suit for the clergy, of which she was the only one. The deep pink was covered in some dirt from use, and the gold fixings—which clearly used to shine brightly—were tarnished.

Lark did her classic cough before pulling onto Robin's arm. "Say hello, Robin. Don't be rude."

"Hello, Elder, and good morning. What's in the tower?" Robin muttered and smiled while cocking their head to the side. They used their arm to shield their eyes from the glare of the tower, mimicking the posture of their mother.

"Ha-ha-ha," chuckled the elder loudly. "You really do have a one-track mind, young one. I believe you asked me the same thing last time you were here?" The two then made their way to the door of the church, and now Aria loomed above them. "Come up, come up," she beckoned as she pointed to the stairs that sat on the outside of the building. The stairs were large and irregular, made with much less care than the tower or house itself. Though Lark was able to walk up them normally, Robin required a little bit of their mother's help, a small pull, to climb them. After a few minutes the two made their way to the porch, where the elder gleefully met them.

"Welcome! Welcome. Here! Come here," called the elder. She led them out of the sun and under the shade of a tall palm tree growing on the porch. "Lark, I must be blunt. I need you and your husband's help with…" Her request was interrupted by Robin, who was absentmindedly picking at the bark on the tree.

"Is it magic that lets you sparkle like a diamond?" Robin had always been entranced by the effect. Like the tattoo, Robin thought it was beautiful.

"Robin, another…inappropriate question." Lark shook her head and began to apologize to Aria.

"No worries, children are always so probing," said Aria slowly while grabbing hold of Lark's hand. "I don't think we'll get much talking done with this one's inquisitive mind." Aria then turned and faced Robin. "Do you have any other questions I can answer, Robin? Before I speak with your mother?"

"Yeah! Of course!" Robin ran over to the two and excitedly danced. "Okay, how is it that everyone is so pale, and yet you're so dark? Why don't you look like us? If you are the oldest of us, why are you so young and beautiful looking? I thought my mother said we get brighter as we age." Robin began trying to ask another question but was stopped by Aria.

"That is a very good question. You know, just like you, my markings are tattoos." Aria reached out her arm to Robin, who began to run their hand over it. "See, here and here," she pointed at white freckles on her skin. "Those are just like you, a long, long, long time ago I was nearly as bright as you. My sparkle is a happy accident." Aria smiled.

"When was that? I don't remember you ever being bright. It must have been a long time ago?"

"I wish I could tell you. Like you, I don't know everything, especially when it happened. I know that once I found I had a gift, I gave myself what I consider to be a very important job. It's one of the few memories of myself I have. So, I will do it for as long as I can. When someone in our town passes on, I take the small number of memories they have left and collect it. Their brand then joins the rest on my body. I house the history of our people."

"So, you're multiple people?"

"I think many of us are multiple people, multiple souls. Especially you, Robin. But you're right, I am more than most. Who I am fluctuates from day to day, like the phases of the moon. Sometimes I am more feminine and sometimes I am more masculine. Sometimes happier and sometimes filled with grief. Inside myself I feel many people. It's not always pleasant but I hope to keep them alive. For now, I am Aria, she. Who are you, my child?"

"I don't know," responded Robin. They didn't think too hard, but they didn't need to. The only things they knew were what had happened in the last few years. Robin had not had any visions or dreams yet.

"Then we are the same, and you understand me. As my friend, you'll have to help me, and I promise to help you. Deal?" Aria smiled and then held a fist up to Robin, who bumped it. "You might wake up and remember something one day, or you might have a dream that is too real. Then maybe your past will come back. Perhaps you'll even learn about your mother. It comes to all of us differently and in time. It's up to you to interpret it for yourself, but remember, don't wallow in it. If you ever need anything, you're always welcome here. You will hopefully have lots of time to figure out all those parts about yourself. Don't worry, put no pressure on your mind. So, are we done with questions?"

"Uh, one more? Why do our dead people make the ground sparkle?" Robin asked while hanging off the banister and pointing to the grass surrounding the tower.

"That we don't know. We haven't had a scientist in many generations. But simply put, it is probably because our people are magic. Look at yourself, child. Your skin and your life are a gift. So, perhaps with our death comes beauty." Aria then turned away from Robin. "Speaking of which, Lark, that is one of the matters I called you here for. Well, there are two, and they partially concern each other. Did you hear about the new visitor?"

"They arrived two days ago…they are newly born, validated that they have only one mark. They are relatively dull, so it means it was in the last few years," rattled off Lark as if it was public knowledge.

"Amazing how in a town of so many sleepy people information still spreads so quickly. He's actually inside right now. If it is okay, may I quickly grab him? I think he can keep Robin entertained while we discuss other matters. Robin's constant questions might be good for his still developing brain."

Aria walked toward the balcony door and opened it. She leaned into the room and gestured with her hand. She then opened the door fully and let out a man dressed in a set of denim pants and jacket. He had a thin, spiraling tattoo that went around the length of his neck. He had low cheekbones and small eyes, and his hair was parted in the middle. "If you could, would you please entertain our friend Robin over there?" He walked toward Robin, wobbling unsteadily on his feet.

"So, you need us to make a new home for him?" Lark pointed toward the mystery man. "Are we leading the construction or are we joining a team? We could probably start later today."

"You're always so gun-ho. It's always a pleasure to work with you, Lark. That's exactly why I called you, but no, nothing that large-scale. I'll simply need you two to perform updates and maybe some customizations on Mr. Shelley's house."

"Mr. Shelley, why his house?" interrupted Robin.

"Robin, talk to the nice man now," Lark whispered. "But yes, what about Mr. Shelley?"

"He hasn't wanted to worry anyone, but he has been weak for a very long time. It doesn't seem he'll be coming out of this fatigue anytime soon. He is asleep most of the time now and as it seems, very close to death. He asked us to start prepping him for the ceremony and burial. It's very important to him."

"I didn't realize Mr. Shelley was that old," interrupted Robin again.

"Robin, and new boy. You must learn that we do not really age. Once you're an adult most stay the same until they are forgotten. Some live forever, others only a few decades." Robin finally turned her attention to the new man.

"What's your name?"

"I don't know. The first name that comes to mind is Charlie, but it also makes me furious."

"How about we call you something completely different then?" questioned Robin as they looked over the man's neck and tattoo. "It kind of looks like vines. How about Forrest?"

"That seems fine." The man's response was unenthusiastic and apathetic.

"So, what do you remember so far?"

"Nothing."

"Boy, new people sure are interesting," Robin said while rolling their eyes.

"Before you fix up the house, we'll bring Mr. Shelley here to rest before the ceremony, then we'll bury him in the tower. Would Enu be able to help with the burial preparations and you with the last rites?" Lark nodded in agreement. "Perfect, thank you so much. I'll keep you updated but I expect no more than two nights."

As morbid as it was, two evenings later Robin excitedly awaited the ceremony to start. It was the only time that they had ever seen the doors to the tower open. If they were going to find out what was in the tower, they would have to do it tonight. Luckily, both Lark and Enu were away all day working to set up the ceremony and their outfits. It wouldn't begin until sundown. That left Robin the day to plan. To pass the time while they thought, they decided to spend it with their friend, Conway, a twelve-year-old and one of the only other children. Though he could not remember his past lives, he was an anxious and old soul. His clothing reflected that, sewn custom for him by the elder; they had come in a dream. He wore a patchwork cabbie hat and matching overalls; he was a makeshift newsie. His eyes were deep in his face, giving him an almost sad look, even when smiling. His tattoos were a blotch of black along his right hand and a set of stripes along his ribs.

"We should probably head over to the tower if we want to get good seats. The entire town is going to be there. You won't be able to see in the back," Conway said as he watched each step he took on the rocky path they played on.

"We'll go. We just need to wait a little bit. We can't be too early," Robin responded, balancing on one leg and leaning forward.

"Why not? I thought you wanted to see the doors open." Conway was getting worried; the sun was getting ready to set.

"I said that I wanted to see what's *inside* the doors. I've seen the doors open before. I gotta step up the investigation. If we get there too early, then my mother will see us and take us somewhere she can watch us the entire ceremony. If we are a little late, she'll be too busy."

"It's a graveyard, its only bodies. Why do you need to see it? Also, what about your dad?" Conway was always worried about what his parents thought, and really what all adults thought. There was an innate sense of respect in his soul.

"He's actually helping carry Mr. Shelley's body into the tower. We are going to follow them and sneak in. If the ceremony is like last time, Aria will be talking for a while. Are you really not curious?" Robin's soul was much more stubborn and needed confirmation.

"I don't need to know. I believe my parents are going to be very worried. You know they are anxious. Besides, we can't just walk in. Everyone is going to be watching the door. They'll see you." Conway was growing more anxious by the moment. By his account, the plan was not sound.

"That's why you're going to tell them that you'll be with me, and we're being taken care of."

"By whom?"

"The new guy, Forrest. We'll say we're performing a public service."

"Are we really? Also, how does that let us sneak in." Conway was fiddling with his overalls, adjusting and lifting them up.

"No, but it's a good excuse. We won't need to actually include him." Robin grabbed Conway by the hand. "Once inside, we'll explore." Robin pulled out two small hand-cranked flashlights; they had been in Artemis' shop and Robin had taken them without asking.

Conway looked to the ground and grabbed his elbow with the opposite arm—an awkward position he often formed when uncomfortable. "If we do this, can we then play another game? I'm tired of always talking about the tower. Mysteries make you reckless." Robin smiled.

As the sun began to truly set and the sky was filled with a faint orange, Robin grabbed Conway's hand again and began to run. The streetlights began to snap on overhead as they made their way through the center of town and down the hill toward the tower. The electric lights were controlled by solar sensors. Citizens with too much energy could use special workout equipment to provide energy to the community. For a large celebration such as this, someone was most likely biking all night.

The streets were bright but nearly empty. Only a handful of stragglers stood circled in the town center. Everyone else who could move was already down the hill and formed into a semicircle around the tower. They lined up around a series of tall torches staked into the ground. Robin and Conway arrived as the sky grew black and the ceremony was about to begin. The two children pushed their way through the crowd and into the front.

They saw that in the center of the circle lay Mr. Shelley's body, lying on a platform covered in a beautiful decorative sheet; it was a large, handwoven tapestry of gold, purple, and blue. Beyond the makeshift altar stood two groups of people, one with Lark and the other with Enu. To the right stood Enu, a man of average height with a large jaw and a flat head. With him stood three others, all wearing the same outfit. Each had a hood that was draped along their back and over a heavy cloak. Both pieces had a gold trim around the edges and while light, their clothes looked warm and inviting. Their texture was regal and of much higher quality than anything Robin had seen, except for Aria's clothes, of course. To the left stood Lark with four others all wearing the same outfit. Their group's design was more militaristic, though they also had hoods; each wore a set of silver armor over leather made of patches of various animal skins. Lizard scales, fish scales, bird feathers, and animal fur peeped out from under the metal. They were an embodiment of nature and the cycle they were all still a part of.

From the crowd, Robin caught their mother's eye and then waved to establish their presence. Conway waved as well, in a more guilty fashion, refusing to make eye contact. Robin pointed at Forrest, who was located further along the circle, then mouthed a lie. Robin then grabbed Conway's hand and the two disappeared into the crowd. They made their way over to Forrest and got Lark's attention one last time. Once Lark turned her back to continue prepping, the two children rushed back into the crowd. Forrest never even knew they were there. They made their way out of the crowd and into the darkness of the distance.

The ceremony began when Aria lifted her arm into the air. The signal silenced the crowd almost instantly, and they all watched as she slowly made her way to Mr. Shelley's body. Behind her followed Enu and his group, who lined up opposite one another, also around the body. Once they were all in position, Aria walked to meet the crowd and began her speech. "Thank you to everyone for attending. I know all of your presence would be a great joy to Mr. Shelley. While sad, it is beautiful to see everyone come together to honor one of our own. You're a beautiful community. May this not be a moment of sadness for you all but instead one of hope. This ceremony honors those who pass for their service. We hope to aid their transfer into whatever the afterlife may hold."

Aria then made her way over to the side of the body and began to lift up the tapestry. From under, a bright and nearly blinding light shone. The light filled the valley they stood in and illuminated everyone watching. "Though it is scary, as we all near our end we do so beautifully. The sunlight within each of us shines brightest. Each of us is a star."

As she spoke, the entire town was transfixed on her, except for Robin and Conway. From the darkness they sneaked along the mountainside and found their way behind the church and along the long side of the tower. Once there they made their way around the tower, between its stone and the mountain, toward the other side. From there they watched the crowd watch the ceremony.

Aria leaned down to the body and from under the tapestry she pulled out his hand. The light in the valley increased even further as the hand was presented to the crowd. She held it while she continued. "It is my honor to partake in this special ceremony, though we don't each know who we are. We know we are something, and that something is enough. It is my honor to hold onto Mr. Shelley's discoveries. The few memories he had made over his life. I honor him as a text of his progress." Aria then kissed his hand and whispered, "It is my honor to hold your memories." She then placed his hand on her forehead. From deep within her, a glow of light began. It shined through her skin like rays out of her tiny freckles, shining like a disco ball. As she did, her light glistened and danced over the faces and bodies of the crowd. Then a few of her lights went black. "I honor you, Mr. Shelley, and the progress you made—all you did for us, and all you've helped us discover about ourselves."

Aria walked from the body and toward the crowd as Enu and his group repositioned. They then each reached down, and each moved the tapestry to reveal small handles that they grabbed tight and lifted onto their shoulders. As the tapestry fell back over the body, Robin noticed it twitch in Mr. Shelley's hand. "His hand moved," Robin screamed in a whisper to Conway.

"How could you tell?" he questioned. He *knew* that Robin was being dramatic. Aria and the four pallbearers began a march toward the front of the tower, whose doors were still closed. Behind them Lark and her group began their part of the ceremony. They pulled out flutes from under their armor and began to play. The music was slow with a heavy rhythm; Lark played the deepest flute, which acted as both bass and drum, directing the rest. The crowd watched silently.

They all stood in front of the doors as the music reached a crescendo, and with their bellow the lights of the torches on the outside walls of the tower flickered. As the music died, the doors released a large scraping noise as they slowly dragged open. Then the music started again, and the scraping acted as part of the high melody. Somehow, the overall noise was a calming and respectful hymn. The doors opened to reveal nothing but darkness, but after a moment from it a man emerged. He was a mountain of a man, much larger than anyone else in the village, both in weight and in height. His armor was similar to Lark's but made of bright gold. While Lark's was makeshift, the man's was perfectly shiny, an antique well taken care of.

"Who's that guy? His armor is amazing," Conway questioned in wonder.

"What? Did you miss him at the last ceremony? That's Wilhelm, the guardian of the tower. He's the coolest person I've ever seen. I wish I could talk to him. Look at his tattoo—it's like a scar across his eye. I bet his story is so cool. Now they are all going to go inside together, then we'll wait and when he lets everyone out, we are going to sneak in."

"Follow him inside? But then we'll *be locked* inside! Are you crazy?" Conway was beginning to hyperventilate.

"Look how cool he is. If we get stuck inside, we'll just ask him for help. Also, if there were only dead people in there, why do we need a guardian? Especially such a badass one."

"We'll get in trouble! Also, it's out of respect?"

"Ask for forgiveness, not permission. Besides, what are they going to do? Kill us? I'm pretty sure that's impossible." Robin watched as the group entered the tower and the tower doors closed behind them. The music continued until the doors had fully shut and then there was a moment of silence. Lark then blew her instrument one last time and walked out into the middle of the crowd.

"Thank you for coming and helping as a community to honor Mr. Shelley. I know he was so happy to be able to be buried here with his family and others like himself. I hope you all have a great rest of your evening and are safe with your families." Lark scanned the crowd but failed to see her child. She then made eye contact with Forrest, who stood in the crowd talking to someone else. Lark waved with a questioning face. Forrest, confused, smiled back and gave her a thumbs-up before walking back toward town. Lark, now sure Robin was being accounted for, made her way back to her band and began the process of cleaning up and getting changed.

Robin and Conway watched as everyone disbanded, and the band made their way back to their homes. The children then sat patiently and waited for an hour before the doors of the tower opened again. The vibration of the door rumbled, and Robin grew excited, while Conway grew nervous. From the doors emerged Aria, Enu, and each of his members. Behind them followed Wilhelm. The group seemed to exchange pleasantries as they disbanded; Robin could not make out their words. As they left, Wilhelm took a moment to stand outside and breathe in the fresh air. It was a cleansing smell, washing out all the stagnant air of the tower. He spent most of this existence within the tower, rarely ever leaving his post. These ceremonies were nice breaks.

It wasn't long before he turned and walked back into the building—that was their chance. The children pressed their small frames against the wall and hid from the few bright spots created by the torches. Together they snuck into the darkness behind Wilhelm. Immediately after they entered, the large doors quickly slammed shut behind them. Much faster than they had opened or closed for the ceremony. The inside of the building was extremely dark; only a few torches lit the hallway they stood in. Robin pulled out the two flashlights and passed one to Conway. Inside, the tower was freezing. Robin and Conway could feel it as tightness in their muscles.

Without saying a word, Robin signified to Conway to continue forward and to turn on his flashlight. They walked through the dark hallway cranking their flashlights for a few steps, then turned them on. The old things flickered on and off as the kids banged them with their hands to knock the machine into a steady motion. Conway continued to crank his as he walked, and the two shined their lights onto the walls. The inside of the tower was not built of the same beautiful stone as the outside. Instead, it was darker and less shimmery. The walls carried a buzz with them that seemed to echo throughout the tower.

The hallway was decorated with many different tapestries, similar to the one that had covered Mr. Shelley. They were less colorful, instead all monochromatic, but longer, nearly twenty-five feet in length. One hung between each of the large columns along the hallway. At the end, they came into the center of the tower, a large room branched into several smaller hallways. Conway stopped at the junction, afraid to enter the room, but like always Robin grabbed his hand and dragged him in. In the center, there was a large spiral staircase that rose fifty feet in the air before disappearing into the next floor. From a distance, Robin shined their light at the top of the staircase, but the light illuminated nothing, like a black hole. The mysterious darkness sent a shiver down even Robin's spine.

That is when Robin spoke for the first time since they had entered the tower. "Maybe, before we explore…you know…" They swallowed heavily. "The top floor. We should check this floor… I am sure there are plenty of things to see." Their voice was drier than expected and clearly nervous. Conway agreed; he was clearly already in over his head. The two played rock, paper, scissors to decide who *got* to choose the first hallway they explored. After three intense games the results were Robin, Conway, and Conway—much to Conway's dismay. With a large gulp Conway pointed into the distance, at the hallway furthest away. Robin turned around and noticed what Conway had already seen. A bright white light shone down the hallway. "He's probably there, and I figured I could try to ignore it and choose somewhere else…but you're going to make me go down it anyway. So, let's get it over with."

"Great planning, Conway. Way to think ahead." Robin also gulped, just as nervous as their friend. They made their way past the staircase and toward the light in the distance. Something in the air was thick and they could smell it among the dry stone and mold. As they approached the light, something strange began to occur. As they got closer, they grew more and more tired. Even so, they pressed on and made their way into the new hallway.

The hallway was the same as the one they had taken into the center area with one exception. On each side they could see arches and doorways that used to be rooms. Each one of them had a nameplate above them, written in gold lettering, and the children could see they were tombs. Each room was boarded up with cement bricks and sealed tight. "See all the names,

Robin? I told you. Nothing but graves. Thank the gods." Conway tugged on Robin's sleeve. "So, we can go now? Right?"

Robin turned back to him and gave him a big *no* with their eyes. "Look, we haven't even gotten to the light. How could you possibly want to turn around?" Though they had not walked far, the two were now out of breath. As if they had been running, they both breathed deeply.

"Self-preservation. Fear of the unknown. Many things." Conway once again pulled on Robin's sleeve, but they ignored him and pushed forward. Left alone in the dark, Conway ran forward to catch up. The pair made their way to the end of the hall, where out of one of the rooms the bright light was shining. Sneakily, they peered around the corner and saw Mr. Shelley lying on a table, still partially covered in the tapestry. His arm dangled down and out, and his light filled the room. In a chair beside his bedside, Wilhelm sat reading a book. The children waited and watched.

It was only a few moments before the light of the room began to shift as Mr. Shelley moved. He rolled and turned, like someone trying to find a comfortable spot in bed. It was clear that he was not dead yet, merely weak. Robin made a noise of shock and pulled at Conway. "What now?" Conway asked, hoping to hear that they were going home.

"I told you he wasn't dead. Why would they put him in here when he's not dead? That doesn't seem fair. Just because they needed his house?" Robin continued to theory craft. They watched for a few more minutes before Wilhelm got up. After placing his book down, he checked on Mr. Shelley, and then began to walk out. As he approached them, Robin noticed behind them another grave was not yet sealed. The two children ran into it and hid behind the corner of the door, where they continued to watch. Wilhelm walked past them, and as he walked down the hall he surveyed it. When he disappeared into the large center room, Robin and Conway ran into Mr. Shelley's room.

"Mr. Shelley, are you okay? They must have made a mistake. I'll let my mother know you're still alive. We'll get you out of here," Robin said as they ran to his side. His skin was shining brighter than any one of them had ever seen. It was painful to look directly at. Robin stared at the wall behind his head as they tried to get him to respond.

Mr. Shelley merely tried to raise his hand, but it barely lifted off the table before being dropped. He attempted to talk but what came out was only a cough. The children continued to feel even weaker. Not only was the light blinding but it was also draining. "How are we going to move him? What could we do? He's too large," Conway complained. He didn't know how to be helpful, except figuring out what might go wrong. Robin did not respond as the two heard the steps of Wilhelm coming back down the hallway. As they looked over the bed, Robin noticed the table Mr. Shelley was on was actually on wheels. Robin lifted up the tapestry that draped over the table and jumped under it, hiding on the small bottom table. Conway stood stuck in his head until Robin pulled on his arms again and he joined them.

Under the table, the two listened for Wilhelm's movements. They heard him approach; his footsteps were heavy but calm. "Okay, Mr. Shelley, I've cleared the way forward to your permanent room. You are getting very bright, very fast. I don't think we have as much time as we thought. If it's okay with you, I'd like to move you upstairs." Wilhelm didn't wait for a response and walked around to the head of the bed. He adjusted it and began rolling it out of the room and down the hallway. The bed rattled back and forth as it bounced on the uneven floor. The children fought to stay inside, and not to make noise. At the same time, as they sat below Mr. Shelley's body, they grew sicker. Their heads were hurting, and though they could not see the light anymore, it was still burned into the back of their eyelids. They sat holding hands and waited.

Wilhelm brought the cart to the main room and parked it near the staircase. From the back of his armor, he pulled a long thin sword. He walked a few paces and faced the stairs. He raised the sword above his head with one arm before stabbing it into the ground. It clanged and echoed as it wedged in between the rock. He then twisted it, and the sword began to glow, filling it with light like a battery. The ground shook and from the ceiling the floor shifted, and a few bricks drifted down together as a simple elevator. When it had reached the ground, Wilhelm rolled Mr. Shelley onto it, and the four of them rode it up.

The kids could not tell how many, but they rode the elevator up three floors. Then Wilhelm pulled the bed behind him, as he made his way down a long series of hallways. The ground was as uneven as the floor below. There in one of the rooms, he placed the body of Mr. Shelley. It was an empty room covered on one side in jail bars. On his way out, he locked it. "I'll be back to check on you in a while, Mr. Shelley. I need to make my rounds. I'll see you soon," he said in his gruff but gentle voice.

Even after they could no longer hear his footsteps they waited for reassurance. Then finally, the children peered out from behind the tapestry to find they were alone and crawled out. Robin turned to look at Mr. Shelley while Conway ran to the door to see it was locked. Conway surveyed the bars and noticed the lack of a window. He couldn't decide if it was more of a cell or a tomb. Robin surveyed Mr. Shelley, who was no longer moving. "Conway, come here. We need to free him!" Robin yelled as they noticed his arms and legs were now both shackled. "He's tied to the bed."

"How are we supposed to get him off the table now?" Conway asked Robin. His body was burning brighter than ever before, and as they looked at him their heads started to hurt more.

"I don't want to leave him alone," Robin pleaded to Conway. The two then looked again at Mr. Shelley. His head shifted toward them, and they could see he now had pain behind his eyes. His face was expressionless, and his body was still. As they looked at him and contemplated what to do, they ran out of time. He grew brighter and brighter, forcing the children to cover their faces and back away from him. The light could be seen through their eyelids as clear as day and they covered their faces with their elbows but it didn't help. They stumbled backward on groggy legs. They turned their heads away and fell to the ground. Then in an instant, they heard Mr. Shelley screech, like the sound of a dying star, then the light grew brighter one last time. The children saw it through their eyelids, and through their arms, without which they might have gone blind. The sound of the yell echoed through the walls and reverberated through the room they were in.

Then all of a sudden, the light was gone. They opened their eyes to see nothing but black and the small shreds of torchlight that bounced around the room. The light from Mr. Shelley was gone. Robin stood up and offered a hand to Conway, then the pair slowly walked back toward the man. His once bright skin was now black and ashy like coal. The iridescence and white that marked his life were gone. As they looked over him, they noticed his body start to change. His eyes, which were brown, bulged and grew in size. They jumped from his skull and devoured part of his face; then they filled with bright yellow fluid. His face too began to change, his jaw widened, and all the corners of his face softened. His complexion became soft and malleable, like molten rock. His ears then stretched along the sides of his face, forming zigzagging antennae. His body contorted and stretched, his fingers and limbs grew longer and thinner.

Then the body began to rise.

"Mr. Shelley? Are you okay?" Conway asked, as he and Robin held onto each other and started to walk away. The black mass began to slowly roll itself from the bed. Its two legs and one arm easily slipped through the chains, but luckily its other arm remained clamped. As it flowed onto the ground, it got stuck, but that failed to stop it. It tried to pull on its arm, tried to free itself. Instead, it crawled forward, pulling on the chain. Its body wiggled and wobbled, flowing like waves, as it quickly learned to stand up and to walk. Behind it, it dragged the bed, which flipped over and began to scrap against the ground. The barely human shape grew bigger, even thinner, taller, and lankier. Its body and shadow loomed over the children. The fingers of its trapped wrist dragged across the ground.

The children backed their way toward the door. With his off hand, Conway fussed with the cell handle; he tried to jiggle and pull it in every direction, but nothing made it move. The creature continued to come toward them, now on all fours; its one arm dragged the cart, and it used its free hand to help drag its body forward like it was climbing a mountain. The two children pushed themselves to the farthest corner of the room and pressed their backs against the bars with so much force they hoped they would phase through it.

The creature crawled closer and closer, and with every passing moment Robin's head grew dizzier and Conway's heart pounded out of his chest. It wasn't just the bright light. The abyss created by the monster's skin was draining, affecting them each differently. It screeched as it was finally within arm's reach and grasped for Robin. Its noodle-like fingers laced their way up Robin's arm. Robin screamed, their skin sizzled, and the white turned black, like the creature itself. Never before had Robin felt pain like this; it was excruciating. Through Robin's screams, Conway heard the squeak of the cell door open.

The large, gauntleted hand of Wilhelm appeared out of the darkness and grabbed Conway by the chest, pulling him by his overalls. Before he knew it, Conway was thrown across the hall. He slid across the floor; his momentum was only stopped by a wall. Wilhelm reached into the back of his armor and removed another sword. He swung the blade down onto the free hand of the monster. The sound of the sword against its skin clanged like steel against rock. It let go of Robin and swiped at the blade. Robin attempted to scream but they had lost their voice. Their screams were silent, and their arm was still throbbing. Wilhelm continued to swipe at the beast, batting its flailing arm away from Robin. Wilhelm made his way into the room and inched closer and closer, eventually grabbing Robin and sprinting out from the cell.

Once he had cleared the doorway, he dropped Robin to the ground and used his foot to push them across the floor. Robin slid into Conway, and the two grabbed hold of one another again. "Make your way downstairs. Search for the staircase—the elevator is too slow to risk," Wilhelm shouted as he lunged for the still-open cell door. On the other side, the monster finally freed its other arm and lunged at the door as well. Wilhelm used one hand to swing his sword against the prying hands. It failed to sway the monster, who started to peel the door open against Wilhelm's strength. The children sprinted down the hallway and aimed for the center of the room. The hallways were hard to see in; the faint torchlight barely illuminated the floor in front of them. The noise had awoken the other inhabitants, and behind the walls the children could hear more of the monsters scratching at the cement. They knew now that each grave was filled with one.

As they made their way into the larger room, it darkened even further. They slowed their run as they broke out their flashlights and illuminated the floor. In the distance they saw a large stone column, broken by a single doorway and a shining golden banister. The two sprinted forward, and in their haste, they nearly ran into a large hole in the floor. The elevator was still below; they could see it in the light of the sword. They snuck around the hole and made their way into the stairwell.

Robin's arm continued to burn, but the deep black of the scar was now changed. The skin had become course, ridged, and stonelike. In the distance they could hear the clash of Wilhelm's sword and his yells, like that of a tennis player. Each scream was followed by an equally loud clang. The pair began to run down. Each step was long and curved, and though they tried to stay next to the wall they found they always drifted toward the edge. They sprinted down the two flights, getting dizzy in the process. As they came through the doorway and onto the first floor, they saw the hallway that led to their salvation.

This time Conway was the first to lead as he grabbed Robin's hand and pulled them. They sprinted toward the main hallway but were stopped short as they approached the elevator. The monster climbed through the open shaft above and dropped from the sky. Only a short distance in front of them, its body crashed into the ground with a noise like the demolition of a skyscraper. Its body crumbled into a dark mass, once again flowing like water. From the amorphous shape, a long, pink tongue stretched out and toward the children. Like it had eyes of its own, it searched the darkness.

The children inched forward but it began to stand up; a bubble rose from the ground and from it the same humanoid form returned. Its bright yellow eyes stared and its tongues still searched in the darkness. Robin held their breath; it was the only thing they could think of doing to try and hide more. But even still, its yellow eyes quickly fixated on them, and it began to approach. As it walked, all of its knuckles dragged on the floor behind. It made a sharp sound of stone against stone that echoed in the hall and pierced the ears. Robin and Conway each grabbed their ears and stepped back, their bodies shivering against their wills.

Then from above came a yell. Like the monster, Wilhelm leapt down the elevator and landed in front of the children. As he landed, he hit the ground heavily; his shins shot through his knees and out through his armor. White smoke billowed from his legs and filled the floor surrounding him, like a mist. Then as gracefully as he had jumped, Wilhelm stood up and his legs joined back together. His sword was gone but he shouted at the monster anyway. "I'm sorry, Mr. Shelley," he groaned.

The monster turned his attention back toward the children and ignored Wilhelm's grand entrance. Behind it, Wilhelm readied his next weapon. He made his way off the platform and to the sword that powered the elevator. On the ground surrounding it was a large circular sigil, a large fountain with wings, of which he stepped into. Wilhelm dropped to one knee and placed his hand onto the floor. The light from the sword began to spread along the ground and enlightened the sigil. From the shape Wilhelm pulled a single thick bar, nearly four inches in diameter, much too large for the average person to hold. "I said," Wilhelm yelled at the monster, "I am sorry, Mr. Shelley. I mean no disrespect."

As he squeezed the bar with both hands as if it were a baseball bat, the top began to glow and from it sprouted two bright, blue, ethereal axe blades. The monster finally turned toward Wilhelm and let out another ear-piercing scream. Wilhelm charged toward them through the fog of his wounds. As they clashed, the children ran past. Before they entered the hallway, Robin stopped to watch the fight, but Conway pulled them away. Like before, the monster attempted to blindly swing at Wilhelm, throwing its claw into contact with the blade of the axe. When they collided, it let out a new type of cry, a screaming pain, the axe slicing through it. Nothing like blood flowed from its wound, a clean cut.

The fight then became a dance, one where Wilhelm was leading. As he swung his axe with extreme speed, the monster darted back, dodging. The creature bounded back across the floor and made its way to the wall. Its body scraped against the ground with each jump. When its back was to the wall, it instead ran up, using its claw as an anchor. It crawled up and away on three legs. Wilhelm then took aim and closed one eye. With the axe over his head, he chucked it into the air. The monster attempted to leap from the wall down onto him, but its leg was sliced off in the process. Its momentum was lost, and it went toppling to the ground. The axe bounced off the wall and dropped to the ground. The monster attempted to jump, using its remaining two limbs, but it was too slow. Wilhelm ran toward his axe and picked it up, then he rushed the beast. "I truly am sorry," he said as he swung one last time and cut him in half. The shards of the monster dropped to the ground and like an eggshell shattered. Without hesitation, Wilhelm ran toward the children.

Down the hallway, the children stood by the front door, and they watched Wilhelm run toward them. At first the sound of footsteps was terrifying, but then as they realized it was him, they were relieved. When the mountain of a man stood before them, he said, "Are you both okay? Did he touch you?" Robin presented their arm to him. "Oh, you've taken a scar. That will never be the same. It should have been worse. What are you two doing here?"

Robin raised their eyeline to meet him. "I can't believe you killed it! You're so cool! That was amazing! How did you do that? What was that weapon? How are you so strong?"

"I see *you* don't seem to be fazed." Wilhelm then turned toward Conway. "Are you always so quiet? I'm not going to get in trouble, am I?" Conway shook his head no but refused to look up. "How about I do not answer any of your many questions, and I will also not discuss the mess you made me make." With a smile, Wilhelm raised his axe handle to the door. With a few small taps on it, the door began to open. The loud squeal of the door was far louder inside the silence of the tower. The moonlight shined through the trees in the distance.

The two children sprinted ahead, and Wilhelm trudged behind them. Already standing outside of the tower were both the children's parents and Aria. Conway silently ran behind his parents and hid his face against them in shame. They patted his head and back as they waited for an explanation. Enu was the first to speak. "I assume this was you're doing?" he questioned Robin as he picked them up. "We were not able to follow you because for our safety, the tower only opens from the inside. You're lucky Wilhelm is a great guard."

"What happened in there?" Aria directed to Wilhelm in a concerned tone.

"Mr. Shelley turned, and they were caught in the middle. I had to put him down and one of them…" Wilhelm then pointed at Robin.

"Robin, your arm, what on earth has happened to you? Your skin, it's damaged forever. It's stone?" Lark asked, concerned.

"It's okay! It doesn't hurt anymore. You should have seen Wilhelm!" Robin began to bounce in their father's arms. "He was so cool. Mr. Shelley turned into this giant monster, and he fought him." Robin began to pantomime swinging a sword. "He cut him like *pew pew pew.*"

"Mr. Shelley was not a monster," Wilhelm said in his first stern tone. "He deserves a proper burial, like we all do. It was not his fault that this happened. It was very inappropriate for you to disturb his grave." He then turned away and started to walk back into the tower. "Luckily, he's not dead—there doesn't seem to be any way to kill them. That we know of. That's why we had to build this tower, to hide our monsters from the rest of the world. Even the kindest soul becomes one of them in the end. Its pieces will sit there for a while but slowly they will seek each other out. Even if we separate them, they will find each other and merge, then he will come back. I need to go back and clean up. Please keep all unauthorized people and children out next time." Wilhelm disappeared back into the tower and behind him the door shut.

Aria took the chance to address the children directly. "We try to phrase our death as something beautiful, but now you know, children, our deaths are anything but. Death can be painful, scary, and horrible for everyone. We don't want the monsters out and they don't want to hurt people…to have people think negatively of them. So, we help so that it's a less tragic end."

Aria made strong eye contact with Robin and Conway as she continued. "We do not want to worry others. We fear they would be afraid if they knew. Mortality can be such a deterrent to self-discovery. So, we fight to keep the peace. I would appreciate your sensitivity on this. This is a secret you now know. You are both part of a special group. So, you must be adults about this, keep it to yourselves. I am sorry you had to learn this way and I am happy you are okay, but now you are honor-bound to keep this secret for us."

Conway nodded in agreement, still hiding behind his parents. "I'm happy to never talk about it ever again. I hope in my next body I don't remember this at all."

"Robin?" Lark and Enu stared down at their child.

"Of course! I can totally keep a secret," Robin said while running their finger over their new stone scar. "Besides, I *knew* there weren't dead people in there," they boasted.

The Book of Yori

Yori sauntered aimlessly down the street with her hands in her jacket pockets. The long green bridge coat had a small hood and extended to her tights. Beneath it, she wore a simple gray T-shirt and black pants. She was an Asian woman with a captivating gaze and expressive eyes. She wore red over-ear headphones, and her long black hair was up in a ponytail that ran to the small of her back. Her hair had highlights of white and dark purple randomly distributed throughout it—it shimmered under the streetlights. As she stomped down the street in her green military boots, she weaved slowly from side to side, making sure to trudge through each stagnant puddle of water that sat from the earlier shower.

Yori, as always, was blaring music, and through her headphones anyone within twenty feet could hear it—it was a constant and intense barrage of either metal, rock, or reggae. Somehow, she never had to choose, and it played endlessly and, to her, wonderfully. One consistent thing was that it was always a male singer; it was something she found calming. Even the most pleasant female voice awakened a sickness and dread in her; somehow it was reminiscent of her mother, whom she couldn't remember, but that was a different problem that brought its own unique frustration to Yori.

Her wandering brought her out of a side alley and onto the main strip of Dotonbori. As she passed over a small wooden bridge over the tiny canal, the lights of the billboards illuminated the crowds of partygoers she merged with. On the northern side, five spider-men costumed performers stood on the rungs of the bridge posing for pictures. Yori moved through the crowd without stopping and made her way to another cross street. She checked her pocket and felt she still had a few yen left.

In the distance she saw several bars, and she realized she could use a drink. Every shop in immediate view were all crowded with enough patrons to spill outside; each had its own unique loud music booming out and they mixed with the voices of drunkards to create a wall of life that shot down the corridor. Yori walked toward them but had no intention of stopping. That many people were not her vibe. She passed them but scanned; she appeared checked out but was actually hyperaware of everything happening around her. She continued to walk until she found one that was nearly empty, an American-themed bar built into an old home. Yori had walked far enough that all the other buildings were residential, meaning this was a dive bar, a community treasure. Two American flags hung outside on banisters, each with forty-eight stars. Inside, the bartender stood cleaning glasses and watching one of the many TVs on the wall displaying the same concert. He had his hair high and greased and wore a shiny, bright red vest over a white button-down shirt.

Yori entered and could hear the concert playing within the bar. She didn't know who they were, just that it was an American band screaming in English. It was more her style than the other bars, but still she decided to keep her headphones on. She scanned the room and luckily, unlike the other places she passed, this bar was surprisingly empty. At the counter sat a couple on a date. Yori knew because they were wearing matching cowboy hats and had both ordered the same signature, red Solo cup cocktail—they were also laughing more than seemed necessary given the energy of the room. The only other person was a nondescript gentleman at a table. She joined the couple at the bar but sat as far away as possible. Yori began to remove her headphones but the sharp voice of the woman at the bar sent a shock through her body.

Too much.

She quickly snapped the headphones back on and held up two fingers while looking down. The bartender made his way over and tried to ask her what she needed, but she was overstimulated. In her peripherals she could see his mouth moving but she refused to respond. After a moment, the bartender gave up and walked away to get the two cheapest beers he could. She felt the slam of the beer steins on the table and threw her change down. The bartender stared in amazement as Yori chugged the first glass and slammed it down without saying a word. She picked up her remaining beer and made her way to a table in the corner to finish drinking alone. She leaned back against the wall and watched the atmosphere of the bar unfold. As the moon rose higher, the small bar filled up.

Though she remained silent, Yori always had the misfortune of people coming to bother her—it must have been something about her angry face, loud headphones, and distant look that drew people to come talk to her. The one good thing was people would always bring her drinks; each suitor, whether male or female, would come up to her, tribute in hand. She would smile, take the drink, and let them ramble. Yori's music still blared, and she ignored their every word. It impressed her how little attention someone needed to keep talking.

It was only when she had finished her drink, and they asked if she wanted another, did they notice she wasn't paying attention—it's a unique and strange feeling when you realize you don't know the sound of someone's voice. Pleasantly, they would leave out of annoyance to get another drink, and *almost* always they would fail to come back. Most were too drunk to remember and too easily distracted by something shinier near the bar. This meant that even without any more money, Yori was drunk and content.

It wasn't until the end of the evening, when her buzz was really going, that a single man caught her eye; an Asian gentleman in his mid-twenties, like everyone else, sitting at the bar with a half-empty bottle of sake. His right eye was slightly lower than his left. His hair was short and spiky, and he had a perfectly shaped goatee. There was something about the smile lines under his cheeks and the slight thinning of his brow; she found the entire package charming. Yori also enjoyed how he spilled a bit of his drink on himself as he approached her. When he leaned down to talk, she could tell his voice was stammering to find the right words. He was either a little nervous or a little drunk; either way *she* knew, *he* knew, she was out of his league. She liked that. *He'll do*, she thought. Yori lowered her headphones and left them dangling around her neck.

She faked a smile as the complex noise of the bar started to echo in her head. The collective sound of *all* the voices, *all* the noise, was so much more overwhelming than her music. Yori took the stick of pineapple pieces and cherries out of one of the many drinks that were brought to her, tilted her head back, and quickly chugged it. He took a seat and the two flirted in Japanese. After only a few polite exchanges, Yori grew serious. "You're cute. Do you wanna go somewhere quieter?" she offered with a smile. The sounds of the bar continued to pound in her mind; she showed none of it.

The man did a double take and returned back with a large grin and a confidence he lacked before—he was really proud with himself that he had been so charming. "Uh, sure, I'd love to. There's a back porch to the bar. We could talk out there," he suggested.

"Take me," Yori said as she stood and offered her hand to the man. He took her hand in his and the two made their way out. She put her arm on the man's back and ran her nails along his spine. She was playing with him, but also pushing him past the crowd of drunk talkers at the bar. Yori was pleased at the silence outside as they exited, they found the porch empty. Its black banisters framed a poorly lit back alley that was littered with partially filled trash cans. *How romantic*, Yori thought sarcastically. "Phew, it's a little bit colder than I anticipated" is what she *actually* said.

"Well, we could warm you up," said the man as he turned back around and pushed her against the wall. Yori pushed her body back into him and began to kiss him intensely. He excitedly wrapped his arms around her and ran his hands up the back of her shirt. Yori started to push back hard against him and switched from long, hard kisses to many small, fast ones across his face. The two started to stumble away from the wall and against the railing of the porch— they crashed and nearly toppled over the edge. The man let out a snide smile. *She must be so drunk*, he thought. "Why don't we go around the side of the building? This way I won't fall to my death. And that way we can also be a little more private." He chuckled with heavy breath.

The man took Yori by the hand and led her down the stairs to a darker part of the alley, an even more secluded area. He pushed Yori against the wall again, and as he ran his arms up and down her body he tried to kiss Yori's neck, but it was impossible with her headphones still on. "Can we remove these?" he whispered.

"Yeah sure," Yori whispered back. She slid them off with one hand and held them across his back. She used her other hand to reach under his shirt and scratch his back again. He let out an excited groan and started to suck on her neck. He ran his arm along her belt line and dragged his nails across her skin, slowly making his way to her zipper.

He whispered in her ear, "You're *soooo* beautiful." In response, something took over Yori's entire body and she began to tremble. She let go of him and her body stiffened. Her eyes grew wide, and she stared into the distance. "I'm what?" she said loudly but nearly catatonic.

"You're so beautiful," he whispered again. Yori dropped her headphones, and she shook even more violently. "You're so cold, baby, you're shaking so hard." He grappled onto her tighter and kissed her neck; she shook *even* more violently. Her arms snapped back around him and gripped his spine—her eyes were still transfixed in the distance. Her nails began to break flesh and he tried to pull away, but he was pulling against barbs. "You okay, babe? You're starting to hurt me. Maybe calm down a bit?" He attempted to keep his cool as he continued to try and to pull away. Behind him her arms began to break; her forearm bones shattered and pulled from her body. As they each ripped open, her bones bent out and formed the shapes of two blades, scissors, like the arms of a praying mantis. Her blood dripped down his back and soaked his shirt.

"You-you-you-you think I'm beautiful?" Yori's tone shook, not with emotion but like the scream of static as you search blank radio stations. Her face deformed and froze into an inhumanly gigantic smile. He continued to struggle, and luckily, lubricated by the blood, he was able to pull away from her. He ran his arms along his back and stared at his blood-stained palms. He now began to shake as well, and he tried to speak but nothing came out. "You-you-you think I'm beautiful?" Yori repeated. Blood continued to flow down her weapons and onto the floor. Her eyes were wide and absent of any feeling or true thought.

"Uhh, noo noo," the man finally mustered out in fear. He turned and tried to run back toward the bar, but one of Yori's arms extended out and pulled him back. She effortlessly lifted him off the ground and pulled his head close to hers. Her idle eyes scanned him one more time and she squeezed. Her arms slid straight through him, cutting him in half. His lower half dropped to the ground, then she let her arms lower to her sides. His top half slid off and joined the earth.

Yori hovered over the body and studied the man's horrified but motionless face. Absent-minded tears streamed down her cheeks, beyond her control. "I'm sorry I wasn't beautiful enough for you," she whispered vitriolically into his now useless ear as she picked up her headphones and placed them back on. Yori's body wobbled down the alley on unsteady legs; her arms swayed to music in her head. Over the course of two blocks her arms began to reform and the blades disappeared into her flesh. Her jacket stitched itself shut and, except for the pools of blood, it looked perfect. When she finally made her way onto a lit street, she was unaware of what had just happened. She only made it a few more blocks before she wandered into another alleyway and collapsed into the trash.

Yori awoke the next evening, just before dusk, to the screams of her music. Her head throbbed with the well-known pain of a hangover. She had no memory of what had happened after her fourth drink—she assumed it included more drinking. Her coat was caked in a thick and smelly liquid that caused her to wretch; something had seeped out of the trash bags she had slept on and soaked in. Its offense to all her senses distracted her from the blood stains below. She used the trash cans to help herself up and looked toward the direction of the setting sun.

She walked toward it, toward the main strip; the smell of her coat forced her to walk with her shoulders tight and high, as if she was freezing. It was the only response her body could take to the discomfort. The water of the central canal caught her eye as the sunset shined off the slight chop. From the edge of the dock, she hung and dipped her coat in the water. She debated drinking it, unsure if it was fresh or sea or contaminated. Yori rubbed her coat against the rock to wash out the chunks of ooze.

From her position she could see a bus stop in the distance; its bright sign traveled down the alleyway and shined onto her face. Yori wrung out her jacket and threw it over her shoulder.

It was going to be another humid night, and she knew her jacket wouldn't dry. So, she made her way toward the sign. *It might be warmer there—maybe I can wait it out*, she thought. Only a moment after she stepped under the sign did another bus appear. With no one else on the street, Yori stepped onto it.

The bus was warm and comfortable, but a little too bright—Yori let out a small sigh of relief. The warmth helped to ease her headache. She made her way toward the back and noticed it was almost completely empty—only a few scattered souls sat alone, looking down at their phones. Yori sat in the back corner and sank in her seat. She placed her wet coat in a small puddle in the seat next to her. She ignored that and caught her breath. Then she attempted to remember what had happened the night before. She placed her head into her hands and leaned forward onto her legs. She stretched a little and let her arms fall to the ground—then she felt a tapping on her shoulder.

"Arr—re you okaaaaay?" asked Autumn, in stuttering but otherwise perfect Japanese. "Do yyyyyou want a coo—okie? You're looking a little pale. You seem like per—er—erhaps a little hypoglycemic as well. Have you had dinner yet?" Her voice cut through the music still blaring in Yori's ear. It was somehow a woman's voice that didn't hurt, that caught Yori off guard more than the tap. She raised her eyes to see a warm hand extending a Tupperware of cookies toward her. Above them, Yori saw Autumn's smiling face. She was wearing a beautiful purple yukata, and on the seat next to her were her purple scrubs; Autumn had changed after her double shift. Her pleasant and comforting face prompted Yori to grab a cookie. "They are oatmeal raisin, chocolate, and chocolate oatmeal raisin. Take whatever you want—they are all my favorite."

Autumn's candor threw off Yori's defensive instincts and she removed her headphones. She bit into the cookie she had taken randomly, chocolate oatmeal raisin, and studied Autumn as she continued to talk. Her voice was surprisingly calming and sweet. "Thanks for coming and sitting next to me. I'm friendly but a few of the people here are a little mu-uu-uch. I can't believe how busy it is on the bus tonight. I didn't expect everyone-n-ne would be going to the festival but then I look at all the elaborate costumes. It's all kind of beau-u—uuu-tiful but really, it's a madhouse in here, right?"

It was then that Yori looked up from Autumn's smile and an ache shot through her body. Her headache disappeared and was replaced by a searing pain. Yori scanned the once-empty bus to find every seat filled. The few people she had seen before were still there but among them were now dozens of other *people*. At the quick glance that Yori was taking everything seemed normal. The new patrons were all in festive clothing, yakatas, and kimonos. What was strangest was that some of them were elderly; silver hair and wrinkles graced their faces. Every face on the bus was happy and they all glowed with a faint aura.

"Oh, are you okay? I'm sorry, are you allergic to glu-u-ten?" asked Autumn, concerned at Yori's expression. "You don't look pale anymore at least. Maybe you should put that coat on."

"How long have I been asleep?" asked Yori, confused. There was a sudden increase in the noise, and it was starting to drown out Autumn. It was oppressive like the bar, but this time Yori felt like she was swimming through the sound instead of being basing against it.

"I'm not sure what you mean. Perhaps, not enough last night. You only just got on the bus. You haven't even finished your first cookie. I'm sorry if they're not very go-oo-od. I'm still having a hard time finding the ri-i-ggght ingredients at the market. I don't know too much kanji."

"I, uhh, I don't know. I must have been a little drunker than I thought. Hell, maybe…I'm still drunk from last night. Thank you for the snack." Yori sat silently eating her cookie and surveying the bus. Now that she searched more diligently she noticed more about them, more that was inhuman. The first time, the patrons' disproportioned body parts and transparent appearance didn't register with Yori. Most of them were gaseous in nature, and as they chanted with one another, their limbs floated away from them and down the aisle. Some noticed and pulled their heads back to them, but for others, their bodies floated like mist toward the front of the bus and were mixed by the wind. Though they seemed joyful, they did so in an uncomfortably different way. Tapestries of cloth swirled around their bodies and into the air. It was clear where the sounds were coming from; toward the front a group of spirits sang with one another in an unknown tongue.

Her trance was broken as Autumn got up and left the bus; she waved at a few of the *people* as she made her way to the front. Then she patiently waited in line as the spirits in front of her exited the bus. Though no other humans got onto the bus, a few new spirits joined. These ones were substantially less human; the first was a school of koi fish swimming through the air. They joked with the second one that came on—it was a large, elderly tortoise using a cane to navigate.

Yori grew uncomfortable again and pulled her headphones back over her head to drown out the sounds of the creatures. Her skin began to itch, and as she scratched her forearm, she pulled the stop cord. She stood up immediately and dashed her way to the front. She pushed her way through the spirits that were leaning into the aisle. As the bus pulled over to the side, Yori was first in line. She felt that something in her was wrong—there was a bubbling in her body.

She exited onto a mostly abandoned road. Though there were some streets of small houses along the road, the rest of the area was remote farmlands. She could see a few spirits in the distance, distinct from the background by their misty glow. They were animalistic and ghastly. Their large heads buzzed like wraiths in the distance. The most intense were ominous figures floating in the middle of some of the rice patties. The largest spirits floated in the air like clouds.

Yori followed the lights in search of someone, anyone human. She made her way toward the small town's only tavern and looked through its windows. Nowhere inside did she see any spirits, only two men drinking in quiet comfort as a female barkeep in a light blue shirt cleaned glasses. Yori placed her arm on the front door, and as she pushed it open her legs crumbled beneath her and she fell into the room—a gasp came from the bartender and silence came from the men at the bar. The bartender rushed over to check on her, and though she was fine, Yori was too embarrassed to roll over on her own.

The bartender flipped her and Yori shook and held her face with her palms over her eyes. She braced herself to get up, but before she could words came from one of the men at the bar. "What are you doing on the floor there, *beautiful*?" This time, though, Yori did not go catatonic. No, this time was different from the hundreds of other times it had happened in her lifetime. Instead, as her forearms began to bend again, as her bones ripped from her body, she felt everything.

She saw her transformation for the first time and screamed in terror—a form that had mutilated and killed so many others. The bartender leaped back as Yori thrashed on the floor. Her bones creaked and shattered into blades once again. Blood flowed onto the floor and pooled around her. As her body morphed, the music in her head grew louder and the screams overcame her own. The only good thing about the pain was that Yori was stunned and unable to attack those at the bar; each of them raced from the room and left her in the puddle she was creating.

Eventually, Yori was able to stand and made for the front door. The blood seemed to be endlessly flowing from her, and she accidentally threw splatters of blood against the walls as she shifted. With beastlike rage, she swung at the door with her scythe-like arms. Yori failed and failed to open the handle. Instead, in her panic she put her thick boots through the glass and then used her claws to cover her face as she jumped through the ruins. Yori darted into the street and hid in the darkness of an alley, but her path was clear from the stream of blood she was still leaving behind her—as if they were her tears, they flowed unnaturally and constantly.

As she sat in an ever-building pool catching her breath and plotting her next move, she moved her blades in front of her face and examined her arms. She could see the reflection of her face in the metal. Now that they were formed, they didn't hurt; starting to understand her condition began to calm her. They were her bones, yes, but the edges were metal, shiny, dense, and unearthly—something that didn't seem to come from her. Yori swung at a garbage can and her spectral blade cut it like butter. She was a weapon.

Inside her, her normal apathy was replaced with a rage; she couldn't tell where it was coming from. It was a thirst for blood, aggression against...*beauty?* Something in her ached deeply. In her head she heard another voice, and a bolt of pain shot through her spine. In her blood-red memories, she saw flashes of a woman she knew had to be her mother; it was the only female voice she recognized. Maybe her mother would know what caused so much pain in her, but where was the memory and when did it happen? Then Yori wandered throughout Japan, avoiding all other people and spirits alike. She was following some instinct home and just hoped her compass wasn't broken.

Eventually, Yori found her way to the secluded home from her childhood, somewhere in the mountains of Chiba prefecture. She disembarked the train at an isolated countryside platform; no one entered or exited, not even a spirit. The tiny platform sat with two rails, one in each direction, and no other signs. If it wasn't for the gravel, the station would have vanished into the background of the rolling grass and rice paddies. Though the scenery was nothing special, all things she had already seen in other small prefectures, she had a great feeling about this one. This was the right area.

It would be overly generous to say that the small group of buildings was a town; its seasonal population of fifteen barely constitutes a village during some of the harsher months. As such, they had no streetlights, or anything professionally kept up with that would legally constitute as streets—only dirt paths and small, peaceful homes scattered in the hills. Among them were small shrines dedicated to no deity, only nature. Something new had been awoken in Yori, and the small statues, which she had seen a million times, now glowed in the dark. Their lights were scattered throughout the hills like fireflies and acted as nightlights as she strolled the fields.

Among the single-story farmhouses stood one building with a general store sign in the window. Everything else was part of an old farming village that was made obsolete by the invention of better rice and larger farms—making it a relic of time. The few people who happily lived there were all asleep at a reasonable hour. Even though they had their original architecture, none of the houses sparked any memories in Yori. Instead, her head was raised to the horizon,

and she looked at the only small mountain that surrounded the town.

Though the hill wasn't the largest, the side facing the town was steep and impossible for

her to climb. Instead, Yori wandered into the hills and followed the paths she could see, always

aiming her body toward the mysterious peak. Throughout the woods she found a trail of shrines

lighting the way; they created a winding route that spiraled up to the top. The path she followed

was a small but clear one where the trees didn't grow, and though it was overrun with tall

grasses, it was clear that a road, or path of some sort, had once been there.

After over a day's journey, Yori found her way to the top with the sun again setting at her

back; the path gave way to a weed-laden stone road and the ruins of an old house. As she came

over the crest of the hill, suddenly snow was falling from the sky. Before her was a house laced

in snow, as if it was frozen in time. The breaks in the roof made it clear that the inside would also

be filled with snow. The house was larger than the ones at the bottom of the hill, taking up three

floors, but the top floors were destroyed, collapsed in on themselves. The house was guarded by

two small dog statues, which glowed like the shrines below. To her left was a small well. Yori

couldn't tell if it was twenty years ago or two hundred, but she knew she had been there before.

Yori approached the front door cautiously. She was not sure why, but she feared what

would be inside. She ducked under a low-hanging door frame and entered. Inside, snow was

caked on many of the surfaces and a slight wind carried snowflakes off the tables and into the

small side rooms. From above, small strands of sunlight came from holes in the ceiling and

breaks in the walls and called for her to search deeper. There were decorations and dissolved

remnants of family photos littering the ground and walls. Yori entered the first area whose door wasn't broken; the simple room had a short table and seats around it—three bowls and broken placemats sat on it.

Yori stood in the light and pulled off her headphones. The building was silent except for an occasional creak from the shifting winds. From the corner of the room came a shrill and rapid voice. "Oh, oh, oh, my." The voice jumped to another corner of the room. "You're home! It's been so long since we've played. Do you wanna play?" The voice jumped once again, this time within the gap between a doorframe and a closet door—a single eye peered through, fixated on her. "What have you been up to? Where have you been? You've grown since you walked away. Did you come back to play?" The voice jumped into the hallway. Yori peered down the corridor, going deeper into the house, and saw the eye appear across the hall in another doorway.

Yori followed the voice deeper into the building but didn't say a word. The hallway was littered with small piles of snow and the walls were deteriorated, but even so the house was beginning to look familiar—she worried it was just her hope. As Yori walked down the hall and deeper into the house, the walls grew warmer and brighter, as if the sun were just rising instead of setting. As she walked forward, the room grew larger, and she felt as if she was a child. The eye stood still in the shadows. "You never played with me before—I've always been waiting." Its voice was more aggressive this time.

Yori watched as the brightness moved down the hallway in front at its own pace, and she finally talked. "You were there? Do you know what happened?" The eye danced down the hallway between the corners and the broken doorways.

"I've always been here. I was born on this mountain way before you or your family lived on it. It's my home and you just lease it. I saw everything, before…during…after." Though it started annoyed, it became gentler as it finished. Yori continued to walk through the house, and though her memories were filling in the gaps in the broken walls and the floorboards, it didn't fill in any figures of her mother or father. All she knew was that she felt small, she had only ever been here as a child. Yori entered the living room and though it was filled with snow, and she could feel the cold on her feet, the room was warm. It was the feeling you get before you die of hyperthermia; your body is warm and crisp at the end. Her vision was blurred by the shining of rose-colored memories that were taking over. From across the room the eye called from the drawer of a small desk. "It wasn't anything special. Not that I've seen. Typical tragedy." The eye moved to a closet in the back of the room. "Here."

Yori walked across the room toward the closet, and the room began to shake. The warmth of her childhood home and the cold of the snow danced back and forth in her vision. She opened the closet and searched for a light, but the ancient building had nothing like that—the solid ceiling let no sun in. Yori peered in but even the rose-colored memories couldn't illuminate it. She pushed snow out of the way with her foot and forced the door open even more. The moonlight came through a hole in the roof behind her and shined into the darkness. From behind her the voice continued. "Welcome home."

Yori walked into the room and moved her way through the snow. Though there was no break in the ceiling, the snow grew deeper as she moved deeper into the room. Her calves burned with cold as if she was walking up the mountain again. Beneath the snow was rubble and dirt, rocks different from anywhere else outside the house. "Further," the voice beckoned, then the door shut behind her and she was enveloped in darkness. A light began to glow beneath the snow and Yori dropped to her knees and began to dig.

Her hands turned red from the cold as she dug through the snow, though there appeared to only be a small layer it seemed to regenerate almost as fast as she could dig. What was rougher on her hands was the stagnant earth she was clawing through. The land had already begun returning the pile; roots and dense soil separated her from the light below. In the rubble, she moved some wood from the ceiling and below it found a strand of stiff, frozen cloth. She excitedly gripped the cloth, to use it as a trail to the secrets below.

When Yori's fingers graced the pile, some memories began to flood back. The room around her glowed pink and warm; her head felt light, like a valve was being released. She dug faster, following the cloth. The more she revealed, the finer the dark blue dress seemed to be. It was only a few more inches under the ground where her hand come into contact with the first bone—the skeleton of her mother. The flood back of memories became too severe; it stunned Yori.

Her vision was clouded by *rose*, and behind her she could hear commotion. Yori turned and through the now opened door she saw her mother setting the dinner table. The small woman had a round face and large eyes. Her dark blue dress brought out a small hint of hazel in them, and the corners of her mouth were wrinkled from smiling. She moved fluidly as she went from the kitchen into the larger, fancier room. Her joy didn't cease as the front door slammed open. Instead, she excitedly ran toward the noise.

She came back into the room with a much more solemn look on her face. The man, who Yori sensed was her father, entered with a shove. He was much larger and grizzled, and compared to Yori's childlike stature, he was a mountain. He wore a three-piece kamishimo consisting of a powder blue outer coat, a matching kimono, and skirt. The markings on his sword detailed his family name and was graced with a symbol from the Edo period. She could hear his gruff voice break her mother's heart. "We married for love when we were young but now for me that love has died. I have been offered a better wife and more/better land. I believe it is because of you, I have never been able to reach my potential. You were never beautiful enough for me. You must have placed a curse on my heart." Then with no emotion, he used his sword to cut her down quickly. With tears in her eyes, Yori came out of the closet. She lunged at his leg and tried to accompany him; he was the only other person she knew. With a scowl on his face he readied his sword, but when he noticed Yori's bright red cheeks, he instead sheathed it and walked away. He kicked her off his leg as he exited the home for the last time.

"Where are these visions coming from? How did I see myself," Yori cried.

"Oh, that's me! What did you think, you had some special ability? Remember? I was there. I'm just showing you what I saw. I've lived so long, though, sometimes I forget when is when and which is which." The voice was within the vision, and Yori couldn't see the small eye that had been following her before.

"Thank you for breaking my heart. I needed to know. But how did I survive here alone?" Yori rested her weight on her tights and let out a sigh.

"Oh, you should probably keep digging." The voice became timid and sheepish. Yori followed his instructions and began to exhume her mother's body. Within the soil she pulled on the dress and moved the head and arms of her mother into the more comfortable-looking position. It was then, in the dirt within her mother's arms, she found another piece of cloth. This one was a dark green dress, a festively beautiful gown to go with her mother's. When she touched it, the voice seemed to remember more and Yori's vision was taken over again.

Yori returned to the living room and sat over her mother's body. She lost time, and when the sun set something sinister began to occur. From somewhere else on the hill came the Being. Yori didn't know what he was, but she knew to be afraid. She was too young to understand, though, that her mother was gone. In her fear, she dragged her mother's body to the closet. She was able to close the door just before the Being entered the house. Yori touched the little arm of her skeleton, still covered in dress fabric, and remembered falling asleep. She was a child, hungry, and alone in the snow. She cuddled into her mother's lifeless body. Together they fell asleep with the snow—but that peace was a false memory, instead, the voice showed her the truth.

Young Yori watched like the eye from the closet as the Being entered her home. He took the form of a bastardized Hainu, a dire wolf with the wings of an eagle. His large frame pressed against the walls of the home and knocked decorations to the ground. What she didn't know was that he was following her scent and that no matter where she was, he was going to find her. It was only a moment before he made his way toward the closet. Yori dashed from the door and with no other ideas cuddled into her mother. She pulled her arms over her and quieted her breath.

The shadow of the beast cast over her, and from the doorway it breathed deep and began to pull in all of the heartache and fear. Though her mother was dead, the insecurity and the heartache she felt filled the room. Her spirit was still warm and the wound fresh. It mixed with Yori's fear and uncertainty and created a soup of unique flavor. Yori dug deeper into her mother, but it wasn't helpful. She began to fall asleep within her mother's arms. As the fear was drained from her, so was her life. When he was done Yori's body was lifeless like her mother's. "It's been snowing here ever since," the voice called out.

Then time began to speed up and Yori watched as the snow continued to flow onto the house until the ceiling broke and the house began to fill. That is when from the snow, Yori's spirit rose and walked away from its corpse. As it did, it grew and changed. She was now a ghost of love, purity, and betrayal—an avenger of her mother's broken heart. Her pure love was betrayed, and the intense emotion of broken purity created her. "You walked out into the snow, and I haven't seen you since. Haven't had a visitor since."

The vision faded and Yori found herself back in the dark of the closet. The snow sat on her head, and in her arms she held the bones of her mother and herself. "I'm de-e-ad?" she stuttered to herself. "I'm dead, and a monster? A weapon? What…do…I do with that?" she muttered to herself.

"So, are you going to play with me now?" The eye called from the crack in the doorway. Yori ignored him and instead returned her attention to the corpses, and she let out a tear. Even if the real Yori had died long ago, some part of her lived in the raging spirit she had become. She could feel her mother's heart in her as well. Though her hands were wrinkled from the water, and they were also frozen from the snow, it did not stop Yori from again using her bare hands to dig out the bodies. In silence, she gently and diligently spent the next two days moving the bodies from their tortured resting place.

In the back of the house, she found a withered but once beautiful cherry blossom tree. It was sturdy and decorated with snow. Under the base of the tree Yori dug only a small hole. To the side she created a small and constant fire and placed the bodies into it. Over two more days she prayed, to whom she wasn't sure, and watched over the remains. Then she buried the ashes into the hole under the tree; something in her spirit directed her through the respectful ceremony her mother deserved all those years ago.

In the same tradition, as the fire burned, Yori used rocks to carve another rock, creating an altar. Above the ashes she placed the small, three-tiered stone set up with her family name carved into it. She searched the home and easily found the remnants of what she once was, but she took her mother's name, not that of her father; not the name of the samurai, instead *Tanikawa*. Yori stood in morose joy and left another small prayer over the bodies. As she prayed and left her last respects to herself, she heard a new voice. "You know that you're going to have to come back next year, right? And the year after that? Then two more? Then three after? If you want their spirits to rest well? You've started a long ceremony."

From the corner of her eye Yori saw something new, a faint white and lavender light. She turned her head, and her eyes met a reptilian and yet furry face. She screamed and attempted to back away. "Ahhh," the new creature joined in. "Why are we screaming? What's happening!" It panicked. Yori spun and attempted to run but quickly realized the light was still over her shoulder. In fact, the creature was attached to her.

From her back came a long, thin, snake-like body that started somewhere within Yori's back, connected to her heart. The thin body led to a large face, a cross between a dragon, dog, and lizard; it was a strong face with a sense of fluff. "Who are you?" screamed Yori as she swatted through the monster.

"I don't know but stop touching me. It tickles in the worst way. I'm here—I've always been here. Wait, you're actually responding to me? You can see me! That's amazing."

"What does that mean? Who are you?"

"You don't seem to understand so I'll repeat. I don't know and I don't know, but it is great to stretch my neck." The creature stretched its long body and started to float through the air and wrap around Yori and flap its ears like little wings. Its personality contrasted with the sacredness of the ceremony. From within the house, Yori heard the voice of the eye again.

"You are two halves of the same coin. I've seen you two together ever since you woke up from the snow. You're the same. I can only guess it's part of the vengeful spirit that seems to have taken over your body. Let's sprinkle in some conspiracy words about destiny, the inevitable cycles. Do you wanna play?" The eye was in the living room, by its favorite closet once again.

Yori came back to the house and looked around. "Do you know a lot about the spirit world? Why have I been seeing these blue lights? Like the one that led me to my body. I'll play with you if you can answer some questions."

"Oh, I know a bunch. Have you only just started seeing the lights? You're at least part spirit. You should be able to see them all the time. It's a connection the Being gives us." The eye jumped to the crack in a dresser.

"You mean that monster? The Being? It created you too?" Yori followed the voice deeper into the house, slowly creeping and trying to corner it, like a small child. The spirit at her back simply watched in confusion.

"Like you, I was born here, only so much earlier. The Being feeding, lead to my creation, as well as all the spirits you saw on the way here. It's lost souls that leave behind lights. Have you only just been able to see them? Strange. It's the one thing we all have. Do you want to play?" Yori darted around the room and looked through drawer after drawer. With each place the eye jumped after she had left and repeated, "Do you want to play?" Eventually, in one small drawer she found a small journal; a set of pages barely held together by leather and some string.

Next to it was an old quill and ink. Yori dropped to the ground with her utensils and started to take notes.

As she jotted, the pages began to glow with a purple hue. Her memories and everything she had learned were copied out of her and onto the page. She was compelled to draw the Being from her memories and the eye that was tutoring her. As she finished the drawings, their images jumped from the pages and played like a movie. She had a gift. She would record everything. "Tell me, why is this place so cursed? Why are there so many spirits?"

"From what I've heard," the voice began.

"Heard? From whom? Aren't you alone here? For seemingly centuries?" Yori interjected and bit the end of her quill.

"Boy, you're a rude student," the dragon said over her shoulder.

"She was never able to grow up. She'll have some emotional shortcomings," the eye jested. "We are all connected, some of us more than others. Certain places are more magical, most likely because the Being lived there for a long time. When the human world was in the most turmoil, he was at his strongest. Those lands that have undergone tragedy are often also left with remnants of the souls caught in the crossfire. Are we going to play or not?" Yori signaled to the eye to keep talking, and she kept writing. "He leaves a stain. He fed on strong energy in this house and the land was left holding the trauma. You'd think after generations it would all be gone, but somehow it persists through the bloodline."

"I've just been wandering for hundreds of years. Is there anything I can do to remove this curse on my body?"

"Yes, if the other spirits are to be believed, you have killed hundreds and have been wandering for hundreds of years. You're rather scary, I've been told. I still don't see it. Even that new fox thing looks pathetic. I'm not sure if it's a curse, or just who you are. You could try to talk to the Being, but no one's ever got anything out of him." The eyes laughed a disgusting and wet laugh. "Not even his kids. That being said, there are many magical rituals you could try. It's possible with all his victims someone has a solution to your…particular…problem."

"I just want to stop the painful transformations."

"You sure? You sure you don't want vengeance?" the dragon whispered into her ear.

"I can't say for sure you could remove your curse. It's possible killing the Being could do something. Doing a ritual to remove your…issues might work? Then again, killing him might simply take you apart. You might just fade away into nothing. What are we without our trauma?"

"We'll be something new." Yori jotted down a few more sentences, then closed the book and stood up. "Thank you so much for all the help and information…and for keeping our bodies safe all these years. Whatever I do next, I need to go out there for it." Yori began to move toward the front door to leave but was met by the eye at the first corner.

"You're just leaving? You said you would play with me. YOU NEVER PLAYED WITH ME. I've waiting for EVER and did everything for you and you're just LEAVING?" The eye began to scream, and every word grew higher pitched and scratchier. Yori could feel it deep in her eardrums. She threw her quill and notebook into her pocket and dashed for the hallway. With every opening she moved past, the eye followed and its scream became louder and closer to static. She finally made it out of the front door.

The ground was no longer covered in snow but instead it was a beautiful spring day. The light was rosy and warm. Yori sprinted from the house with all her might and made her way down the hill. The loose soil made her stumble, but she was able to stabilize. Behind her the spirit still clung to her back and it searched in the distance for the eye. "I don't see anything; I think we might have gotten away. What a creep that little ocular nightmare was," the spirit said.

The earth shook around them, and they heard the voice of the eye once again. "You may be a spirit but you're weak. I can read your thoughts and they are human. Your imagination is human. It means you're weak and closedminded…and easy to trick." The eye appeared at the bottom of the hill peering through a hole in the universe. It peered through static. Yori was not outside. Instead, her body was still sitting in the cold snow of the house—the eye was controlling her memories, and Yori's mind and soul were fighting back.

"You're a spirit, aren't you?" Yori asked in a stern but worried tone. "What the fuck is going on?"

"First of all, *we're* spirits, *and* I just got here. Why don't you know what's happening? My name is Tomo, by the way." The head floated in front of Yori's face and talked quickly. "If I were to guess, and I am guessing, I'd think our minds are in some sort of phantom universe. We might even be in the mind of the eye."

"He's trying to pull us into him like a black hole?" Yori asked, sadly and half sarcastically. She lowered her head to think. "If he's trying to devour our soul, through our mind…we could fight back?"

"Wait, do you have powers or something?" Tomo asked surprised with a large grin. "I'm thinking the rules here are probably the same as the real world, except he knows every inch, and is probably stronger. Home field advantage. But I'd think we win here, we win there." Then he paused. "And if we die here, we're as good as digested. So yeah, what are your powers?"

Even though Yori's troubled soul had transformed thousands of times throughout her lifetime, she had never done it on purpose. The time she had done it, and been aware, it was a nightmare and a curse. It didn't even cross her mind as an option. "I was hoping you had some type of power. You look all ethereal and magical."

"Why thank you, kid. Yeah, I got a few tricks up my lack of sleeves." Tomo started to extend his body and coiled around her many times. "I can also mean mug like the best of them." The monster's face became angry in an almost unnatural way. Yori didn't see how either of the *tricks* she had just seen would be of much use.

"Kid?" she asked, a little annoyed. "Apparently, I'm hundreds of years old and I don't see how you'll be much of a help. Maybe we can find something here we can use against it."

"Sure, *maybe* you are hundreds of years old, but whatever you are, I am *SURE* I am older. It's a feeling thing…kid." Tomo unwrapped and the two turned toward the large eye in the distance. It drifted across the sky, raining static bolts of lightning from its portal on the buildings below. The eye itself searched the horizon.

Yori surveyed the landscape and noticed there was very little to work with. The hill was the same one she had walked up, but as it was many centuries ago. The hills were still littered with small farm buildings and the trees were cut down to make room for more and more rice. Though there were some buildings, the area was now mostly exposed—which left Yori nowhere to hide.

"Maybe we can just run in the other direction?" Yori questioned Tomo. "I think going down this hill will get us spotted." Tomo extended his body and flew over the small hill on the opposite side and searched the horizon. Instead of the rest of the town, the house stood on the edge of a cliff that fed into the sea. Below them was nothing but crashing waves.

"There is a raging sea past the house. It looks like there is nothing we can do but to find a way forward."

"How is that possible? How old is this monster? Could there really have been a sea here so long ago?"

"No, I don't think so. I'm assuming the sea is a gap in its memory. Perhaps it never saw past this mountain and has nothing but open questions about it." Tomo shifted his eyebrows back and forth while thinking.

"So, if he doesn't know everything, he probably doesn't have control of everything in his mind." Yori paused.

"I know I don't." Tomo whispered in agreement. "What are you thinking?"

"I'm not sure, just taking stock." Yori started to make her way down the hill. She headed toward a group of fences and a large barn on her right. She wondered if she could hide in the tall but dead grass. Either way, she had to get off the road. She dropped down into the rice bed, which was still flooded with water. Yori crouched into it and though her boots kept her feet dry, her coat dipped into the water. To hide, Tomo ducked down into her coat. She stumbled in the mud and then moved among the grass. The dry, unharvested stalks cracked under her pressure. She didn't know where she was headed, just that she needed to get somewhere and do it secretly. The earth surrounding the field rose above and Yori lost sight of the eye.

What she didn't know was that with each crack of the grass, the eye grew closer to hearing her. When she had reached the barn, she was too close to be making that much noise. Yori crawled over the small, muddy hill and pulled herself onto the softer grass surrounding the building. The eye spotted her and turned its attention from the houses below to Yori on the hill. It no longer spoke; instead, it shrieked a hungry yell. The large portal closed for only a moment before it reappeared over the barn and let out another unearthly scream.

Out of the portal the static lightning struck the ground, only now it came to life. With each blast that hit the ground, a small monster crawled from the smoke. Their bodies too were static, but among their unclear shapes were small teeth. Though their screams were higher-pitched, they were just as hungry—they yelled as they charged her position. Yori stared up at the eye that was now focused on her. A bolt of static dropped out of the sky and directly toward her.

Yori attempted to get up from the ground, but her hands slipped on the mud below her. The ground was gooey in a way that was not naturally possible. She was getting up but slowly. Too slowly. Yori closed her eyes and braced herself for the blast by throwing her forearms over her head. A large crash drew her attention next. When she opened her eyes, Yori was surrounded by the spectral body of Tomo. When the lightning bolt came down, he wrapped around her and used his body to protect her. It bounced off of him without a care.

"Wah! What!" Yori yelled as Tomo unwound from her. "I guess you're more helpful than you seem." Tomo smiled.

"You can praise me later. Get up, kid." Tomo stretched away from her as if he was trying to pull her up. Yori noticed the mobs of small creatures running toward her and rushed to get up with new vigor. She finally managed and raced towards the barn. The front door was open, Yori rushed in and slammed the sliding door shut. She dropped a large plank of wood in front and pressed her back against it.

The little monsters fell onto the roof above and the two of them could hear the sound of their little feet as they scattered across the surface. Then began the sound of their little claws as they attempted to get in. Yori's eyes darted from corner to corner to look for weak spots. The only one she saw was a single open window above. Tomo instinctually went toward it and pulled it closed. They could now hear the scraping of the monster's claws as they slid down the side of the building, and the splashing of the mud as they started to dig under the building's walls. Yori did not have much time. "What are we going to do? It's going to be like being torn apart by an army of toddlers," panicked Tomo.

"My nightmare," responded Yori. "I don't know, I don't know." Yori was attempting to remain calm but with nowhere to go, she couldn't pay attention to anything but her heartbeat and the sound of the claws scraping against the walls; each sound felt like it came in but never died out. As if it was a pool filling with water, the building bulged with noise. It began to shake as the small claws broke though the wood for the first time. Then all around them, small pieces were removed, and the monsters made their way in.

As the small static bodies began to rain from the ceiling, Yori's heartbeat reached its peak. She couldn't take all the noises around her. It was too much to bear; beyond all the other stress, her senses were overwhelmed. Like in the past, her body began to take over and change. Yori's arms began to break, and this time was not any easier on her than the last time. Her forearms bent back, and the razor-sharp claws emerged from her flesh. Tomo closed his eyes and hummed a strange song, long tunes of alternating octaves. The sound soothed Yori and she could no longer feel the pain of her shifting body.

Yori rose from the ground, once again a weapon, and readied herself. She looked around and saw a second door on the other side. She would exit there. The static monsters dripped down the walls and into the room. Some leaped from the air, and others sprinted on the ground, but all came toward her. Yori threw her arms back and readied them like pinchers in front of her. On her back, Tomo formed a wall behind her. Yori rushed forward.

She swung her arms and cut through the tiny creatures who burst into nothing. Tomo protected her from the ones that continued to fall from the sky. The small creatures clung to him but then he snapped his body and they all fell through him onto the ground behind her, then he would solidify again. As Yori ran, Tomo swung his body and swatted at the creatures that approached. Yori swung her arms as if they were dislocated and created a swirling wall of death. When they came to the barn door it, like small creatures, stood no chance. Yori swung a few swipes with her arms and cut through the hard wooden door with ease. Then she covered her face and charged through the ruined wood. She burst through the door and back into the countryside.

The eye stared at her and began to let out even more creatures, and the rain of static increased. Yori mercilessly continued to swing her arms, cutting every creature that came down. The rain of minions was nothing. The eye grew bloodshot and angry and growled. The portal closed and the eye disappeared, and the sky opened. The sun shined down onto Yori, and it felt great on her skin. The monsters that were on the ground began to explode in the sunlight with a sizzle and a pop.

From the side a rising shadow was cast over Yori. She turned to see the giant eye over the horizon. It's bloodshot gaze fixated on her and shook with frustration. It let out another howl and its pupil dilated. It grew large and then shrank like it was focusing on her. Instinctually Yori began to run toward the eye, darting between the trees and small buildings. Where the eye focused burst into flames, and the stream followed behind Yori as she zigged and zagged closer and closer. Soon, though, she stood behind a small shed and was met with a big issue. There was a giant eye on the horizon and no more coverage. She poked her head out to look for somewhere else to go but drew the rage of the eye. He focused and it too burst into flame.

Yori had no choice other choice but to try. Tomo wrapped around her and Yori darted out from behind the building. She would rush toward the eye; if she could puncture it, maybe she could escape. The eye focused on her as she ran, and a flame built up. As she charged, she became a fire ball. Shortly, though, Tomo was not able to take any more of the invisible laser. He retracted into Yori's back and left her guarding herself. She continued to run but the pressure of the flames grew heavier and harder to fight as she got closer. Her blades were beginning to glow in the heat of the fire, and she was brought to her knees.

Yori's arms gave way, and she was thrown backwards into the air. Her jacket was on fire, her sleeves were gone, and the flame was spreading up her arms. Tears began to come down her face, and she grew angry. "Thank you for playing with me," the eye finally spoke, and chuckled. "What a sweet treat after all these years." The eye focused again on Yori, and she started to burst into flames; Yori screamed as she was engulfed.

Below the flames Yori's soul was being drained from her body. In the real world her body was fading out of existence. "I wanted to break the cycle, to end the curse. This wasn't the happy ending I was hoping for." Yori was speaking to Tomo, yes, but mostly herself. Her blades continued to heat up, and though she was ablaze she felt she was being drained more than she was being burned. Something deep inside her began to boil, a deep will to survive. Yori was not the type to die sad; no, she was filled with rage. She clenched her teeth and smiled. She remembered her music. She was not going to die in silence. Yori slid her headphones on and the music kicked back in.

As the heavy metal music started to pump through her body, Yori forgot about the flames— she was filling with rage. Her body began to violently shake and Tomo was pulled out from her. "What is that RIFF," Tomo commented as he began to expand. "This feels…GREAT." The music vibrated through him, and he started to glow and expand. Yori began to gain an aura and it pushed back against the fire.

It took a few moments but eventually Yori was surrounded by a protective barrier; the fire from the eye's gaze was deflected off. The eye screamed in frustration. "How dare you—what is this nonsense?" He focused harder on her, and she began to burn again. However, Tomo continued to grow. He grew and grew until he stretched four stories tall. Then his body began to transform.

Tomo's head transformed into a enormous and majestic purple manta ray. His body swam through the celestial sparkles that came from Yori's body below. His tail drifted back in the air like a tiny ponytail. From the mist he grew arms, and they mimicked Yori's. He stood as a juggernaut, with two bladed mantis arms. Tomo let out a loud laugh and swung his giant blades at the horizon. His arms sliced through the giant eye and from inside it spewed static. The eye began to drop below the horizon like the setting sun, and the world around them began to fall apart.

The false walls that contained them fell apart and they were released back into the real world. With the eye vanquished, Yori's consciousness returned to her body, and she was able to move again. "Well, kid, what's the move? Where are we heading now?" asked Tomo. It wrapped around her, floated up to her face, gave her a phantom lick, and chuckled.

"I don't know, but we'll need to find some trustworthy people—or *spirits*—to get some more information from. I'm going to compile everything I can. I want to stop hurting people, but ultimately just want to be able to live." Yori stepped out of the house and into the snowy night. In the distance, she saw a sea of stars shining over Japan. She didn't know where to start her adventure, but her journey was only beginning, and the world finally seemed open.

www.ingramcontent.com/pod-product-compliance
Lightning Source LLC
Chambersburg PA
CBHW070445300726
48975CB00007B/2047